the
decoding
of
lana morris

Also by Laura and Tom McNeal

Crooked

Zipped

Crushed

Laura & Tom McNeal

the
decoding
of
lana morris

Alfred A. Knopf

New York

The authors will donate 10 percent of net royalties from the sale
of this book to The Arc of the United States, an organization that advocates
for the rights and full participation of children and adults
with intellectual and developmental disabilities.

THIS IS A BORZOI BOOK PUBLISHED BY ALFRED A. KNOPF

Excerpt from "Hiawatha" by Laurie Anderson copyright © 1989
by Difficult Music.

www.randomhouse.com/teens

Educators and librarians, for a variety of teaching tools, visit us at
www.randomhouse.com/teachers

Library of Congress Cataloging-in-Publication Data
McNeal, Laura.
The decoding of Lana Morris / Laura & Tom McNeal. — 1st ed.
p.   cm.
SUMMARY: For sixteen-year-old Lana life is often difficult, with a flirtatious
foster father, an ice queen foster mother, a houseful of special-needs children
to care for, and bullies harassing her, until the day she ventures into an
antique shop and buys a drawing set that may change her life.
ISBN 978-0-375-83106-5 (trade) — ISBN 978-0-375-93106-2 (lib. bdg.)
[1. Foster home care—Fiction.   2. People with disabilities—Fiction.
3. Drawing—Fiction.   4. Supernatural—Fiction.   5. Nebraska—Fiction.]
I. McNeal, Tom.   II. Title.
PZ7.M47879365Dec 2007
[Fic]—dc22
2006023950

Printed in the United States of America
May 2007
10 9 8 7 6 5 4 3 2
First Edition

For Sam and Hank

And for Jane Morris

the
decoding
of
lana morris

There is nothing more properly the language

of the heart than a wish.

—Robert South

Part One

1.

*N*ebraska, June, the sky white with heat.

The dust devil begins with a pocket of unstable air where a farmer's field of irrigated beans meets the heated asphalt of Highway 20, sending up a sudden rush of warm air that swirls and stretches higher, increasing speed. The twisting funnel of dirt and debris moves east through fields of alfalfa and wheat and corn toward the town of Two Rivers, where, in a two-storied foster home, a girl named Lana Morris lives.

Lana is sixteen and slim, with watchful dark eyes, brown hair that falls in straight lines down her long back, and a slot between her two front teeth that was once called her most charming feature by one of the least reliable in her mother's long line of unreliable boyfriends. He said she was pretty, too, but the truth is Lana doesn't think anything about herself is charming or pretty, only that the slot between her front teeth is the exact thickness of a dime, something she learned by trial and error.

Slipped into the crease behind Lana's left ear, where some people might store a pencil or even a cigarette, you will normally find a tightly rolled two-dollar bill. With use and with time, this bill has been worn soft as cloth. Lana believes the bill was left to her by her father, believes that by unrolling it and holding it flat in her hand, she can sometimes feel the presence of the person he must have been. Lana has always believed in things. Fortune cookies. Horoscopes. That one of these days her mother (whereabouts unknown) would stop drinking, get a steady job, and buy them a little house somewhere. That her father, before he died, was nicer and less foolish than people said he was.

Lana stares down at her open hand with mild surprise. A minute before, she'd been drawing on a yellow legal pad, and now, without remembering doing it, she's smoothing the two-dollar bill across the flat of her palm.

Lana rolls and fastens the bill, then tucks it behind her ear. *Today will be okay,* she thinks, *if I can just get out of the house.*

Always a big *if*.

It's Saturday morning, for one thing. School is out for the summer. Whit Winters, her foster father, is upstairs asleep. His wife, Veronica, is in the backyard hanging sheets. Lana makes a point of being where Veronica isn't, so she's sneaked out to the front porch and sits sketching on a yellow legal tablet and eating Froot Loops from a box with a foster girl named Tilly, who is also sixteen. With her curly brown hair, green eyes, and round body, Tilly looks almost normal, but she isn't.

"Look, Lana!" Tilly says, and Lana looks. Tilly holds open her pudgy hand to display a dozen or so Froot Loops, all pink. "Look! Look!"

"Pink is definitely your favorite," Lana says.

Tilly says seriously, "Pinkies are better than yellows, Lana. You bet."

They both fall quiet in the thick heat. Lana goes back to sketching Whit Winters's face from memory. She can do his wavy hair, and she's never had trouble with his eyes, but there's something wrong with the chin, and if the chin's wrong, everything's wrong. He looks sharp and bony instead of smooth and boyish. She erases quickly, whisks the pink rubbery dust away with the side of her hand, and starts again.

Cicadas are whirring in the cottonwood, and a crow descends on the front lawn. Lana, lost again in her drawing, presumes this is a Saturday morning like any other Saturday morning, but in this she is wrong.

2.

"Look, Lana!" Tilly says. "A slinky winky!"

Lana follows Tilly's gaze. "That's just a dust devil," she says, frowning. "I hope it doesn't come this way."

This has no effect on Tilly's position. "Slinky winky!" she says with a hint of truculence in her voice, and why not? Lana thinks. What does somebody like Tilly have other than her half-baked opinions? Tilly goes into the house, and when she comes back, she's wearing one of the red backpacks that are kept in the hollow part of the living room window seat. The backpacks are for emergencies—to put on if there's a tornado and they have to evacuate.

"It's not a tornado, Tilly," Lana says. "Are you scared?"

"No, Lana. I'm not scared. No."

Lana isn't sure what's wrong with Tilly, but Lana's being of sound mind and body is the exception here—the rest are special-needs kids, or Snicks, as foster mom Veronica calls them. Lana thought it was some kind of slur until she saw the way Veronica wrote it out on receipts and accounting forms: *SNKs*.

Six months ago, on Lana's first day at the Winterses',

she called her caseworker, Hallie Simpson, and without bothering to say hello announced that there'd been a mistake. "And not a little one," Lana said. "As mistakes go, Hallie, this one is stellar."

Hallie in her low, rich, mellifluent voice said, "Hello, Lana. And how are you? Are you well? Because I hope you're well."

Lana likes Hallie. She is the best caseworker Lana has ever had and one of the few adults she can trust. Still, Lana said, "You put me in a home for retards is how I am, Hallie."

"Special needs," Hallie said evenly. Hallie Simpson is six feet tall, black, and—Lana knows this for a fact—unflappable. Lana has tried it all; Hallie cannot be flapped. Hallie said, "The correct term is *special needs*."

Lana was using the house phone at the time. She lowered her voice slightly. "Does that mean they each have a special need to be packed off to outer space?" she said, and when Hallie said nothing, Lana said, "Did I mention that one of them has his mouth open all the time? And he keeps walking up to me and touching my shoulder and walking off. Touching my shoulder and walking off. Again and again. Have you ever spent extended time with someone who does that, Hallie?—because I have to tell you, it's a little creepy, and every one of the rest of them is . . . just . . . as . . . *special*."

"Special needs," Hallie said smoothly, "is a category into which you arguably now fit, Lana, although yours is really more of a compound category. Let's call it . . . special needs and limited options." She paused and softened her voice. "Look, Lana, the Winterses are decent enough fosters, and they said they'd try you." Another pause. "As for the other, less fortunate kids who live there, I'd suggest a small dose of compassion."

Which was easy for Hallie to say because she didn't live in Snick House, where all the faces were a little too big and a little too flat and a little too elongated, like, Lana thinks, jumbo eggs drawn on a page without shading or shadow.

Lana kept her purse with her every minute after the boy named Alfred Mobilio took it off to a corner and ate all her Life Savers and Tic Tacs and started to eat her earplugs because they were packaged like mints in a cellophane bag. He stole her Little Walter CD, the one that her mother gave her because it was her father's favorite, or so she said. Alfred kept it in his canvas tote bag for a whole day. When Lana told Veronica it was missing, Veronica had gone right to Alfred's bag, fished it out, and said nonchalantly, "Pilfering's part of his makeup. Keep your stuff out of sight."

Lana kept her distance, fingered her two-dollar bill, and watched television. She washed her own dishes before she ate because the Snicks, who had rotating dish duty, usually had to be reminded to wash their own hands when they left the bathroom. There was a lock on the fridge to prevent food-stealing. A lock on the medicine cabinet. Behavior charts everywhere.

Then one night about a month into her stay, Alfred Mobilio, who for sure had Down syndrome, sat down on the sofa beside her and said, "Jamha far yesterday."

"You want to try that in English?" Lana said. Alfred at least could talk, but he wasn't easy to understand.

"J-J-J-Jamha farted yesterday," Alfred repeated, more clearly this time.

Lana didn't know who Jamha was, so she said, "Did Jamha say excuse me?"

"Naw," Alfred said cheerfully, "Jamha's a dog," and Lana had to laugh.

She got used to Alfred first. He was like a fifteen-year-old middle-aged man. Every day he wore a green golf shirt, blue slacks, and polyester socks with loafers. When nothing else was happening, he copied words out of magazines and ads, sometimes for hours, rubbing his teeth together to make a sound that reminded Lana of a purring cat or a croaking toad, depending on her mood. "Bruxism," Whit called it. "All part of the Down's deal." If Alfred didn't have a special kind of black pen and paper, he rocked or hit himself. The strange thing was, after he filled a whole piece of paper with copied words and phrases, he wadded the paper up and threw it away.

Then she got used to the others, too. She learned their full names—Carlito Guiterrez, Garth Stoneman, and Tilly Oates—and the peculiarities that went with them.

Carlito, an enormous, blocky boy of fourteen, was the shoulder toucher—he repeatedly walked up and touched your shoulder and quietly walked away, as if this was his job—and his favorite snack was dill pickles with Tabasco sauce. It was Tilly who said that when Carlito touched people's shoulders, he was blessing them. "Who told you that?" Lana had asked, and Tilly stared at her a second or two and said, "Nobody. I just know it, you bet."

Garth was twelve and he wore superhero T-shirts every day—Superman, Batman, Spider-Man, or the Hulk—and he was so skinny he wore suspenders to keep his pants up. He always carried a plastic Popeye doll, kind of like a Barbie, and he twisted the head when he was nervous, which was a lot of the time. He didn't like anyone to touch him, and if you got too close, he'd scream. ("Give him his inches!" Veronica would yell if she was anywhere nearby at the time.)

First thing every morning and every night right after supper, Garth took his Popeye and sat in a chair by the front door. Whit told Lana that Garth was waiting for his mom to come and pick him up. He said that one day about three years ago, Garth's mom came to the house with Garth and a social worker and introduced him to Whit and Veronica. Garth carried two shopping bags, one in each hand. One bag held all his clothes and the other was full of plastic action heroes, including Popeye.

Garth's mother, according to Whit, seemed like an average woman, not too skinny or fat or short or tall or pretty or plain. But hidden by all the averageness, Whit said, was a hardness like nothing he'd ever seen. After introducing Garth to Whit and Veronica, Garth's mom went down on one knee and said, "This is your home now, Garth. I'm not coming back today or tomorrow or anytime after that. I won't be sending birthday cards or Christmas presents, and you shouldn't expect me to. This is your home now, in this house with these people." Garth's mom stood up. She didn't hug Garth or kiss him. When he tried to follow her, she pushed him away. She took his hand, shook it firmly, and let go of it. Then she went to the door, opened it, and, without a look back, closed it behind her. Garth had gone to the closed door and stood by it until at last he was tired of standing and then he sat on the floor and finally he lay down and fell asleep.

Whit and Veronica had carried him to bed, but when they woke up in the morning, Garth was again sleeping curled by the front door. He wrapped himself in a rug and clung to his Popeye doll and didn't eat or leave his spot for three days, except to go to the bathroom. After a week, he began to eat with the others and began to fall into the routines of the house, but he'd never stopped his waiting hours, which were between eight and nine in the morning and six and seven in the evening. "Guess that's when his mother picked him up when she left him places overnight or during the day," Whit said. "So that's when he thinks she'll pick him up now."

Garth and most of the kids moved toward and away from Lana in casual, unpredictable ways, but Tilly Oates was different. After a week of watching Lana from a safe distance, Tilly began to move ever closer to Lana, and then, once close, she didn't leave. She followed Lana from room to room like a shadow. At first it was unnerving, but then Lana grew used to it and realized there was no obligation to talk or listen to Tilly in the usual ways. They fell into easy company.

Tilly liked to wear pink pants with lots of pockets—her favorite pair had a pocket total of ten—and she liked using the pockets for the special objects she found—a small, smooth red rock, a stick resembling a fork, a leaf shaped like a heart. And any kind of feather. Feathers were her specialty, and nests, though she didn't put these in her pockets—she always hand-carried the nests. Often she presented them to Lana as gifts, and Lana made a point of arranging them along the windowsills in her room.

One day Tilly said something strange. She'd been sitting

with Lana in the backyard watching her draw, and out of the blue Tilly said, "I'm a big mistake."

Tilly was normally cheerful, but her tone now was forlorn. Lana looked up from her drawing. "What?"

"I'm a big mistake. No one should have had me." Tilly's lower lip began to tremble like a toddler's. "That's why no one wants me."

These words sent something like an electrical shock through Lana's system. She herself had thought this very thing of all the Snicks, and more than once. "Who told you that?" Lana asked.

"A girl at my school," Tilly said.

Lana thought it was one thing to think it, but saying it was worse. Much worse.

She leaned forward and took Tilly's hands in hers. "Well, I want you, Tilly," she said. "I like to be with you." She hadn't thought this before, but once she said it, it felt more or less true. Tilly needed somebody, and, well, Lana was somebody.

That night when they were all watching TV, Tilly yawned and put her head in Lana's lap and took hold of Lana's hand and almost immediately fell asleep, and Lana hadn't minded having this odd, stocky, cuddling creature snoring gently against her. From then on, Tilly slept on the other twin bed in Lana's room, which was fine by Lana. Tilly wasn't bad company. It was true she brought with her a pink Cinderella alarm clock, a pink Cinderella bedspread, and her pink shoe boxes full of feathers and nests and rocks and smashed bottle caps. But she didn't steal. She wasn't devious. She said thank you, please, and excuse me more than most people. And most of the time, she saw the sunny side of things, even when there wasn't much sunny to see.

Now, on the front porch, on this normal-seeming Saturday morning, Tilly shouts gleefully, "Slinky winky coming after us!"

3.

*T*he swirling dust devil has swept along the street, lifting leaves and candy wrappers, moving past Chet's house next door, veering north and now, suddenly, it is whooshing toward the Winterses' house, toward the front porch, toward Lana and Tilly.

"We'd better go in," Lana says, snatching the two-dollar bill from her ear, clapping a hand over her drawing tablet, and standing up.

But Tilly stays where she is, grinning, exultant, wearing her red tornado pack and sucking on a Froot Loop.

Lana hunches over the sketch pad, closes her eyes, and waits. The hot wind pours through her clothes and goes right inside her, finding all the little corners, sucking up stray thoughts and idle notions, and then abruptly it is gone, leaving behind a feeling Lana can't remember feeling before. A lightness, she thinks. A pleasant emptiness that makes her feel strangely hopeful.

She opens her eyes.

Papers litter the yard, the Froot Loops box is upside down on the driveway, and Tilly is still grinning. Sheer pleasure beams in her face. "We were in the slinky winky!" she says.

Lana nods and wipes at her skin to see if she's dusty. She is, a little. She slips the rolled two-dollar bill back into place behind her left ear. The odd elation still fills her.

Tilly says, "Did it carry us away?"

Lana thinks she *did* get a little carried away by the dust devil, but not in the way Tilly means, so she says, "We're still here, aren't we?"

Tilly nods. Then she smiles her usual satisfied smile and says, "It was *fun!*"

Lana thinks that in a way, it was. If Tilly hadn't been here, she would have gone inside and missed the whole thing. "You weren't scared?"

"No!" Then, "You was here!" Then Tilly opens her tornado pack, takes out one of her emergency granola bars, and starts to eat it.

Lana says, "You'd better put your pack in the window seat before Veronica sees it."

Tilly evidently sees the wisdom of this—she starts zipping up the pack's compartments. Lana folds open her tablet to the drawing of Whit. There's nothing wrong with doing a portrait of him, she tells herself. She's drawn faces before, though not of men, certainly not her guardians.

But Whit is different. Back in December, at Lana's arrival, Whit smiled and said, "Well, hello, Miss Morris," while Veronica stared with cold gray eyes at Lana for about a minute. Lana stared right back. Veronica's lips, unglossed, had a faintly bluish tone.

Finally Veronica said, "One more L.M.A."

Don't ask, Lana thought, but she couldn't help herself. In a sullen voice she said, "What's that supposed to mean?"

Veronica seemed pleased that Lana had taken the bait.

"It means one more Little Miss Attitude," she said in an icy voice. Then, "We've seen a few, just so you know. They come and they go."

And Lana, feeling something close down inside her, said, "F.U." She made a small, stony smile. "But just so you know, F.U. doesn't mean anything personal toward you—they're just my adopted middle initials." She kept her hard little smile. "They stand for Faith and Unity." She narrowed her gaze on Veronica.

Veronica, satisfied that her worst expectations had just been confirmed, gave a cold, knowing nod and walked away. But Whit Winters just stood there with a loose grin on his face.

He was a man, Lana knew, but his look was boyish, and he had narrow hips and skin so smooth Lana wondered if he ever had to shave. His eyes were frisky and deeply brown and exerted on Lana what felt like an actual pull. Still, he was connected to Veronica, so Lana stared at his mouth and said, "I would call that grin moronic." A word her father had liked to use.

Whit Winters seemed actually amused. "You're kind of a desperado, aren't you?"

Lana stared over his shoulder, away from his eyes.

He said, "Lana Morris. Is that what you said your name is?"

Lana wouldn't even nod. She kept her eyes drilling into the wall behind him.

In a mild, almost playful tone, he said, "Well, you know what? I'm going to make it my personal mission to learn the Morris code."

These words affected Lana, but she didn't want to

show it. She said sullenly, "That's the *Morse* code. My name isn't even spelled like that."

Whit Winters shrugged. "Didn't say it was." He waited until she was looking at him again and then, when she was, he said, "Everybody's got their own secret code and then one day"—his grin slid up on one side—"along comes the Decoder."

That was how it all started.

Now, six months later, Lana puts her pencil lead on the line of Whit's mouth and begins to make a shadow. Tilly, who has stopped eating her granola bar and recovered the Froot Loops box from the driveway, reaches into it, rummages, and says, "I like Froot Loops and Trix, Lana. But I don't like Kix and Chex. Not really."

"Okay by me," Lana says, and sneaks a glance at the house next door. Chet's house. The blinds of Chet's bedroom are still pulled.

"Chet's a sleepyhead!" Tilly says, and Lana realizes Tilly is on to her.

"He keeps late hours," Lana says, and—does she actually hear Veronica approaching or just sense it?—she casually folds back the page on her yellow legal pad and quickly begins a crude sketch of the dust devil. A few seconds later, Veronica pushes open the screen door.

"You're lunch duty, Lana," she says.

In fact, Lana has already made the sandwiches— bologna with mayo and mustard for everyone except Carlito, who screams if you give him mustard—but she doesn't say so. She doesn't want to give Veronica the satisfaction.

"Did you hear me?" Veronica says with an edge to it.

Lana says, "I nodded, didn't I?" though she knows she didn't.

"It's bologna and cheese," Veronica says, "but we're out of cheese."

"Then it's not really bologna and cheese, is it?" Lana says. She knows it'll go on Veronica's report as bologna and cheese, or maybe ham and cheese.

"Technically, yes, it is," Veronica says. "We're just out of cheese."

Lana gives Veronica a look, but she's not going to argue. She herself wouldn't eat the cheese even if they had it, because what Veronica buys is a horrible, Velveeta-like knockoff she gets at some big-box store in Rapid City. This isn't anything unusual. Veronica's always whining about money, and Lana's noticed that Veronica makes a habit of cutting corners on the Snicks' food. Once she bought a cheap Froot Loop knockoff and put the stuff in real Froot Loop boxes, but none of the Snicks would eat it.

"And no mustard for Carlito," Veronica says, and Lana under her breath says, "Thanks for the mighty advice."

A mistake, because Veronica must've heard it. She steps out onto the porch, and when Lana glances up, Veronica's eyes are on the drawing paper.

"What is that?" she says in her cool voice, and then, "No, don't tell me, I already know. It's a pathetic doodle. But that's okay, because I'm sure that out there in the real world, there are all sorts of really great opportunities for pathetic doodlers."

"Faith," Lana says in the droning, stretched-out voice

she imagines to be in the style of a chanting Himalayan monk. "Unity."

Veronica presents a frosty smile. "What exactly is that behind your ear?" she says. "Is it a dollar bill of some kind?"

Lana says, "Of some kind, yeah."

"What denomination?"

Sullenly Lana says, "I can't recall."

Veronica's eyes brighten slightly. "Really? Isn't it a two-dollar bill? Isn't it a two-dollar bill that you unfold and hold flat in your hand when you want to feel the presence of whoever it was who was once, ever so briefly, your father?"

These are things Lana has told Whit privately and confidentially, and when they come back at her from Veronica's lips, the sensation is that of a puncture wound. How could Whit have passed these things on to her?

It's as if Veronica hears the thought, because she smiles and says, "Whit can't keep secrets from me any better than you can."

This is a typical Veronica exit line, and the screen door flaps closed behind her.

"F.U. squared," Lana says under her breath, and Tilly, who's been through this drill before, says in her happy, thick voice, "F.U. cubed!"

This produces laughs from both of them, and afterward, when it's quiet and Lana looks over at Tilly, she sees something surprising. Tilly is gazing sedately out, calm and still. From this particular angle and in this particular light, she looks pretty and normal-seeming, and Lana has the eerie feeling that she's being given a glimpse of the other Tilly, the Tilly that would've been here today if there just hadn't been the genetic bungle.

And then, abruptly, Tilly's head cocks. "I hear something, Lana. Do you hear something, Lana?"

Lana does. It's a car without a muffler, a car Lana has ridden in before and hopes to ride in again.

4.

*T*he emerald green LeSabre turning the corner and coming this way is old, enormous, and belongs to a slackly handsome boy named K.C., who at Two Rivers High is the magnet around which kids of a certain type collect. It's the type Lana has always been: not normal enough to have kids over after school, not hip or competent or confident enough for cheerleading, sports, or student government. She could tell these kids at a glance, the ones whose parents had died or gone to drugs or just plain cut and run, but in Two Rivers, when it came to weirdness, Lana is in a league of her own: she is the one who lives in a foster home for retards.

As he rolls up to Chet's house next door, K.C. leans on the LeSabre's horn, which has been tricked out for exceptional loudness.

Lana says, "There's Chet's eleven a.m. wake-up call," which might've gotten her a laugh in quicker company, but all Tilly says is, "I like Chet, Lana. Yes, sir."

"Chet's okay," Lana says. *Okay,* in her mind, is a term that slides on a loose line between bad and not so bad. Chet is a lank, straw-haired boy whose looks aren't helped by the dark bulbous mole tucked into the side fold of his nose. Last night, around two, when she went down the hall to pee, Lana looked out the hall window and saw that Chet's light was still on. Through the open windows of his upstairs room she could see him pacing, wearing earphones, and talking, or singing along, or something, because his mouth was moving. Now, though, the blinds to the two windows are shut tight. Sleeping.

This isn't the first time she's noticed Chet's pattern of staying up late and snoozing till noon. "What do you do up there in the middle of the night anyhow?" she asked him one afternoon.

Chet had given her one of his distant grins and said, "What goes on in Chet's room is between Chet and his larger public," which didn't take Lana far in terms of explanation, so she said, "What's that supposed to mean?"

Chet's gaze had drifted to the far reaches. "Chetteroids mean what we mean," he said, "but . . . we don't always dot our *i*'s."

Lana had looked exaggeratedly around and said, "You talking to me or to aliens hiding in nearby trees?"

Chet's eyes widened for a moment, and then he'd begun nodding lazily and chuckling to himself. "That's it, all right, in and out of the nutshell. The Chetster's talking to aliens hiding in nearby trees."

At which point Lana had left him to his own amusements.

K.C. leans again on the megahorn. His girlfriend, Trina, is sitting sideways on the front seat with her back against the passenger door. Trina has dyed red hair that she wears with bangs that make a perfectly straight line across her forehead. She goes in big for jewelry: rings for her ears, nose, toes, and fingers and brightly colored fake jewel necklaces that draw attention to her cleavage and creamy white skin. ("You have to admit," Chet once said of Trina to Lana, "her breasts *are* majestic." To which Lana responded that she didn't have to admit anything.) When Lana first enrolled at Two Rivers High, Trina was so obviously the queen of the outsiders that Lana expected—hoped for—kinship. For a while, Lana even tried big jewelry, but the only thing Trina ever said to her was, "I have a cousin who was raped by a retard. I'd be scared shitless if I was you."

Poking up behind Trina and K.C. is somebody else's head. Probably Spink, is Lana's guess, based on the gelled, vertical do. He'd dyed it white a while back and now, with the brown roots growing out, the stiffened hair looks like porcupine quills.

Next door, the blinds on the upstairs window go up and Chet pops his head out to say he'll be right down. He's been asleep, all right—his hair is sticking up in ways even more than normally weird.

Lana folds her tablet closed and hands it to Tilly. "Stay here," she says. "I'm gonna check this out."

As she approaches the car, she sees that Trina has her ringed toes in K.C.'s lap, her knees bent so her short skirt has nowhere to go but up. Spink is on the far side of the backseat staring out through the slits of his bulgy, half-closed eyes. Nobody even looks at Lana, and Lana doesn't ask any questions because she knows they won't answer her. They have a policy.

K.C. leans on the horn one more time (it really is

loud—Lana would cover her ears if it weren't such a nerdy move), and Chet comes out in an unbuttoned shirt carrying his comb and smokes and wallet in his hands. He passes on Lana's right, so she gets a good view of the mole ballooning from the crease of his nose. He gets right into the backseat opposite Spink without even asking where they're going. On the theory, Lana supposes, that anyplace is better than here. A theory she believes in herself.

"Can I come, too?" Lana says to Chet, and Chet says to K.C., "Lana wants to come."

This is the procedure. K.C. and Trina and Spink won't talk to Lana, but Chet, because he's her next-door neighbor and sometime friend, will, so he acts as the go-between.

K.C. says, "Who's Lana? You mean Foster?"

Foster, as in foster kid.

"Yeah," Chet says. "She wants to come."

K.C. glances at Trina, who gives a who-cares shrug and says, "Trunk only, though."

"Tell her okay," K.C. says, "but trunk only." He leans forward to punch the trunk release. The trunk door springs open.

Spink says in a monotone, "The LeSabre's capacious trunk accommodates all your cargo needs."

Lana looks at the trunk—empty except for a couple of old cushions she's never seen before—and says, "When can I ride in the seat?"

Chet repeats the question to K.C., who says, "When she grows tits," which gets a good snort from Trina, and Lana's face burns. She tries to remember what Whit told her once—that thin girls stay pretty longer, that the Trina types turn into Pillsbury doughgirls—but it doesn't help much. She thinks of saying, *F.U., K.C., and your slutty buddies, too,* but the truth is, she believes that even if K.C. and his friends are scummy, they at least have a look of their own and they stick close, and Chet is okay, so maybe if she pays her dues, they'll see she's got something to offer and let her into their creepy club, so she just stands glaring at Chet's nose mole, which always makes him self-conscious.

"I threw in some cushions the other day," he says. "To make it a little softer in there."

Lana glances at the frayed and faded red cushions—patio discards, without a doubt—and says, "Thanks heaps."

From inside the car Spink says, "How 'bout we move on dot-com?"

"Tell her she's got five seconds to get in," K.C. says. "This train's leaving the station."

Lana runs halfway to the porch and says to Tilly, "Lunch is all made, it's in the refrigerator, and if Veronica asks, I went to the library," then she runs back and climbs into the trunk. When Chet comes around to close it, he looks at her and his eyes go gentle and he whispers what he always whispers.

"Don't worry, okay?"

Then he closes the trunk tight.

5.

*I*t's hot in the trunk, but not so much once you get moving, and otherwise it's not bad. It's roomy enough, and the cushions actually help with the sharp corners. It's true the trunk is pitch-black, and it gives off an oily smell, but there isn't any oil or grease that actually gets on you, and if K.C. plays the music loud enough, you can hear it through the backseat.

Lana has been out with K.C. and the others maybe a dozen times, and the drives always divide into two types. Either they're out to break into a house and steal stuff (Spink calls this "a wealth redistribution action") or they're just out cruising. Lana can tell which it'll be by the way K.C. drives. If it's a break-in day, he stays on the surface streets, slow-driving, checking out houses from a list they buy from a paperboy telling the addresses of people gone on vacation.

Lana doesn't like the housebreaking stuff, but there's one part of it she doesn't mind. K.C., Spink, and Trina are the ones who actually go in and bring the goods out, while Chet walks up and down the street with a cell phone in his pocket so he can give the others a quick heads-up if anyone shows at the house. When Lana's along, she walks with Chet, but it looks funny, them just walking up and down the street like stiffs, so on one of their first times doing it, Lana said, "It'd be better if we looked like a couple or something," and Chet said, "What do you mean?" and Lana said, "Well, we could just hold hands or something," which is what they'd done, and is something she now more or less looks forward to, not that she'd say so to Chet.

Today, it turns out, they're just cruising—Lana can feel the car wheeling onto Highway 20, picking up speed. If Chet and the others talk loud enough, Lana can hear what they're saying, which can be interesting in a secret-agent kind of way, but on the highway the road noise swallows up most of the conversation. Up front, they're passing a hash pipe—a trace of its sharp smell seeps into the trunk—and Lana hopes it won't soak into her clothes and hair because Veronica has the nose of a police dog. In another way, though, she's relieved. These trips are aimless. Chet and the others just get on the highway and smoke their stuff and drive until they find something that in their altered state they think is worth stopping for— someone painting a WELCOME TO LAKE LITTLETON highway sign with five-foot-high ducks gliding onto the water, for example, or a livestock truck unloading old horses at a rendering plant (which K.C. and Spink, in particular, found hilarious). Usually, though, they will drive an hour or two or even more before stopping at all, most often for food.

Suddenly the car slows enough for Lana to hear Trina say, "Whoa, check it out! That's one maximum dust devil," and Spink adds, "Or one mini-tornado."

Chet in his stretched-out voice says, "Let's follow that dudester to wherever it takes us."

The LeSabre lurches right and Lana's head and shoulders thump against the side of the wheel well as the car slides down onto a dirt road. Gravel pops the undercarriage. Lana wishes she were somewhere else, even Bible camp, which was where one of her mother's boyfriends was always joking about sending her.

"You better crank it," Trina yells. "That sucker's *moving!*"

The car bounces down the road and in the trunk Lana's whole body feels like chattering teeth. "Hey!" she yells. "Slow down!" but nobody hears.

Finally the car slows slightly and she hears K.C. say, "Where's it at?"

They're all quiet and Lana thinks maybe they've come to their senses, but then Trina says, "Thataway, buckaroo—by the butte!" and the car races off again, Trina laughing like an idiot and shouting, "Ride 'em, cowboy!"

To keep from bouncing around, Lana pushes against one end of the trunk with her legs and against the other end with her hands. It helps, but it's tiring, and she's about to give out when the car slows again and in the relative quiet she hears K.C. say, "We lost it."

The car moves slowly ahead and then Trina says, "Anyone know where we are?"

Spink says something that has "uncharted territory" in it, which makes K.C. peevish. "No, I mean it. Does anyone know where we are?"

Chet seems amused. "In the hinterlands is where we are."

After a silence, Spink says, "There are weeds growing in the road. I don't think there are weeds growing in your well-traveled roads."

K.C. says there are weeds growing out of every crack in Spink's brain, and Lana has to laugh.

Up front, Trina says, "There's a sign that says Hereford that way, eleven-point-two miles."

Spink says, "How do we feel about the practice of installing mileage signs for upcoming cows?"

After a second or two, Chet says, "I call it badly thought out." Then: "I mean, what if the cow decides to *move*?"

Lana smells the sulfur smell of lighted matches followed by the more intense smell of burning hashish and the riders fall quiet. The car turns and climbs onto a slightly smoother dirt road. Lana runs a hand over her body, searching the sore spots for blood, but finds only the tenderness that she supposes will turn to bruise. She scooches the patio cushion up behind her and makes herself comfortable. There is the low drone of the car rolling along the road, the occasional tick of gravel on metal beneath her. Otherwise there is nothing to hear, nothing to see, nothing to do, nothing to think. She feels again the pleasant emptiness she'd felt after the dust devil swept over her this morning.

She yawns and yawns again.

Then she is asleep.

6.

*D*oors slam.

Lana's eyes shoot open.

The car has stopped; the engine is off.

This is the worst part. Trina would never let her out—she wouldn't give Lana the satisfaction—and K.C. and Spink never give Lana a thought, so it's up to Chet, and one time he forgot for a few minutes, which threw Lana into a screaming-kicking-sobbing panic, so now, whenever they stop and the engine falls quiet, she screams, "Chet! Chet! Chet!" until he opens the trunk.

"Okay, okay," he says today when he pops the trunk open.

The light is harsh. Lana climbs out and straightens herself and looks blinkingly around. She feels sweaty. Wet hair sticks to her forehead. A half block away, in a patch of grass installed in the middle of the wide main street, a brown and white cow stands staring forward. It isn't moving. "Is that a statue of a *cow*?" she says.

"Welcome to the historic town of Hereford," Chet says, "a town named in honor of a large and not-smart animal."

Beyond him, all Lana sees is another deserted podunk town, except this one seems even more deserted and more podunk than the rest. "Whose mighty idea was this?" she says.

Chet, grinning, says, "Trina's, mostly. She said she felt the urgent need for a cheeseburger, and hey, if you can't find a cheeseburger in a town called Hereford . . ."

Lana looks at the boarded-up movie theater and the silent shops and wonders about that. Two Rivers is small and a bit on the shabby side, but at least you saw people walking in and out of the grocery store.

Chet starts off in the direction of Spink, K.C., and Trina, who are already far down the block, but then he turns and says halfheartedly, "Wanna come?"

He knows she won't. It's not that great sitting at a table with people who have a rule against talking to you, for one thing, and for another, all she's got is small change. (That's the norm with Lana. Sometimes when K.C. and Trina get tired of calling her Foster, they call her Unfunded Foster.) "Naw, you go ahead," she says, and Chet slides off to catch up with the others.

Lana notices the LeSabre is the only car parked on the entire street and yells, "Tell K.C. that was staunch luck finding such a fine parking space."

Staunch is a word one of her mother's boyfriends used—Lana didn't like the boyfriend, but she likes the word. She thinks it's funny, but almost nobody else does, so it's a nice surprise when Chet throws a grin back over his shoulder.

As he walks off, Lana realizes the two-dollar bill isn't behind her left ear and feels a surge of panic until she sees it lying there in the trunk, unrolled and flattened. This isn't the first time she's done this in her sleep—unrolled and flattened the bill, then lost track of it in the blankets—

and she often awakens afterward with a vague sense of dreaming of her father. Today she can't find the little rubber band she uses to bind the rolled bill, but she always keeps a spare in her pocket (they're orthodontic rubber bands—she pocketed a whole handful in a dentist's office a few years before and they've lasted ever since).

Lana rolls the bill tightly, secures it with a new band, and tucks it behind her ear. Then she looks around. Chet and the others have disappeared from view, and no one else is out and about. Except for heat vapors rising from the blacktop, nothing moves.

Lana crosses to the shady side and walks along with the idea of window-shopping, but there isn't much to see. There's a post office, a craft store, a barbershop, a feed store, and a defunct market. One scrawled sign in an insurance office says, *Gone to Town Picnic,* and after that Lana starts noticing yellow flyers announcing the Hereford Roundup and Barbecue, Live Music & Boat Races, Main Bower at Lake McElheny.

Lana turns the corner and heads away from downtown, scuffing her shoes across the fine dirt of an alley where a cat watches her from a trash can lid with such blandness that Lana points a finger and says, "Bang." The cat pulls its paws under its white fur, unimpressed, and Lana walks on.

At the corner of First Street, an old stone hitching post sticks crookedly out of the grass, and Lana sees that the houses here are old, high-peaked, and handsome, with wide porches and massive doors. It's the sort of street her mother used to drive them along when she had a car and enough gas, a good street for playing the House Game. In the House Game, you looked over the contenders. You considered size, color, and features. Then you settled on the one you were going to buy just as soon as it came on the market. Her mother always picked one with a sun-porch full of wicker and potted plants. Lana always picked one that had bicycles, sleds, or baseball equipment strewn on the yard and driveway, as if the sale of the house would include children.

The houses on First Street both cheer and depress Lana. The yards are green, there are flowers here and there, and in one front yard a beach ball floats in a blue wader pool. Beyond the little pool is a porch with enormous wavy glass windows, and sure enough, inside it, among the potted plants, there rests an empty wicker love seat, the sort she knows now her mother was never even close to owning.

Lana crosses the street to get away from the house and finds herself in front of a green-roofed Victorian with two, maybe three floors, the topmost roof crowned with iron filigree and lightning rods. The porch is open to the weather, not glassed in, and it has two wooden rocking chairs on it, turned slightly so that if two ghosts were sitting there, they could speak. Lana puts her hand on the little curlicue iron gate that's attached to a curlicue iron fence. Somebody has the right to open it, walk up the sandstone steps, and plop down in the rocking chair, then open the carved wooden door to what is probably a carved wooden staircase. Somebody does that every day, she thinks, and probably never considers that it's anything special.

A dog's bark carries from down the street, and a squirrel whisks here and there on the front lawn. Worked into the iron swirls on the gate is the capital letter *H*.

Lana lets go of the gate, then walks on past a white cottage, a blue two-story, a yellow house that is plainly the one with the fun mom (sports gear everywhere), and a plain white corner house, from which she can see downtown again. The emerald green LeSabre's still parked alone on the street, but Chet and the others are nowhere in sight. Lana puts her hands in her pockets and is walking back to Main Street, wondering what to do next, when she sees something reflected in the window of the insurance office, a movement in the shop across the street, and she turns for a better look.

It's an upstairs shop, and hanging from the roof eave above its door is a wooden sign that says MISS HEKKITY'S ODDMENTS & ANTIQUES. Below that, in crackled gilt lettering, it says,

WHAT YOU DESIRE
MISS HEKKITY PROVIDES

And here's something. There, in the window where Lana thought she'd seen a moving shadow, an OPEN sign has appeared.

7.

"*H*ello?" Lana says once she's climbed the outside stairs and stepped into the shop, but no one answers. Sun shines through the windows, but the lights in the shop are off. Much of the shop is dim, and the corners are dark. "Hello?"

Nothing.

"Miss Hekkity? Anybody?" For no good reason, she imagines Miss Hekkity as someone young and pretty, like her kindergarten teacher, Miss Marsh.

No reply.

Lana fingers her two-dollar bill and stands adjusting to the dimness. In the center of the store, the glass cases are full of family artifacts—engraved sports trophies, felt pennants, awards for school achievements. Around the edges of the shop, antique furnishings have been arranged in a semblance of tiny, packed rooms. In the nearest one, a blue-and-white-painted doll crib holds a stained Raggedy Ann beside a miniature aqua high chair, a rocking horse, and a display of hand-smocked dresses. Beside that, a crazy quilt covers a red wooden spool bed just big enough for Lana to lie down on, an idea that Lana has to resist, it seems so welcoming.

Lana goes idly from one tiny roomlike space to the next, picking things up, putting them down. What always makes Lana wonder are the things people are willing to leave behind. There are awards and ribbons and old books with personal notes written inside (on the title page of one, someone had written, *See p. 131 for hiccup cure,* and another book was inscribed, *To Jamesy, Papa's Little Lump of Love*). Lana wonders what happened to the girl named Betty Jean Coker who took home the second-place award from her sixth-grade spelling bee or to the person whose rabbit won a blue ribbon at the 1954 Dawes County Fair. Lana is holding a soft green felt pennant bought by somebody to commemorate a trip to Banff National Park when suddenly a voice close behind her says, "Find what you're looking for?"

Lana turns, and a single overhead lamp suddenly illuminates the woman who, by means of a string pull, has just turned it on. She isn't young and tall, like Miss Marsh in kindergarten. She is small, thin, and old, her face wrinkled like tissue paper that's been folded and unfolded many times. Her white hair is cut short to frame her face, like it might have been cut when she was five, ten, twenty, and forty. She wears plain girlish clothes: a gray cardigan with enormous buttons, a white blouse with a round collar, and navy blue pants. But her shoes are a surprise, red leather, definitely stylish, the kind of shoes Lana hasn't seen on the feet of many small-town shopkeepers. And behind her glasses, her eyes are keen and kindly and a beautiful luminous blue.

The woman had been knitting—she holds four short wooden needles linked by red yarn—but now she waits patiently for Lana's reply.

"I like everything," Lana says. "I'm just looking, though."

The woman, resuming her knitting, seems slightly amused. "That's what they all say."

For some reason this annoys Lana. "Well, the reason I say it is I'm fresh out of loot."

The woman's expression doesn't change at all. It's as if she hears, but doesn't hear. Lana sees that what's emerging from the knitting needles is a mitten, a really big mitten. Gigantic, even. The woman shifts the stitches along one needle with her index finger and seems to count. A silence develops, and Lana notices a neatly printed poem taped to the back of the cash register:

> Borrow from your father
> Borrow from your mother
> The price you see
> Is the price it be
> Don't ask me for another
> —Miss Hekkity

Not that this matters to Lana. She wouldn't be buying anything unless the label said FREE.

Lana says, "How come nobody's home in this town?"

The woman barely looks up from her knitting. "Town picnic."

"And everybody goes?"

"Just about. There's a cranky old misanthrope named Friedrich who doesn't. He keeps his café open every day of the year."

"Every day?"

"Every day." The knitting needles keep moving, *click click click.* "There are a few of us who live alone and are grateful for a place to go on Thanksgiving or New Year's. He does German dishes." The woman smiles to herself. "I'm one of a small group of Americans who actually associates Thanksgiving with potato pancakes and wurst."

Lana picks up a tea towel that has a cluster of cherries and the word *Tuesday* stitched into it with cheerful red embroidery floss. "How come you don't go to the town picnic?" she says, and then without thinking it through, she adds, "Are you cranky, too?"

The woman laughs a surprising laugh. It's quick, bright, *young*-sounding. "Not *too* cranky, I hope."

But the woman doesn't answer the question, so Lana says, "I guess you don't like the picnic, then?"

"I used to go," the woman says, and her expression seems to dry up and hollow out and her voice, too. "I just didn't feel like it this year." She glances down at the jumbo mitten she's knitting and seems to be deciding whether to go on explaining or not.

She goes on.

"Last year," she says in the same dry, hollow voice, "I was taking care of someone who was fond of the picnic. My nephew, actually. He looked forward to it every summer, especially the boat races. He liked to cheer them on. He'd pick his favorite on the basis of color. If there was a red one, he'd always root for that. Then a little committee came to ask me if I could keep him home. They said some mothers had complained that he was dangerous, that he scared their children. They said they hoped I would understand and wouldn't be offended."

Lana's guessing the nephew is a Snick or has AIDS, one or the other. "What happened?" she asks.

"Well, I *didn't* understand, and I *was* offended. I had to lie to my nephew and say it was canceled. But he saw the boats on people's trailers, headed out of town. He saw the flyers. He may have been different, but he wasn't an idiot."

So he's a Snick, or at least was, Lana thinks. "What do you mean, *wasn't?*"

The woman hitches her chin a half inch. "He died a few months ago of heart failure. In March. He was fifty-two." She looks off toward the line of windows facing the street. "His father died about six years ago, and then his mother passed, and no one else in the family wanted him." Something touches the woman's face, Lana can see it, some soft touch of a hand no longer there. "His name was Quinn," she says.

"I'm sorry," Lana says. She could say more, but something keeps her from telling the woman about Tilly and the rest. Maybe it's because she knows in her bones there's a difference. She doesn't mind the Snicks, sometimes she even halfway likes them, but she can tell that this woman's feelings for her nephew went way beyond liking and Lana isn't sure her feelings for the Snicks go beyond liking, or ever will. So Lana just says she's sorry and waits.

"Well," the woman says, picking up her yarn to wrap and knit again, her voice again composed. "What would you be looking for if you weren't . . . fresh out of *loot?*"

"Sometimes I like old photograph albums," Lana says, and the woman nods and says, "Well, look around to your heart's content. Sometimes people find what they're looking for."

Lana wanders down the aisle, staring into the little rooms with all the wares on display—shaving brushes, class rings, hat pins, thimbles, commencement programs, perfume bottles, ribbons for prize Herefords. The rooms are so full of abandoned things that Lana feels a strange kind of longing to move into them. There is everything a person would need to live here: beds, quilts, lamps, pots, dishes, even clothes, all of them smaller than modern things and more fragile, as if the people who owned them were a different people altogether, smaller, simpler, more careful with their things. Until of course they outlived them, and others found them useless and sold them or gave them away or just left them where they lay when they closed the door for the last time.

Lana kneels to look through a box of women's clothing, white cotton chemises and petticoats and drawers, inset with lace and layered with dust. She holds up a full-length gown—it is far too short—and when she glances back toward the register, the woman quickly looks down at her knitting, a dead giveaway that she's been watching, not that Lana cares. She folds the gown and sets it aside.

And then, at the bottom of the stack of clothes, under a heavy wool skirt, Lana sees something: three wide, flat black boxes covered with black leather, pebbly yet soft to the touch. Her hand is drawn to the box at the bottom, and with that first touch a sudden expectant feeling moves through her.

She slides the box from beneath the other two and turns a tag that's been strung from a side-buttoning flap. In tiny print it says,

Ladies Drawing Kit
$2

She unsnaps the side flap, and as she lays open the cover of the box, a pleasant musty smell blooms into the air. Lana feels light-headed, and then that same pleasant hopefulness she'd felt earlier in the day comes over her again.

The loose sheets of paper are thick, coarse, even, with particles of red and pink embedded in them, and Lana loves the feel as she lifts one and runs her palm across its surface. Something is embossed along the top of each one, and when she holds the paper to the light, *Morpheus & Co., St. Louis, Missouri* appears as an imprinted shadow. The set comes with a bundle of sharpened charcoal pencils, tied with a leather thong.

It is truly beautiful paper, more beautiful than anything Lana has ever seen, and though she's not especially acquisitive or covetous by nature, these sheets of paper take hold of her and don't let go. She wants them. She wants them more than she's ever wanted any object in her entire life.

Except she can't pay for even one box of the paper.

She thinks of stealing one, but the old woman is just down the aisle, knitting for the world's largest human, and besides, the woman's never done anything to her.

But Lana can't set the box of paper down. It's under her arm. It's meant to be hers. It feels like hers.

And then a sudden thought: *Borrow from your father, borrow from your mother.*

Lana touches the two-dollar bill rolled behind her ear.

She goes to the cash register and sets the drawing kit beside it.

She unrolls the two-dollar bill worn soft as cloth. *I'll come back,* Lana thinks. *I'll pay now and then come back with two dollars and exchange it,* an idea she explains to the old woman. "Could I do that?" Lana says.

The woman looks at the bill with her keen and young-seeming blue eyes, then shifts her knitting to one hand and slides the bill under the cash drawer within the register. "I don't see why not," she says.

It's not a foolproof plan—and Lana knows it—but it's enough of a plan that she can savor the pleasure of knowing this leather case and the paper inside it is hers. Not somebody else's to look at or even somebody else's to borrow, but hers.

Hers.

The woman's blue eyes are on her. "I'm glad you came in," she says, and Lana can tell she means it.

"Me too," Lana says.

"Come back now that you know the way. Your two-dollar bill will be waiting."

Lana says good-bye, but something occurs to her as she reaches the door, and she turns back. "You are Miss Hekkity, right?"

The woman smiles at the question. "I am indeed."

And then Lana has one last question. "So, are those mittens you're making for the Jolly Green Giant?"

"No," Miss Hekkity says, laughing. It's the laugh Lana likes most. It's a laugh that makes her feel amusing. The old woman holds up the mitten and regards it. "They're not going to be as big as they look now," she says. "At least, I hope not. The pattern tells you to wash them afterward so they'll felt up tight and not let the snow in."

Lana thinks this is going to be all, but then Miss Hekkity says, "They're for the nephew I told you about. I was making them for him, and he died before I could finish. I couldn't even look at them for a while, then about a week ago I picked them up and I had a very strong feeling that he would've wanted me to finish them and give them away. He was always giving things away. 'Here,' he would say, sometimes to perfect strangers. 'Take this free.' " She smiles. "Once he gave a set of my prize china thimbles to a little girl down the street, and by the time I caught up with her, she was using them as seats for a mouse's tea party and I couldn't bear to ask for them back." Miss Hekkity stares off toward the windows that overlook the street. "Sometimes I thought Quinn was turning my life upside down, making a complete chaos of it, but now I think he was just trying to *reorganize* it." The blueness in the woman's eyes gleams as she turns to Lana. "I mean, which is the better place for a set of china thimbles—gathering dust in a curio cabinet or providing seating at a mouse's tea party?"

Lana knows this isn't a question meant to be answered. "Bye," she says softly, and Miss Hekkity says, "Thank you, and come back," and her gaze drifts again to the windows.

Lana is halfway down the wooden stairs with the Ladies Drawing Kit under her arm when she hears hard raucous laughter from somewhere on the street and then, ahead, between two buildings, she sees K.C. streak by. Lana hurries out to the walk and nearly collides with Chet, who's loping along and doesn't stop.

"C'mon," he yells back, and his face seems a strange mix of excitement and fear. "We're being run out of town!"

Following Chet are Spink and Trina, who's holding her breasts to keep them from jouncing so much, and although Spink's face is its usual blank, Trina's is manic with merriment. "Little Betty coming through!" she yells.

Lana has no clue what this might mean, but Trina finds it hilarious, and even Spink breaks out a reptilian grin.

Behind them, maybe fifty yards up the walk, an old man half trots, half stumbles after them wearing a big white apron and waving a piece of paper. His face is red and bulging with anger, and he's yelling so loud and fast that it seems like a foreign language and then Lana realizes it *is* a foreign language. The red-faced man is shouting in German. No translation is needed. It's like the buzz of an angry hornet.

A sound from the other direction: K.C. has started the LeSabre, and Chet is opening the doors.

Lana takes one last look at the old man—his red face seems about to burst into flame—then she turns and sprints off to the car as fast as her legs will take her. She's the last one there, and she knows it's only because Chet stands outside the car waiting with the door open that K.C. doesn't just drive away.

Chet steps aside, she jumps into the backseat, and, before Chet is fully in beside her, K.C. has the car squealing and fishtailing down Main Street, past all the locked-up shops, past the statue of the giant Hereford, and out of town.

8.

*U*p front, K.C. drives, grins, and occasionally whoops. The car is loud with excited accounts of their experience— from which Lana learns that the old man who chased them is the very same Friedrich who keeps his café open every day of the year and who Miss Hekkity called a misanthrope and who, today, while serving them cheeseburgers, fries, and lemon Cokes, kept sliding glances at Trina's cleavage and talking about someone called Little Betty, who, he said, "was big in the *Büstenhalter*" and was "the kind of Fräulein who keeps Herr Doktor jolly." Friedrich didn't go away either. He kept hovering close and saying weirder and weirder things to Trina like, "Little Betty knows all about it, don't you?—all about the big bouncy *Büste?*" and Trina kept saying, "She does, she surely does," and then when they all finished eating, Trina went to the bathroom in the back and came out in a rush yelling that there was a live kangaroo rat in the ladies' room and when the old German went back to investigate was when K.C. and the rest of them all ran for it.

"I didn't stiff old Friedrich," Trina says. "Little Betty did." Which gets a laugh from everybody in the car except Lana, and so does Trina's mere repetition of *big in the*

Büstenhalter or *the kind of Fräulein who keeps Herr Doktor happy.*

"I thought you said *jolly,*" Lana says, the first words she's spoken, and all at once Trina swivels her eyes to the backseat. "What?"

Lana says, "I thought you said he said Little Betty was the kind of fräulein who keeps the doctor *jolly.* Not keeps him *happy.*"

As she stares at Lana, Trina's pupils shrink to small stones. She says, "Chet, you better tell Foster that if she forgets the policy again, we're stopping the car and she's taking the long walk home."

Lana glances outside. It's hot, and there isn't a cloud in the sky or a tree within miles.

Chet nods but doesn't speak.

"Tell her," Trina says in a seething voice, and Chet does.

Then, from up front, not loud, but loud enough to hear, Trina says, "Jesus. No wonder nobody wants to be around her."

A minute passes in silence, and it's clear that the party mood has slipped from the car and isn't coming back anytime soon. Trina gives Lana one last withering look, then lays her head in K.C.'s lap and curls for a nap, and before long a kind of communal sleepiness overtakes the car. Spink, in the back at Lana's left, leans against the door and is soon asleep. On Lana's right, Chet stares ahead with drooping eyelids. Up front, K.C. yawns and leans forward over the wheel. Occasionally he gives his head a quick shake to keep from nodding off.

"You okay up there?" Chet says.

K.C. in no way acknowledges the question. The car drones on.

Chet says, "You going to fall asleep and kill us all before we're grown?"

K.C.'s eyes rise heavily to the rearview mirror. "The front-seat passengers would be a loss to society, the backseat assholes not so much."

Chet shakes his head and gives Lana a sleepy, amiable shrug. In a low voice, he says, "So what's in the box?"

Lana glances down at the leather box lying across her lap. "Something called a Ladies Drawing Kit."

Chet leans over, and Lana opens the box to give him a look.

"Nice," he says. "Wha'd you pay for it?"

Lana thinks of the two-dollar bill. "Too much, probably."

There's a moment of quiet, and Chet says, "That guy Friedrich scared me."

Lana is dubious. "He looked about a hundred and four."

Chet shook his head. "I don't know. He was really creepy, and then when he was yelling at us and so mad he could hardly make words, he reminded me of Donald Duck."

Lana considers this. "Donald Duck scares you?"

"Oh, yeah, totally. When I was little, whenever the Donald started going off on somebody, I'd have to hide." He pauses. "My personal feeling is that duck could use some anger management training."

Lana looks at him for a few seconds and says, "Chet, you're not a normal thinker."

Chet's expression loosens. "That's a compliment, right?"

"A person who thinks like you do might think so."

Chet nods sleepily and shifts a little so he can lean into his door. Lana wants to tell him where she got the drawing kit and how she paid for it, but Chet's eyelids droop, flicker open, close for good.

He looks peaceful and, except for the mole beside his nose, almost handsome.

Lana slips a pencil from the bundle within the box, then removes a single sheet of paper and lays it on top. She takes a long look at Chet in silhouette, and she begins to draw.

9.

*F*rom the moment her pencil touches the paper, Lana feels improved, skilled, inspired, even. *It must be the paper,* she thinks, *or the softness of the charcoal pencil.* Her hand sweeps over the page in easy, fluid strokes. At the side of the sheet a tree takes shape, a leafy friendly tree with outstretched armlike limbs, on one of which—the one extending across the length of the page—Chet reclines, natural-seeming and cozy. Lana's hand knows where to put shadows, where to make lines. Chet's slouchy clothes take on texture and depth, his hair shoots off in every direction, and his body seems to move with the slow, subtle breathing of sleep. The line rolls into low background hills and rises into a distant water tower, then bursts into thunderclouds and a distant flash of lightning, and all at once Lana is done.

She lays the pencil down.

She blinks, inhales, exhales. Her skin is damp, her heart is pounding, and the drawing is better than anything she's done before, so much better that she can hardly believe it came from her own hand. The tree seems almost more than a tree, the sleeping figure on its outstretched limb seems more than just Chet, and the lightning-brightened countryside beyond suggests a land far, far away, and all of it, together, allows you to see the enticement of sleep.

There is only one thing wrong. In drawing Chet's left side, she's forgotten the dark mole snugged into the crease of his nose. She wonders why she's left it out, and she thinks of adding it now, but she's too tired. She'll do it later. She slides the drawing into the box and settles the box on her lap. She thinks of resting her head against Chet's arm—she wants to—but she doesn't. She crosses her arms, leans forward, and closes her eyes.

10.

*T*hip thip thip.

Lana, awakening, hears the gentle rhythm of the LeSabre's windshield wipers. *Thip thip thip.* She opens her eyes and lifts herself from Chet's shoulder. Outside, the world is dark and the rain is steady. Low thunder rumbles and, off to the north, sheet lightning throws a crackling light over distant buttes. For a moment she thinks she's somewhere else, and then she realizes that the storm they're in is much like the one she'd drawn in the background of her sketch of the sleeping Chet, which is strange, she guesses, but not that strange.

The others in the car are stirring now, slowly coming to life, looking around. "What day is this?" Chet says, and Trina says, "What's with the rain? Did any of the weather chicks predict rain?"

Spink says, "I don't think the weather chick selection process is brain-based."

Nobody laughs. Nobody offers another comment, even though this rain seems to have materialized out of nowhere, without even a hint of the usual darkening advance of black clouds. The radio's off, the windshield wipers click back and forth, back and forth. For K.C.,

Trina, and the others, the drive, the adventure, and the day are over. They're silent when they turn off the highway, and they're silent when they pull up in front of Chet's house. Chet gives the others a quick nod, then throws open the car door and ambles toward his house without any concessions to the downpour whatsoever. Whereas Lana, following him out, slams the car door closed, tucks her box under her arm, lowers her head, and runs for it.

On the porch of her house she shakes herself doglike, then looks around for a rag. She is wiping the wet from her black leather box when Tilly pushes open the front screen door.

"'Ronica wants you," Tilly says, "and she is mad!"

"Veronica's always mad," Lana says. "It's her reason for living." But after stashing her box under a chair cushion, she says, "Mad about what?"

"Dunno," Tilly says. "Something, though."

Lana glances into the lighted house and instinctively raises her left hand to touch the two-dollar bill that isn't there.

11.

*A*s Lana steps inside, Veronica is in the living room putting in a video, and when the Snicks hear this, they're drawn to the TV like metal to magnet, Tilly included. Lana glances at the screen: it's Clifford, the big red moronic dog.

"Sit," Veronica says when Lana follows her into the kitchen, and the first thing Lana notices is that there's a fire going in the wood-burning stove at one end of the kitchen. It's been raining, yes, but it's June and there's no need for a fire. Lana, seating herself at the kitchen table, finds herself staring at a sealed manila envelope propped against the napkin holder. It's unmarked, but as far as Lana's concerned, it might as well wear a label saying OMINOUS.

The fire makes a ticking noise. Veronica, tight-lipped, keeps working on dinner. She pours a huge box of generic potato flakes into a mixing bowl, adds hot water, and lets it sit. She goes into the pantry and comes out carrying a package of brownish ground meat wrapped in blood-stained butcher paper, which she lays into a bowl along with two boxes of Hamburger Helper. From a bin by the stove she breaks off a clove of garlic, lays it on a cutting board, and only when she is through mincing it does she say, "Where is it you went this morning?"

"Who says I went anywhere?" Lana says, a standard delaying tactic. She knows who said, of course—Tilly. She couldn't help it. What came into her mind went out of her mouth. Most of the time it was endearing.

Veronica measures oatmeal into a cup, then reaches for the salt and says, "You're saying you didn't leave without permission in the trunk of a boy's car?"

A sudden shift and crackle from the woodstove. "No," Lana says. "I did leave. But not in anybody's trunk and I just went to the library."

Veronica lets her eyes fall on her. "The library, you say."

Lana doesn't like lying, but she knows enough about it to know that if you're going to lie, you have to sell it. "That's right," she says in a firm voice. "The one at Tenth and G." The only library in town, actually.

"What did you check out?"

"Nothing," she says. "I just sat there at a desk along the north wall and read old newspapers."

"For five hours."

Lana glances out the window, which is slightly ajar. The rain has stopped. "It was interesting," she says. "One weird thing, though. The weather report didn't say anything about rain."

Veronica stares at her a second or two, then says in a cold, hard voice, "Open the envelope."

Lana points to the manila envelope in front of her. "This one?"

Veronica gives her a don't-play-stupid look.

Lana unclasps the envelope, tips it, and six or seven

sheets of yellow paper slide out. They are sketches of Whit. *Her* sketches of Whit.

"How . . . ," she starts to say, but stops. There is no how or why. Foster kids have no safe zones.

Veronica, all ice, says, "I thought since you were gone, I might as well tidy up your room. I noticed the high spots especially needed cleaning. Do you know what I thought when I came upon your primitive little drawings of my husband? I thought, *Well, well, well.*"

Veronica is quiet then, but there's more; Lana can feel it. There's more and it's worse.

Veronica wipes her hands on her apron and pulls a small sandwich bag from her pocket. It contains a half-dozen red capsules, which she pours onto the table. She smiles at Lana. "Familiar?"

"No."

Veronica simultaneously nods and smiles. "I found them on the same top closet shelf, right along with your little drawings of my husband."

Lana knows this is a lie. She's seen pills like these—they look like methamphetamines—but they aren't hers. "You planted them," she says.

Veronica blinks a calm blink. "Ah, *you planted them.* The familiar first line of defense for those caught red-handed. Which is what makes it so fortunate that my friend Louise happened to be here when I found them. Louise was so surprised. She said she thought you seemed like such a nice girl."

Louise, Lana knows, is a born-again who sees Veronica as a potential convert, one that, for degree of difficulty, would earn Louise more than the usual number of conversion points. In other words, Louise is the kind of person who can be easily duped.

Lana goes to the living room, pulls Tilly away from the Clifford cartoon, and leads her into the kitchen. She points at the pills. "Have you ever seen me with these pills?"

Tilly, face white, closes her eyes and shakes her head no, and Veronica laughs a harsh, derisive laugh. "Thank you, Tilly," Veronica says. "Go on back to the show now."

Tilly is happy to be set free, but she doesn't go back to the show. She carries a pink shoe box into the backyard, where Lana can see her walking back and forth on the worn, wet grass, looking for prize specimens. The window is still ajar, and Lana knows that Tilly can hear every word Veronica says.

"Let's see. Three years ago I was Citizen of the Year in this twerpy burg. Louise is the president of the Angel Society, and her husband is a church deacon. Now who do you think is the credible source here?—Louise and me, or a shoplifting, foul-talking foster kid and her little half-wit friend?"

Lana stiffens and glances toward the window. "She's not a half-wit."

Another hard laugh from Veronica. "You're right. It's more like a quarter."

Lana wants to ask why Veronica is in the foster-mothering business instead of doing something more suited to her skills, like, for just one example, becoming president of the Sizzling Bitch Society, but she just clamps her lips and watches Tilly scanning the grass, her head tucked low.

Veronica moves close to pick up the pills, then the drawings. Her hands leave behind the smell of garlic.

"These," she announces, holding out the drawings, "go into the fire."

She opens the front door to the wood-burning stove and shoves them in. For a moment Lana can see Whit's face on one of the curling sheets, and then it's turning black as Veronica closes the door.

She holds up the plastic bag of red pills. "And these will go downstate to social services with an affidavit signed by Veronica Winters and Louise Booker. If laboratory analysis shows they contain an illegal substance, you'll be getting a new address." She smiles and drops the bag into her blue purse, which she then locks into the cupboard over the fridge. "When it comes to drugs, this house has a zero-tolerance policy."

From overhead, Lana hears the sound of footsteps, hard-heeled and snappy. Then the flushing of the toilet, the running of water. Lana can tell Veronica hears it, too, because her eyes shift and her face takes on a listening stillness. Whit's been napping, Lana bets, and now he's getting ready to go out. That's his pattern.

"So what are those pills you planted in my room?" Lana says, and Veronica, snapped free of her listening, says, "What?"

"The pills you put in my room. What are they?"

"Oh. Those." A smile. "You tell me—they were in your room. Not that what you say matters. What counts is what the lab says."

Lana wonders how long this will take. With the state you never knew, but she has the feeling drug analysis goes to the front of the line.

A staccato click of quick steps on the wood stairs and then Whit breezes through the kitchen on his way out.

He's wearing a faded Huskers baseball cap, which he tips to say grinningly, "Night, ladies, using the term loosely." Then he stops at the computer set up on a desk in the corner and does some clicking. The computer has programs on it for the Snicks, but Whit mostly uses it to download sports events and radio shows that he listens to while he drives or paints houses.

"Where're you going?" Veronica says, and it secretly pleases Lana that she uses the same icy tone on Whit as she uses on her. One more thing she and Whit have in common.

Whit grabs an apple from the kitchen counter and says, "Got to see a man about a dog," then throws a wink past Veronica toward Lana.

"You're not going anywhere, Lucian Winters," Veronica says.

This affects Whit not at all. He takes a crackling bite of the green apple. "Oh, I'm going somewhere, all right," he says, and jangles his car keys. He begins to sing as he crosses the yard to the garage. "Some enchanted evening," he croons in an exaggerated, comic way, but still, it sounds pretty good, "you will meet a stranger . . ."

Lana has the sudden sensation that she is locked into a dream, a dream that goes on and on and moves easily from the real to unreal, from the house here on Cedar Street to Miss Hekkity's shop and back again, a sensation so unsettling that she pushes a fingernail into the palm of her hand until she feels actual pain. And—she runs a finger over her left ear—the two-dollar bill is gone.

So she isn't dreaming.

12.

*B*efore dusk that evening, when Veronica's in the backyard fiddling with her hollyhocks and trying to ignore the Snicks, Lana sneaks to the kitchen phone and dials Hallie's private number.

"Hallie?" she says. Over the line, Lana can hear voices, clinking sounds, the happy shrieking of children, which is strange because Lana knows Hallie doesn't have children. It was why, when Lana lived in Omaha, Hallie could occasionally take Lana to the movies, the mall, or the ice rink. "It's me, Lana," she says now into the phone.

"Ah," Hallie says in her smooth, silky voice. "It's Lana calling my private cell number . . . in the evening . . . after hours, and here I am at my niece's eighth-grade graduation party wondering, Why would Lana do that?"

Lana sighs. Hallie is friendly when being friendly is her own idea, but it's a different story when Lana's doing the calling. "Veronica planted pills in my room," she says anyway. "They look like meth."

Calmly Hallie says, "By Veronica, I'm presuming you mean Mrs. Winters?"

"Mmm." Through the window Lana watches Veronica pulling off her gloves and stepping into the garage.

"And why would Mrs. Winters plant pills in your room?"

"She says she's going to mail them to a lab downstate and have them tested and that it will be my word against hers. Hers being like God's, I guess."

"Why would she do that, Lana?"

"Because she wants to get rid of me."

Behind Hallie's silence, Lana hears something new: the low throb of dance music. She stares across the lawn at the garage. Behind the grimy garage window, Veronica seems to be getting something from a cupboard.

Hallie says, "Why would Mrs. Winters want to get rid of you?"

Because she thinks I've got the wild eye for her husband, Lana thinks, but what she says is, "I have no clue."

Hallie doesn't respond. Outside, Veronica emerges from the garage with a handful of bamboo stakes and a ball of twine, but they wouldn't've come from the cupboard. Lana pulls hard on the stretchy coil of phone cord. "Hallie?" she says. "You still there?"

Hallie says quietly, "If she just wanted you out of there, all she would have to do is file a five-day notice with us. Which means that if what you're saying is true, she not only wants you gone but wants you gone *with cause.*"

"Which means?"

"That you've regally ticked her off for some reason."

For some reason seems to hang suspended in the silence between them.

Outside, Veronica looks at the sky, then the street, then her watch. *Whit,* Lana thinks. *Veronica's worried about Whit.* And what she's doing to Lana is just one patch in the blanket she wants to wrap around Whit.

These are strange, alarming thoughts and Lana says with sudden vehemence, "So what are you going to do about this shit?"

"If I hear another vulgarity," Hallie says evenly, "I will hang up," and Lana knows she will, so she says in a softer voice, "Well?"

"Let's see if anything goes to the state lab. Then we'll go from there."

Lana says, "That sounds like a mighty plan."

"Cynicism is not a winning quality, Lana." Then, "Fortunately, I know that behind the cynicism, there's an endearing young woman of whom I'm fond."

Lana doesn't speak, and after a second or two, Hallie says, "Lana, you'll have to excuse me, but I've just been asked to dance by a young man too handsome to refuse."

After one last look out the window—Garth is sitting morosely against the fence, twisting Popeye's head, and Veronica is tying a drooping purple flower stalk to a bamboo rod—Lana tiptoes through the house to the front porch, but the minute she gets to the porch and slides her hand under the chair cushion to remove the drawing kit, Tilly comes to find her, the old shoe box in her hand, her fingernails grubby from scavenging. Her interest in the kit is immediate. "That yours, Lana?" she says in her thick voice.

Lana nods.

"Where'd you get it?"

"A shop."

"Good," Tilly says with finality.

It's warm out, but the setting sun makes everything seem beautiful and benign. The crickets are at it—laying down a dense reassuring track of sibilant sound.

"Did you find anything in the grass?"

"You bet," Tilly says, and shows Lana a plastic square that Lana guesses used to close up a bag of bread. It's faded enough to be pink.

"Good color," Lana says.

Tilly says, "How come 'Ronica wants to get you a new dress?"

Lana turns. "What?"

"She said she'd get you a new dress."

This makes no sense at all, and then suddenly it does. "No, Tilly, she said she was going to get me a new *address*, not a new dress. She wants to send me somewhere else."

Tilly looks stricken. "When?"

Lana shrugs. "I don't know."

Tilly holds tightly to the bread fastener.

"Don't worry," Lana says quickly. "I'm not going anywhere. Veronica's just trying to scare me." Then she says what she wants to believe. "Whit won't let it happen."

Tilly seems satisfied with this, and then her face hardens. "'Ronica's the devil!" she says, and Lana has to laugh, but the devil doesn't seem like quite the right type for Veronica.

"More like Ms. Blizzard," Lana says.

She opens the flat leather box, slides out a piece of paper, and takes a pencil in hand. She gazes off for a moment or two and then, all at once, her hand begins to move across the page as before—easily, fluidly—and in perhaps two minutes the living line has created someone who both is and isn't Veronica, an icy, epic figure on her own ledge of a sheer frozen cliff, comfortable in the cold, happy with it, in fact, her white body wrapped in blankets of snow parted to show her creamy cleavage, and then the living line surrounds and shades a quiver of dartlike icicles that she tosses down at ant-sized humans who, in the valley below, run for their lives. . . .

A sudden, sharp tapping.

Lana blinks. She's glazed with sweat—it's as if she's been suddenly returned from hard labor under a hot sun. She turns. A foot away, on the other side of a window, Veronica stares out at her with eyes that seem about to explode. And then she disappears for a moment before bolting through the screen door and onto the wooden porch.

"How dare you?" she says through clenched teeth.

"How dare me what?" Lana says, and as she looks at Veronica, it registers that she's changed out of her gardening clothes into heeled sandals with tight black pants and an open shirt over a tight, stretchy top. Definitely not her house clothes.

"How dare you do *that*," Veronica says, pointing at the drawing. "It's me. It's me made ugly."

"No, it's not. It's Ms. Blizzard. The jolly Ice Queen." She turns to Tilly. "Right?"

Tilly nods. "You bet. 'Ronica the Ice Queen."

"It's not Veronica," Lana says quickly, but when she looks at the drawing, she knows it's a lost cause. The fierce frozen eyes are Veronica's eyes and the thin bluish lips are Veronica's lips.

"Erase it," Veronica says.

Lana gives an okay-okay shrug and reaches for the eraser. Veronica unzips her little beaded party bag, checks for something inside, rezips it.

It is during the rezipping that Lana thinks something important: *If she's taking her beaded party bag, she won't be taking the blue purse. And the pills are in the purse.*

Lana says, "You going somewhere?"

Veronica ignores this. "Every line of it," she says. "Erase every line of it."

Lana starts with a hand and is working her way up the Ice Queen's quiver-holding arm when a car pulls up to the curb. It's Louise and her church deacon husband. They're wearing their Snick-tending clothes—white sneakers, creased unfaded jeans, and T-shirts—and they've got their little bag of *VeggieTales* videos for doing the Lord's work on the disabled.

So Veronica's definitely going out.

"Where're you going?" Lana says.

Veronica doesn't answer. She walks out to meet Louise and her husband on the front lawn, where they talk briefly before Veronica departs.

Lana stops erasing. She's almost to the Ice Queen's elbow.

"Hi, Leeze," Tilly says. "Hi, Marvin. Did you bring Bob the Tomato?"

"Yes, Tilly, we did," Louise says. Bob the Tomato is the funny one in *VeggieTales*, and, Lana has to admit it, Bob can be funny.

"So where's Veronica going?" Lana says to Louise's husband, but it's Louise who answers. "I believe she said she was meeting her husband for dinner."

"Well, that's a good one," Lana says. "Because her husband left two hours ago and wouldn't say where he was going. I heard Veronica ask him."

"Oh," Louise says airily. "He probably called."

"I suppose you're right, but then if he called, you might think the phone would've rung."

"I imagine it was prearranged, then," Louise says. "Some

kind of little secret." She lets her eyes settle on Lana. "It's one of those aspects of matrimony you'll learn someday— the tender little secrets between a wife and her husband." Louise glances at her husband. "Am I right, Marvin?"

Marvin nods, and Lana wants to say, *You don't talk much, do you, Marv?* but instead she turns to Louise and says, "You've got a point there, Louise, and I don't mean the one on your noggin," and lets loose a big laugh to make it seem like just a joke and nothing more, no offense intended, none whatsoever.

They both stare at her, and then Louise manufactures the stiffest smile Lana has ever seen and says, "Jesus' forgiveness is roomy, Lana, roomy enough even for you."

Lana despises Louise. From her clean white Nikes right up to her gold cross earrings, she despises Louise, and yet an image flows unbidden from Louise's words, an image of an enormous gilded ballroom filled with all the people Lana has ever disappointed—her mother, Hallie, a whole assortment of foster parents and foster kids and teachers and coaches and headshrinkers. They are all there in beautiful dresses and suits and ties and in smooth slow motion they are dancing to perfection the dance they are doing, which is the dance of forgiveness.

The screen door slams shut.

Mr. and Mrs. Louise have gone inside, and Tilly has gone in, too. Lana hears her shout to the other Snicks, "Here comes Bob the Tomato! Yes, yes, yes!"

Lana looks down at her sketch. She likes it—it has the same loose, free flow to it that her sketch of Chet had— and even with her lower arm erased and gone, Veronica still looks like an Ice Queen, which, in Lana's book, is exactly what she is.

She slides the sketch back into the black box and secures the lid. She smoothes her hand over the box's pebbly leather cover. She closes her eyes and tries to imagine again the Giant Ballroom of Forgiveness, but it won't come. She wants to see if she can find Veronica among the dancers, but the vision of the ballroom won't come. It's like a face you might recognize if you saw it on the street someday but that you can't otherwise remember, like, for example, all the faces of her mother's boyfriends.

13.

A half hour later, up in her room, Lana goes to the closet and sees how easy she'd made it for Veronica: the shelf high overhead but the empty milk crate—a handy step—sitting there below her clothes. Obvious. And stupid. Beyond stupid. *Pilfering isn't just in Alfred's makeup,* she thinks. *It's in Veronica's, too.*

From downstairs the sounds of cartoon voices carry, then raucous laughter from the Snicks at something or somebody. Bob the Tomato, is Lana's guess.

She pushes the drawing kit under her bed and slides out one of the three cardboard boxes stored there. Probably Veronica went through all of these, too, and probably she pushed them all back under, wondering what she'd just looked at.

The boxes contain old photograph albums, the smallest of which is an almost empty souvenir book with black pages and a leather cover celebrating the completion of the Hoover Dam. On the first page of this book, Lana keeps a picture of her father at seventeen. *Dee Morris catches dee most!* someone had written across the front, in the sand below the bare feet of her father, who was holding a string of trout. Dee's face was lean and sweet-looking, and his grin was so goofy and wide that you'd think he could never die or hurt people. When Lana was in kindergarten, learning her letters in Miss Marsh's class, her father was in the House of Corrections. Lana wasn't supposed to tell people, so she didn't, but then they came to the letter D. *"Bad little, sad little* d*"* was the rhyme for remembering which way the *d* faced—toward the wall, ashamed of something, and Lana heard it as *Bad little, sad little Dee* and thought somehow Miss Marsh knew about her father.

Things changed in her father's life, but he never got over fishing, and now, staring at the photograph of her father, Lana remembers how one day instead of taking her to school, he drove her off to a deserted lake where they ate egg salad sandwiches and drank cocoa from a thermos and fished and talked and fished until Lana looked up and saw her mother striding their way wearing a look that meant things were going to get bad and get bad quick. Lana gauged her mother's position against that of her father's car and realized that if they made a break for it, her mother would never catch them. "Run for it!" Lana yelled, reeling in her line as fast as she could, but her father took hold of her arm and looked into her eyes and said, "We don't run, Lana. And we don't hide." He smiled. "That's not who the Morrises are."

Which was very much a big fat laugh. It seemed like all Lana and her mother ever did after her father was gone was run and hide, hide and run. And now her mother had run and hidden who knew where. . . .

Shame and sadness. This is what Lana almost always

finally feels when she looks at the Hoover Dam souvenir album, shame and sadness, which is probably why she prefers the other albums, the ones full of photos of families Lana doesn't know. The books are old, with triangular corner pockets for the black-and-white photographs to fit into—Lana has purchased most of these albums at secondhand stores. The pictures Lana likes are the ones of families on their picnics and Christmases and vacations to Yellowstone or Yosemite. Lana only buys an album if the photographed family seems friendly and happy and has some other indefinable quality she likes. She now has seventeen such albums in the boxes under her bed.

One day a few weeks earlier when she was sitting on the edge of her bed paging through one of the albums, she looked up to find Whit standing just beyond the door staring in at her. He took a step forward and said, "Can I come in?"

The rule was foster fathers didn't come into the room of a girl without someone else there, but Lana didn't care. She nodded, and in he came.

"So what're these?" he said, sitting on the edge of the bed a full three feet beyond her. A safe distance, but she could smell the faint lime scent of his shaving cream.

"Old photograph albums," she said. "I kind of collect them."

Whit leaned closer to look.

"I call this one the Vee family," Lana said. "The father's Victor, the mother's Virginia, and the two kids are Victoria and Virgil." The picture in front of them showed the boy and girl muggingly opening their mouths in preparation for first bites of huge hot dogs and was labeled *Victoria & Virg eating footlongs at the Great Salt Lake.*

"Funny," Whit said, and Lana nodded. Then he said, "So, they're your grandparents?"

Lana shook her head no, and paged through the album while he watched. "I mean, I buy them at shops."

"Oh," Whit said. A bit later, he said, "Victoria looks a little like you."

This pleased Lana, but what she said was, "She's prettier."

Whit without looking at her said matter-of-factly, "No, she's not."

They went through two more albums page by page and then several more albums quickly. As she closed the last one, Whit said, "Well, I think I finally broke the Morris code."

Lana looked over at him with open curiosity.

"All the families in these albums are happy-seeming. And they all have a girl with hair like yours."

This surprised Lana. She'd never looked at them this way. But still, even if it was true, what did it tell you? "So?"

Whit was smiling now, an encouraging, generous smile. "I think you just want to belong." A pause. "Which isn't so strange. It's what we all want to do."

Lana started to put the albums away, and Whit picked up the little Hoover Dam book, which had slipped to the floor. He opened it, and they looked in silence at the photo of her father, which unlike all the rest was in color, faded yellows and browns and greens that looked muddy now.

" 'Dee Morris catches dee most!' " Whit read. "I guess

this one's somebody you know." He glanced toward Lana. "Your dad?"

Lana nodded.

"He died in an accident, right?" Whit asked.

"Sort of. It happened when he was in jail. I was six."

Whit didn't say anything, just as most people didn't. It was like she'd shown them a disfiguring scar.

Then she heard herself say to Whit, "How come you never had kids?" A question she'd thought before but never expected actually to ask.

He looked at her for two or three seconds, then he said, "Veronica can't is all."

Whit pushed himself up and started to go but turned back. He let his eyes settle on her eyes, and he touched a finger under her chin, tipping it lightly up, and leaned forward and gently kissed her forehead, so gently that, in speech, it would've been a whisper. He left the room then without a word, but she knew he knew it would mean something to her, and it does.

Lana folds closed the photograph album she's been looking at, tucks it into its box, and slides the box under the bed. *The pills and the purse,* she thinks. She needs to stop thinking about Whit and focus on the pills.

The pills are in Veronica's blue purse.

Which is in the cupboard over the refrigerator.

Which isn't quite as secure as Veronica thinks it is.

Lana goes quietly downstairs, past the living room (the Snicks, sprawled on the floor and sofas, stare raptly at the talking vegetables on the TV screen) to the kitchen cabinet where the spices are kept. Toward the back of the cabinet, among several dozen tin boxes, she finds the one marked *Ground Cumin.* This is where, Lana learned one day while experimentally dipping a finger into various spices, Veronica hides extra keys to the cupboard and her car. Lana slips the cupboard key from the mustard-colored powder and wipes it clean.

"Hello?"

It's Louise, calling from the living room.

"Just me," Lana calls. She looks around. "I'm just eating some grapes."

Which is beyond-belief lame, but it seems to work: Louise doesn't investigate further. Lana actually eats a few grapes—they're collapsed and pulpy, some week-old crap Veronica picked up cheap is Lana's guess—then when it seems safe, she quietly unlocks the cupboard, eases open the door, and stops short.

It's not there.

The blue purse isn't there.

But it has to be somewhere, because Veronica didn't have it when she left.

Veronica's room. Maybe she left it in her own room.

Lana grabs a bunch of the horrible grapes and in passing the living room she pokes her head in, chewing, smiling, letting Louise know everything's fine, then she heads back upstairs. She opens and closes the door to her room but doesn't go in. Instead she tiptoes toward Veronica and Whit's room.

The door, at her touch, swings silently open.

Stacks of clothes lie on a nearby chair, pants and blouses in layers of complementary colors, outfits Veronica must've tried on and discarded before going out. On the unmade bed, one pillow is plumped, the other flattened. She picks up the flattened one and brings it to her face—it has on it the mixed smells of Whit's hair oil and lime shaving cream—and she doesn't want to put it down, but she has to. She has to find the purse.

She looks around. Tries to imagine Veronica's idea of a hiding place. Lies on her stomach and peers under the bed, pokes into every corner of the closet, eases the corner cabinet away from the wall. Pulls open every dresser drawer deep enough to hold a purse.

In the cabinet under the bathroom sink, she doesn't find the purse, but she discovers something else. Toward the front, there is a large glass bottle of something called T.L.C. Primera, and before she puts it back in place, Lana unscrews the cap and smells it. It smells like alcohol. She looks at the label, where T.L.C. Primera is described as "a skin restorative blend of oils of sensimilla and clove." Lana pours a little on her hand. It's clear and thin. It isn't body oil at all. She touches her tongue to her wet palm. It's alcohol, one of the clear ones, gin or vodka.

Well, well, well. This is like the keys Veronica keeps in the cumin box. Something worth knowing.

Lana recaps the bottle, sets it back into its place, then, standing still in the doorway, her gaze, as if guided or drawn, lights upon the heat register in the floor.

And then she is there, leaning down and looking through the grill. She gets to her knees, but still, she can see nothing, she needs light, and when she straightens and looks around the room for a lamp or a match, she sees Louise and her husband standing in the doorway, staring at her.

"I thought I heard something in here," Lana says.

Louise and Marvin just keep staring.

"Something gnarly," Lana says. "A rat, I think. I could hear it all the way from my room."

Louise and Marvin don't say a word.

"I can't relax at all with a rat in the house," Lana says, and when Mr. and Mrs. Louise remain quiet, Lana decides this is as good a time as any for her exit. She walks toward the door where Louise and her husband are standing, and as she approaches, they part and she passes by.

Nobody speaks. It's as if the silence is the solution required for Louise and her husband to preserve Lana's behavior in their minds. Lana walks as unhurriedly as she can back to her room and closes the door behind her.

At once she hears footsteps down the stairs and back up again, then the squeak of something being pried free. She cracks open her door. The lights are on in Whit and Veronica's room, and she can see the thrown shadow of a standing person. She drifts close and when she reaches the open door, things suddenly change in the room.

"It's her," Louise hisses, and beyond the bed her husband, who has set the register grate on the floor and is kneeling beside the open vent, both straightens himself and slides something behind him, but Lana has glimpsed the blue purse, she's almost sure she's glimpsed it.

"Find the rat?" she says.

Marv, at a loss, looks from Lana to Louise, who says, "We certainly did."

Lana knows what this means. It means the rat they've caught goes by the name of Lana, and she can tell by the brightness in Louise's eyes that she's excited by her catch and can't wait to report the news to Veronica and her PTA friends and church friends and God knew who else.

"Need any help?" Lana says as gamely as she can, and Louise in a cool voice says, "None whatsoever."

Lana glances at Silent Marv, whose eyes say, *Sorry,* and she realizes that he is a nice man, which would only mean something if he was in charge, which he unquestionably is not.

14.

*A*n hour or so later, after pajamas, toothbrushing, and peeing, Tilly crawls into the bed beside Lana's. "Love *VeggieTales*!" she says, and then she snugs her head into her Cinderella pillow, smiles, and falls asleep. This moment, repeated almost nightly, is the only moment of the day when Lana feels truly envious of Tilly.

After the afternoon thunderstorm, the skies have cleared. There is a waxing moon, and it silhouettes the ash tree branches that reach past Lana and Tilly's second-story window. The leaves move under a gentle breeze. *Doomed,* Lana thinks. *I am unquestionably doomed.* She's had wild-eye thoughts about the foster father. She's been accused of hiding pills in her own room. And now she's been caught in her foster parents' room. She knows that all these things are connected, that, starting with the wild-eye thoughts, one thing has led to another. That no matter how horrid Veronica the Ice Queen and her Jesus-freak friend Louise are, it is her own Lana self, or maybe her own Lana heart, that has put it all into motion.

Lana's thoughts float through the shadowy tree and off toward the moonlight and then return again.

Doomed. Unquestionably doomed.

Lana slides two fingers into the crease between her ear and skull, between the soft on one side and the hard on the other, where the last gift from her father had always rested, except now it lay in a dark drawer of an old cash register in a town so small no one had ever heard of it. She needs to go back there. She needs to get two dollars and go back there tomorrow. Maybe Chet could borrow a car and take her.

Or, better yet, Whit.

And just like that, there she is, thinking of riding down dirt country roads sitting on the smooth bench seat in the cab of Whit's old Dodge truck, listening to Little Walter, just riding along with neither of them saying anything because, deep in their hearts and deep in their bones, they both already know everything they need to know.

Lana gives her head a quick shake. This is just the kind of dreaming that will doom her and Whit, too. She looks down at Tilly, who, fast asleep, seems in the moonlight to be smiling.

15.

*F*rom deepest sleep, Lana becomes aware of a ringing telephone. Finally it stops, and Whit's voice, as if at a great distance, can be heard saying, "Hello?" and then, "What? What?"

The Cinderella clock says 2:22. Tilly is gently snoring.

Whit's voice again comes muffled through the wall.

Lana gets up, puts her ear to the wall, and hears Whit's voice grow loud with alarm. "When? But how? Where? No, I can come. About ten minutes."

Whit stops talking, and there are the sounds of rapid movement within his room, then his door creaks open and Lana barely has time to get back into bed before he opens her door and pokes his head in. "Lana?"

Lana sits up in bed.

The moonlight still pours into her room, and she is wearing just a sleeveless white T-shirt. She pulls the sheet up around her.

"Veronica's been in some kind of accident," he says. Something hangs from one of his hands. Veronica's blue purse. Louise and her husband must've given it to him when he got home. But maybe not the story that went with it. Louise would've wanted to save that for Veronica.

"Wasn't she with you?" Lana says.

"What?"

"Wasn't Veronica with you?"

"When?"

"She told Louise and Marvin she was meeting you for dinner."

He seems distracted. "Yeah, that's right. But we had two cars."

Lana waits, but he doesn't say more. "I don't get it," she says. "You had dinner but didn't come home together?"

Whit seems exasperated. "Look, Veronica gets things in her head, goes looking for me. It's just her way. Last night she found me, we had dinner, did some bar-hopping, and I was ready to come home before she was."

"And she stayed out at a bar?"

A strange look, a look that seems to hint at private misery, passes across his face, and then it's gone. "This isn't the time, Lana. She's been in a car wreck. I've got to go."

Lana glances again at the bag hanging from his hand. "You're taking her purse?"

He nods. "Women always need their purses."

"Not in the hospital," Lana says. "They'll probably just ask you to bring it home."

But he seems barely to hear this. "Look," he says, "if I'm not back, can you take care of breakfast? There's slow oatmeal in the Crock-Pot."

His knowing there's slow oatmeal in the crock is a little surprise. When it comes to food preparation, he's always passed himself off as clueless. "Sure," Lana says, "I can do breakfast."

"And I left something downstairs by the computer for you," he says. "I was going to give it to you tomorrow."

When Tilly stirs, both Lana and Whit look at her, but she resumes sleep, and then, for a long moment, she and Whit are looking at each other in the moonlit room until finally he says, "Thanks," and turns and is taking the stairs two at a time.

Lana lies in the dark listening to the sound of his Dodge diesel roaring off and has a string of thoughts. *Maybe this will keep Louise from ratting on me. Maybe this will keep Veronica from sending the pills downstate. Maybe this will put Whit in charge of the house.* And then these and other smaller thoughts are gathered together into one large thought so horrible it shames her.

I hope she dies.

She knows this thought is terrible, worse than terrible, so she tells herself, *No I don't, no I don't, no I don't.*

16.

*L*ana can't sleep. She lies on her back, she lies on her stomach, she turns up the cool side of the pillow, but she still can't fall back to sleep. She keeps thinking of Whit staring at her in the moonlight, and the longer she thinks of it, the longer and more meaningful the brief scene seems, when in fact it meant just slightly more than nothing, she knows that, she absolutely knows that.

The tender little secrets between a wife and her husband, that was the phrase Louise had used. So what do you call Veronica going out to hunt down her husband, suspecting the worst? And what do you call them having dinner together and then going bar to bar until he comes home and she doesn't? Tender little secrets? Lana doesn't think so.

Then she remembers the present from Whit. The thought of it fills her with a childlike pleasure, and she wants the present now, not tomorrow. She goes downstairs nearly as fast as Whit had, and there beside the computer is an iPod. It's connected to the computer. She's used iPods before—other fosters had them or, more often, the biological kids of foster parents. She's never had her own. She slides on the tiny earphones and sits down in the blue darkness of the kitchen and starts turning the dial, reading the names of albums, songs, and shows, none of them very interesting. She sees three podcasts in a row called chiefchetteroid@2rivers.com and clicks one.

"Greetings, Citizens of the Otherworld, this is kay-ess-oh-dee, and that's K-SOD, and that's us, and if you know us, you know we have issues to hyperventilate, so let's just bang out of the bull chute with issue uno, which is a little issue we happen to have with those folks over at the Disney Company. We have just one question and the question is, WHAT IS IT WITH THIS DONALD DUCK GUY? I mean, what was old Walt thinking?—*THAT WHAT THIS WORLD REALLY BADLY, URGENTLY NEEDS IS A SPUTTERING DUCK?*"

Lana has heard this voice and this peculiar paranoia before, but Chet doesn't seem like the sort of person who would start his own talk show. There is a long pause, so long Lana wonders if the recording somehow got cut off. But then the voice is back.

"Well, I'd take Walt's money and build myself a beach compound in Tobago and I'd do it tomorrow by four p.m., but that doesn't mean old Walt wasn't WAY WRONG ON THE DUCK THING." Another long pause, and then in a calmer voice: "And how about the little guys, Huey, Dewey, and Louie, and their little Hispanic cousin Chuy, always going to their little *Junior Woodchucks Manual* every time they get themselves in a pinch?" Pause. "Okay, Walt, I can see where that would be useful if you want to get, you know, a real-life version of the *Junior Woodchucks Manual* in our hands for use next time we get in a little fix, then, okay, you can say you actually finally did something for the global community." Pause. "But in the meantime the very best next thing you can do, Walt, is to OFF THAT SPUTTERING DUCK."

Pause.

There's something oddly interesting about the pauses, Lana thinks, the way it makes you wait for the next thing.

"Okay, Chetteroids," the voice continues, "issue numero two. We've got the Olympics coming up. We've talked about this. We've expressed our opinions. We know, for example, where we stand on the pentathlon. We need alternatives; that much we can all agree on. And your good Chief Chetteroid has in mind something cyberspatial that he in his Chetness has anointed"—here the speaker seems to thin his lips to expel a sibilant trumpet-like introduction—*"the Oddball Olympics."*

Chief Chetteroid? He in his Chetness?

Lana pulls her earphones from her head, goes to the front window, and stares across at Chet's house. Through the upstairs window she can see him pacing back and forth with his mouth moving. His Chetness, the Chief Chetteroid, is doing his next show. She can't stop grinning. It's weird and kind of endearing and definitely blackmailable. She slips the earphones back on.

"That's correct," the voice says. "The Oddball Olympics. And the first event in the Oddball Olympics is"—another trumpety intro—"SPUTTERING DUCK EXPUNGEMENT." Pause, then more calmly: "I don't need to tell you, there are no rules for this event. Bare hands, buck knives, or AK-47s, we Chetteroids don't as they say give a fig, AS LONG AS SOMEBODY BRINGS DOWN THAT DUCK." Pause. "Okay, enough on the Disney segment. It's time for—"

Lana is no longer thinking about her bad evil heart. She is grinning at the thought of not-normal Chet podcasting his not-normal thoughts at three in the morning, thoughts to which she now has access.

She goes back to bed and listens while Chet does a segment on finding your cat's purr spot and one on statues of animals and in particular cows and then finally what must be his signature sign-off, "This is kay-ess-oh-dee, K-SOD, where no subject is too small for lengthy and uninformed consideration. You know who we are. We're aliens hiding in nearby trees, where we can see it all. Good night, Chetteroids and Chetteristas. Keep those cards and letters coming. And please don't call again." And then he plays a song sung by a woman with a high, haunting voice:

> *Good night, ladies*
> *Good night, gentlemen*
> *Keep those cards and letters*
> *Coming*
> *And please don't call again.*

Lana walks to the hall window. The lights are off in Chet's room. Past his house and down the street, all the houses are dark. She can hear the distant drone of a truck on the highway. In the same direction, beyond her sight, is the hospital, where Veronica lies and Whit sits waiting.

17.

"**G**et up, Lana."

In her dream, it had been Whit asking her to get up, and because in her dream she'd been completely naked, she didn't know if she could just get up with him standing right there, but now, as the words were repeated—*Get up, Lana*—she realizes it isn't Whit's voice, and she isn't naked, and she opens her eyes.

It's Tilly, and just behind her, in the doorway, stand skinny Garth and big Carlito. Lana remembers suddenly the accident of the night before, and the message she sees in the Snicks' expressions is of something else having gone terribly wrong. "What?" she says. "What's happened?"

"We're hungry, Lana," says Tilly. "It's morning. We're hungry. You bet."

Lana looks at Carlito and Garth, who stare blankly. Alfred's there, too, standing behind the others in his green golf shirt and blue slacks, grinding his teeth.

"I'll be right down," Lana says.

She washes her face, combs her hair, and then glances out at Chet's house—his blinds are closed—before heading down to the kitchen.

Lana races from one task to another, and nobody wets

himself or starts screaming or spills juice, so the Snicks are nearly done with their oatmeal (Lana's been much freer than Veronica with the raisins and brown sugar) when Whit's diesel chugs up the driveway. Lana stands just back from the window to watch. It's surprising. Only hours have passed, but he looks older as he walks toward the house with a handful of papers.

Veronica's blue purse is not in his possession.

As Whit steps into the kitchen, the kids somehow know to fall quiet. He looks at them and tries to smile but can't quite do it. He stands before them all, glancing at them, then down at the papers in his hands. Finally he says, "Veronica's been in a bad car wreck."

A silence follows until Tilly in her loud voice says, "Is she dead as a doornail?"

Whit makes a dry laugh. "No, Tilly. Veronica isn't dead as a doornail. She isn't dead at all." A deep breath. "But she did lose part of an arm."

They are all quiet for a few seconds, then Alfred says, "And they c-c-c-can't find it?"

"No, Alfred. They can't. It's lost for good." Again he tries to smile. "But she's alive and that's what we need to be relieved about."

Lana in fact does feel an odd sense of relief. If she'd wished that Veronica would die and then she *did* die, Lana would always think she'd had something to do with it, which was something she'd just as soon not live with. "When will they release her?" she says.

"A week or so," Whit says.

Lana feels her spirits rise. *A week without Veronica in the house.* "I can take over the kitchen and cooking if you want," she says.

"That's good, Lana," he says, and smiles a tired smile. "Now if you kiddos can keep it down, I'm going to get a little sleep."

Lana lets him go upstairs but can't stop herself from following a few minutes later.

"Whit?" she says from outside the partially closed door.

No answer. But she can hear water running in the bathroom, then the bathroom door opening.

"Whit?" she says again.

The sound of his footsteps coming toward her makes her mouth dry.

"What?" he says, poking his head out.

"Can I ask you something?"

"Sure," he says. He opens the door to let her in, but she looks at the unmade bed and the stack of Veronica's clothes on the chair and stays where she is.

"Thank you for the gift," she says. "I didn't know we had a podcaster in the neighborhood."

"Yeah, our boy Chet's more interesting than you'd guess from meeting him in the street." He smiles. "Of course, most people are."

"I guess," Lana says, but her mind's on what she wants to say next.

Whit sits down on the edge of the bed, begins to unlace his shoes, and Lana blurts, "Did Veronica tell you about the pills?"

"Pills?" he says, standing up again to remove his wallet, some change from his front pocket, and a packet of folded papers, all of which he dumps on the nightstand.

"She claimed she found drugs in my room. She said she's going to send them to a lab and get me shipped out of here."

Whit sits again on the bed. He rubs his eyes. He doesn't look shocked or upset. He just says, "Why would she want to do that?"

The same question, more or less, that Hallie had asked. But this time, instead of saying she doesn't know, Lana says, "She found some sketches of mine."

Whit cocks his head slightly. His expression says, *What?*

"They were sketches of you," Lana says.

His weary expression becomes one of mild amusement, which annoys Lana.

She says, "What Veronica doesn't understand is that I sketch everybody. I have one of Chet, too. That doesn't mean I have a thing for him."

If anything, Whit's amusement deepens. "Ronnie thinks you have some kind of thing for me?"

Lana lowers her eyes and feels her skin warming. "She might think that, yeah."

"And what do you think?"

She wants to look into his eyes and say, *I think maybe I do, I'm not sure,* but she keeps her eyes down and shakes her head and says, "I don't think anything."

"You're a funny thing, Lana Morris," he says, and she looks up, and when he lets his tired eyes settle into hers, the desire to tuck herself against his body is like an undertow. She would like to use his chest as a pillow, listen to his slow heartbeat as he sleeps.

"What about the pills?" she says, and this breaks the spell, which both relieves and disappoints her.

He shrugs and says, "You worry too much." He pivots and stretches onto the bed fully clothed. His voice is low and tired and gentle. "It's not just you, Lana. Everybody worries too much. It's a widespread affliction." His eyes fall closed, then he forces them open and makes a little smile. "Someday I'll help cure you of it."

He crosses his feet at the ankles and then, just like that, he's asleep and Lana, looking upon him serene and still, feels something surprising. She feels the weight of her worries lift away.

18.

*A*fter breakfast, Alfred, Garth, and Carlito go to the library with a cheerful job coach named Mrs. Arnot in order to clean plastic book covers with spray bottles and rags, one of the unpaid, low-skill jobs that's supposed to prepare them for independent living. Tilly goes sometimes, but today she says, "Going to help *you*, Lana!" so Lana leads Tilly next door, where Chet's in the yard trying to start a red Toro lawn mower.

"Hey," she says.

Chet is kneeling beside the mower, unscrewing a lid to something. "Hey," he says, and Lana can tell by his voice he isn't happy. He lays aside the lid and pulls out something that looks like a dirty sponge, which he regards morosely. Something about him seems different, but she can't put her finger on it. She and Tilly follow him to his garage, where he begins sloshing the sponge around in a coffee can filled with gasoline, a process Tilly regards with interest.

Lana says, "So what you're doing there—would that be something you learned from your *Junior Woodchucks Manual?*"

Chet doesn't flinch, grin, or respond in any way. He just keeps working.

"Because I figure that's where his Chetness would learn something like that."

Chet keeps sloshing the sponge and doesn't utter a word.

Lana says, "So how is his Chetness?"

Chet without looking up says, "Who?"

"His Chetness. The Chief Chetteroid."

Chet says blandly, "I have no idea what you're talking about."

Lana picks up an oily wrench and regards it. "Well, that's too bad," she says casually, "because I was hoping to meet the Chief Chetteroid, you know, in the flesh."

Chet continues to pretend the sponge takes one hundred percent of his attention. His face is stone, and Lana wonders if maybe this is public Chet and the funny, ranting, K-SOD Chet is private Chet. And for a second time, she thinks there's something else, too, something actually different about the way he looks, but she isn't sure what.

She whistles a few bars of the song he'd closed his podcast with, but Chet's face doesn't register a thing. It's like he's got some kind of Dr.-Chet-and-Mr.-Chetteroid thing going here. Lana decides to stop inquiring about the weird broadcasting. She'll just listen in again and see what's on the air tonight.

They walk back into the yard and Chet sets the sponge back into the lawn mower. Lana says, "I guess Veronica did some drinking last night and wrecked her car. She lost an arm."

Chet seems unimpressed. He says, "Should I be grieving about that?"

"I'm just making conversation," Lana says.

Chet says, "Yeah, well, on my party list, Veronica's just below a rabid dog."

This is Chief Chetteroid funny, and Lana wouldn't mind using it herself. "You make that up?" she says.

"Naw. It's K.C.'s line."

Then Lana would forget it. She looks up and down the street. She looks at the blank blue sky. She doesn't know what she's feeling. So many things have changed since yesterday, but everything looks more or less the same. She plucks a dandelion and prods at the downy seeds so that they float off a few at a time.

Suddenly Tilly says, "Your spot's gone, Chet. You bet it is," and Lana turns to Tilly, who's staring at Chet but pointing at her own nose.

Chet nods. "Yep, that's right. The mole is gone."

"The mole is gone?" Lana asks, but even as she speaks, she sees it's true.

Chet says, "I've been using this ointment my dad bought for me and then—*bam*—it's gone." He glances at Tilly—she's gently picking her nose—then turns his gaze back to Lana. "Go figure. My dad didn't notice it, you didn't notice it, but"—here he hitches his head toward Tilly—"one of the village idiots does."

"Don't call them idiots," Lana says, and Chet directs an apologetic look Tilly's way. "Sorry."

Tilly doesn't acknowledge the apology. She walks over to a dry birdbath that stands in the corner of Chet's yard. She begins scraping out hardened bird dung with her fingernails and Lana makes a mental note not to share snacks with Tilly in the foreseeable future. Chet abruptly stops tightening a wing nut on the mower and turns a serious expression to Lana.

"Which would you rather lose—a leg or an arm?"

Lana gives it some thought. "An arm," she says, "as long as it wasn't my drawing one."

Chet nods. "Yeah. Me too." Then he says, "Okay, which would it be—an eye or a foot?"

They both agree an eye, as long as they can see out of the other one, and they go on with this game until Chet says, "Okay, your boyfriend's eyes or his so-called member?" which just about ends the conversation as far as Lana is concerned.

As she turns away, she says that most so-called members would be less missed by the average girl than the average guy supposed.

Chet gives a grin and says, "Oh, and I'm sure you're an expert on the subject," which Lana isn't, not by a long shot, but she isn't going to tell him that, so she just keeps walking. But then something occurs to her and she turns back.

"You're going to use this as a bit, aren't you? This whole which-body-part-would-you-rather-lose routine—you're going to use it on K-SOD, aren't you?"

Chet blinks once and says, "I have no idea what you're talking about."

Lana gives him a long, cold look and turns away. "C'mon, Tilly. Let's vaminose." As she waits, she says, "Which would you rather lose, a big black mole or the idiot whose face it was growing on?"

"Funny," Chet says deadpan, and Tilly and Lana move off.

As they near their porch, Chet gives the lawn mower cord a pull, the engine suddenly sputters to life, and just as suddenly goes dead. Lana expects to hear swearing. When she doesn't, she turns and finds Chet standing motionless over the mower. His shoulders droop, his eyes are closed, and he suggests a statue meant to represent the weary contemplation of life's little trials.

A statue that, Lana has to admit, has a faint and unexplainable attraction to it.

19.

The rest of the morning Lana doesn't know what to do with herself. Tilly is doing a child's wooden puzzle and the other Snicks are still with Mrs. Arnot and a little while ago, through the window, Lana watched Chet walk off toward town pushing the lawn mower in front of him, so Lana tries to keep busy. She goes from cleaning to reading to snacking to staring out the window wondering what's going to happen to Veronica and what Louise is going to tell Veronica about Lana's snooping in her room and what's become of the blue purse and the pills. Through all of this, Lana's aware she's doing something else, too: she's listening for sounds overhead, some little indication that Whit is awake.

When Carlito, Garth, and Alfred come back, Lana ignores the scheduled menu (Pasta with Green Vegetable, which, Lana knows, just means Top Ramen with a handful of frozen peas) and makes them all her favorite lunch—egg salad on toasted white with a side of boysenberry Jell-O and diced pears—and after feeding them all and putting on a video, she does what she's been dying to do: she takes a tray up to Whit.

The door is only partly closed and she pushes it open

with her elbow. He doesn't stir and she tiptoes across the carpet and stands with the tray for a few seconds, watching him sleep. What's strange is how closed down his face seems—it's clamped tight as a walnut—though when Lana whispers his name and his eyes blink open, his face at once relaxes into a smile.

"You missed breakfast," she says. "This is lunch."

He glances at the tray, then back at her. "Don't know which looks yummier, the sandwich or the long, tall waitress."

Lana sets the tray on the nightstand beside him and wonders if he can tell she's blushing. The remark both pleases and unsettles her—she decides to say nothing.

"Guess you think I say that to all the waitresses," he says.

"So . . . do you?"

Whit grins and takes a bite into the sandwich. "Nope. Only the yummy ones." He chews and grins and looks at Lana so frankly that she feels discombobulated.

"So what happened to Veronica?" she says. "The accident, I mean."

Whit keeps chewing but looks away. "She was driving home and ran a light. Car coming the other way was doing at least forty." He frowns and picks up a fallen piece of egg white. "At the hospital she told the cop it was because she's color blind."

"She's color blind?"

He shrugs. "A little bit." He looks at the sandwich in his hand and purses his lips slightly. "More so whenever she runs a red light."

"Wouldn't a color-blind person know that the top light is red and the bottom one is green, or whatever it is?"

"Well, if you was talking about a *sober* color-blind person, the answer would be yes. But we're not." His gaze drifts. "She'll lose her license over this one, guaranteed."

Whit takes another bite. The room is quiet. Through the open windows a breeze moves the pale cotton curtains in a way that makes Lana think of ghosts. She says, "When Veronica left, she seemed worried about you."

He turns. "Worried?"

"As in jealous."

Whit had stopped chewing, but now he resumes. "Oh, that."

"Oh, that?"

"Veronica's always been the jealous type."

Lana remembers Hallie's phrase: *with cause*. She says, "With or without cause?"

Whit picks a crumb from the bedspread and drops it on his plate. He seems to be choosing his words. "You're getting in a little over your head here, Lana." He makes a smile that seems sad. "I'll say this much. I'm no saint, and neither is Veronica." He looks into Lana's eyes. "But I've sworn off the extracurricular stuff. If I'm with Veronica, I'm with Veronica, just like if I was with you, I'd be with you."

For the second time in this conversation, she wonders if he can see her blushing. "Do you mean that you want to adopt me but Veronica doesn't?"

Something registers in his eyes, and she can't say for sure what it is. Pity? Concern?

"Maybe we should talk about this another time," Whit says. "I'm not making sense."

She says, "But you *are* with her. She's who you're married to."

"That's right," Whit says quietly. "She is."

Lana can't think of what to say or even what to think. "I've got to go now," she says.

Whit pushes a last bite of sandwich into his mouth. "Me too."

"You're going to the hospital?"

He nods. He sets the plate on the tray and throws back the covers. He's still wearing his street clothes from the night before, except for his feet. When he sits up and swings them out, she sees they're bare.

Lana retreats, but as she closes the door, she can't help glancing back. Whit has slipped out of his shirt and is walking toward the bathroom with his back to her. Lana has guessed that Whit is small inside his clothes, but that doesn't prepare her for what she sees. The joints of his spine look like fingertips pushing through the smooth white skin, and from within each of his shoulder blades a hand seems to be pushing out, palms first.

Lana quietly pulls the door closed, but she has the feeling that what she's just seen will alter her feelings about Whit Winters. Alter and complicate them.

Because now she has an image she can't get rid of—the image of a person trapped inside him trying to get out.

20.

*L*ana closes the door to her room, sits on the bed, and tries to stay perfectly still, as if by doing this she might become a rock or stick or bone, something free of thought and feeling, but she isn't rock or stick or bone and through the walls she hears a toilet flush and then she hears the water pipes tremble and whine as the shower starts.

So he's taking a shower before going to the hospital.

Wanting to look good for Veronica.

Well, why shouldn't he? He's her husband. She's his wife.

Downstairs, the Snicks are suddenly talking and moving, which means the video must be over. Lana should go down, but she doesn't. She slides the black box of sketching paper from under the bed. She's thinking of drawing Chet standing over the lawn mower, or Whit eating in bed, or maybe even Whit walking across the room with his shoulder blades like the hands of someone trying to get out, but she knows that would be death squared if Veronica found it, and finding things is Veronica's specialty.

The sketch lying on top of the other paper is of Veronica the Ice Queen. The more Lana stares at it, the more

97

she thinks it really does reveal the coldness in Veronica the world can't see. It captures the deep-freeze cruelty that Veronica keeps hidden even from photographers. The drawing is good, Lana sees that plain as day, but she feels no particular pride in this fact. She feels only vaguely connected to the sketch, as if her sister had drawn it or maybe a cousin.

As Lana gazes at the drawing, she suddenly realizes something that stops her cold: what she'd erased the prior day was Veronica's left arm to the elbow.

Lana feels in her bones that this means something but doesn't know what—it's as if she's just received a telegram but can't open it.

She stares out the window awhile, until in fact she hears Whit's hard heels on the hallway floor, down the wooden stairs. A question occurs to Lana, a question Whit can answer. He's already out the kitchen door and on his way to his truck when she catches up. "Whit?"

He turns.

Lana can't quite speak.

"What?" Whit says. He's not exactly impatient, but she can see he's ready to go.

"I was wondering," she says, "which arm was it Veronica lost?"

Whit looks down and raises first his right hand, then his left. "Left," he says.

"You're sure?"

He cocks his head. "Sure, I'm sure. Why do you ask?"

"No reason. I just wondered."

Whit is staring at her. "You okay, Lana?"

She nods.

"Okay, then. I'd better go." But he doesn't go. He stands looking into her. "I've got to tell you . . . a little while ago, when I woke up and you were there . . . I know I was joking around with you, but . . . laying eyes on you before anything else"—his expression turns oddly serious— "it was like waking up in my own little corner of heaven."

For the third time in less than an hour, Lana wonders if he can tell she's blushing.

And then he is gone.

Lana goes back into the house trying to figure out what she is feeling. Tilly is swinging on the front porch with Carlito. Alfred is writing and creaking his teeth. Garth is wearing his Hulk shirt and twisting Popeye's head.

In the kitchen Lana takes a Tanya Tucker CD out of the computer, puts in disc two of Little Walter, then begins rinsing the lunch dishes and arranging them in the dishwasher. In her mind she goes through the things that feel like facts.

On a sunny day she sketches a storm and then it rains.

She leaves the mole off Chet's face and suddenly his mole medicine works and the mole disappears.

She erases part of Veronica's left arm from another sketch and then Veronica gets in a car crash and loses part of her left arm.

Well, what of it? Lana thinks. Didn't unexpected thunderstorms come along? Didn't mole medicines sometimes work? Didn't people get in accidents and get hurt? And it didn't snow, did it? In the drawing, Veronica was wrapped in a snow robe and not a single snowflake had since fallen in Two Rivers.

Came home this morning about half-past four, Little Walter is singing. *Found that note lying on my floor.* And then a long riff on the mouth harp.

"Little Walter's the guy that brought the mouth harp from the country to the city." That's what Whit had said about him when he heard Lana playing his songs.

And then Lana is thinking of Whit, of him looking into her and calling her his own little corner of heaven. She knows that what she feels for Whit is love, helpless and deep. Standing near him is like standing waist deep in the Niobrara River. He's married. He's fifteen years older than she is. He's what the state calls her father. And pretty soon Veronica's going to separate them for what Lana has to admit is pretty good cause.

Don't send no doctor, Little Walter sings. *He won't do no good.*

Lana doesn't have much time. Any second one of the Snicks will need her for something. She wipes the counters and goes quietly up to her room. She stares at the drawing of Veronica, especially at what remains of the left arm. She's had an idea, a strange idea that scares her a little, but finally she decides she will do it.

She takes out the eraser and carefully rubs out the left arm up to that point where it converts to shoulder.

A meaningless act, she tells herself, because erasing something from a picture can't make it disappear.

That isn't how things work in the real world.

21.

That night, Whit comes home with the news that there's been an infection and they are going to have to take a bit more of Veronica's arm.

Lana, at the dinner table, stills a spoonful of creamed corn. A strong surge of bile shoots up from her stomach. She puts her spoon down and takes a sip of water.

"What's that mean, a bit more of her arm?" she says.

Whit has seated himself and is spooning rice and gravy over his hamburger steak. "Up to the shoulder," he says. "They were talking about it yesterday, so it wasn't totally unexpected."

This time the bile is thicker and surges into Lana's mouth. She runs for the bathroom, where she throws up everything she's eaten. Her body trembles, and her skin is slick with sweat. She's on all fours, and when she glimpses herself in the full-length mirror, she thinks of a human in some myth being turned into a small groveling beast.

Behind her, the door eases open and Tilly sticks her head in. "Okay, Lana? All right?"

But Lana's eyes are fixed on the sweating, girl-like creature in the mirror.

A creature with the power to make true what isn't and to erase what is.

"Lana okay?" Tilly asks again.

Lana doesn't know what to answer. And then she doesn't have to. Whit is behind her now. "You through?" he says, and when she nods, yes, and wipes her lips with the sleeve of her shirt, he puts his hands under her arms and helps her to her feet, but trying to stand, her legs go rubbery. As they fold closed, Whit catches hold of her, one arm fully across her chest for a moment before he spins her slightly, and, throwing one arm beneath her knees and the other under her arms, he lifts her into the air and carries her upstairs. He is not a big man and even in her sweaty, nauseous state she is aware of the ease with which he manages this, and she thinks, *I'll bet he's a good dancer.*

He lays her on the bed and pulls a sheet around her. He asks Tilly to bring a glass of 7UP or ginger ale. Lana has her eyes closed but feels Whit's weight when he sits on the side of her bed. She opens her eyes. He's staring off. He looks like a man peering out from solitary confinement. When finally he takes a deep breath and begins to turn toward her, she closes her eyes.

"Lana," he whispers.

She doesn't open her eyes. She pretends she doesn't know why, but she does. She senses that her having her eyes closed will make it easier for him to say what he wants to say but knows he shouldn't. She thinks when she hears these words, they will be spoken with the voice of the person inside him, the one wanting to push his way out.

"Lana," he says again, but abruptly stops. Tennis shoes squeak on the stairs. Whit Winters doesn't say another word. Instead he takes up her clenched hand and unfolds it. With the soft tip of his finger he writes four letters on her palm, each letter sending through her skin ticklish feelings that flow to the furthest and most intimate parts of her body. She knows what letters they are and what word they spell. *L a n a.*

The squeaking footsteps move closer. He closes her hand over the invisible letters.

The tinkling of ice and glass becomes audible.

"Soda and snack coming right up, you bet!" Tilly says, and when Lana opens her eyes, Tilly is holding a tall glass with ice and a can of root beer inside. That's in one hand. In the other hand she is carrying a bowl of strictly pink Froot Loops.

Lana makes a weak laugh. "Pinkies are better than yellows," Lana says, and Tilly nods beamingly.

On his way out, Whit stops at the door and, looking back at Lana, he smiles so small a smile that Lana guesses that she alone in the world would know that it is one. She reaches up to feel for the lost two-dollar bill and then tries to remember how long it's been since she thought of it or of the man named Dee, who had been her father.

Part Two

22.

*A*lmost a week has passed. Lana had hoped in a half-guilty way that in Veronica's absence the house would be theirs, hers and Whit's, but Whit has hardly been home—he's been at the hospital a lot and out bidding a whole slew of painting jobs (though he hasn't landed any of them)—and when he has been home, the Snicks have been greedy for his company and have followed him so closely he's been like a man with four shadows. Five if you counted Lana.

Every now and then, he would catch her eye and hold it in a wistful-seeming way, but then one of the Snicks would say, "Play ball, Whit!" or " 'Eed 'elp, 'it!" and the moment would be gone. Hardly a full minute passes by without Lana's mind returning to the sketch paper and the powers it seems to contain. Repeatedly she thinks of getting out the paper and making a drawing of Whit and herself, with absolutely nothing else on the page, nothing and no one else to interfere, but whenever she thinks of it, she wonders if it might mean that they'd somehow be dropped into a blank, bleak landscape without food or shelter or even hope or, just as bad, if she drew only her and Whit, somehow something bad might happen to Tilly and Garth and Carlito and everybody else she leaves out of the sketch, and the one thing she doesn't want to do with the paper ever again is accidentally hurt somebody, so, in the end, she has just kept the drawing kit hidden away and not drawn anything at all.

The night before, Lana heard Whit come in late, and when he didn't come upstairs, she put on a robe and crept down. He was sitting at the kitchen table reading the *World-Herald* sports page, which he tipped to pick up the dim light from the single overhead lamp. He didn't see her and she just stood silently watching him for maybe a minute, aware and yet not aware of her tongue in the tooth slit, until he rattlingly turned back the paper and started scanning the headlines of the next page.

"Hi," she said.

His hand jumped. Then, "Hey, you. Did I wake you up? I was trying for quiet."

"You didn't wake me. Your diesel did."

He laughed and laid down his paper.

She slid into the chair opposite him. "Tired?" she said.

"And then some."

"Were you at the hospital?"

He nodded. "She says she can't sleep if I'm not there." He made a rueful smile. "Problem is, *I* can't sleep when I'm there. A nurse took pity and had a chair brought in that reclines a little bit, but still . . ." He arched his back to demonstrate the stiffening effect of it. He was quiet then for a second or two, staring at her in the shadowy light, and then he extended his arms onto the table. "Lemme see your hands."

She slid her hands forward. He took them in his, gently turned them over, and began smoothing his thumbs over her palms, slowly, in a way that sent sensations through her arms to the most secret parts of her body. "It's clear you're working way too hard," he said in a soft voice.

She didn't reply. She didn't want to speak. All she wanted was to keep receiving the sensations she was now receiving.

"You doing okay?" he said.

She nodded.

He let his thumb stray from her open palm up to the softness of her inner wrist, and if at that moment he'd asked her to follow him to any room of the house, she would've risen and followed, she couldn't have done anything else, but he didn't ask that. He let go of her hands and said, "You know what? If I don't go up to bed now, I'm going to fall asleep on this table and then our Snickledy friends will get up in the morning and eat me for breakfast."

She laughed, but the truth was, she was annoyed he could touch her skin and swell her with feeling and then, with just a joking word or two, disappear on her. When he pushed back from the table, she felt such a desperate need to keep him there that she heard herself blurt, "What would you do if you had three wishes?"

He chuckled. "Easy. Ask for three more."

"No, really," she said, because she knew that would keep him. One of the things she liked about Whit Winters was that he would think about things. If you asked him something and he saw you were serious, he'd give it his best serious thought.

Now he said, "You ever hear the story of the fisherman and his wife?"

Lana had, but she couldn't remember the specifics,

and besides, she wanted Whit to stay, so she shook her head, no.

"Well, this fisherman and his wife are peasants, poor as can be, living in a dirt-floor hut, eating fish head soup every night for dinner. And then he catches a holy mackerel, or something like that, and the mackerel can talk. It pleads for its life, and the fisherman decides that a talking fish is too mysterious and powerful to kill. He tosses the mackerel back and runs home to tell his wife, which was bad thinking on his part. She says right away the fish owes them big and sends him to ask the mackerel for a cottage. Presto, they're in one, but after a couple of days she looks around and she's still not happy. She sends her husband back to the fish, asking for a mansion, then a palace, then to be queen, empress, pope, and finally, 'like the good Lord.' "

Whit grinned. "And the moment she asks for this, all the grandeur disappears and they're back where they started, in a dirt-floor hut."

Lana thought it served them right. "I would've stopped at the cottage," she said, thinking about those drives through nice neighborhoods with her mother, playing the House Game.

Whit smiled. "That's because you're a better human being than your average citizen."

Whether this was a compliment or mild sarcasm, Lana wasn't sure.

Whit rose and stretched. "I think of that story from time to time. Know what I think the moral of it is?"

"That being pope is plenty good enough?" Lana said, hoping Whit would laugh.

He did, politely, and then said, "That nobody ever

knows when to stop." He yawned and grinned. "So, to answer your question, I suppose if I was a smart guy, I'd just say no to your three wishes. But since I'm not that smart, I'd probably say yes and hope I'd have enough sense to be careful with them."

He came around the table, leaned forward, and kissed her forehead in the same whispery way he'd kissed her that first time, in her room. He smelled faintly of lime soap, and she wanted to reach out and hold on to him for dear life, but she didn't. She knew that her three wishes used to be that her father was alive, that he was working in a normal place you could tell people about, and that he was coming home every night to one of those houses with a porch. She assumed that if she made those wishes, everything that was wrong with her mother would no longer be wrong.

But now Lana smelled the sweet scent of Whit's body and tried very hard not to wish for him, him, him. Then he walked away from her toward the doorway.

"Night," he said, and that's what Lana said, too.

|||

23.

*G*arth Stoneman is sitting on the front steps, waiting. It's eight twenty-five, almost halfway through his morning waiting hour, but he seems more anxious than usual today. Lana can see him from her place on the porch swing, where she's making pot holders with Tilly instead of washing dishes and vacuuming, two chores on the Saturday chart Veronica has drawn up from the hospital and sent home with Whit, who handed it to Lana apologetically. "Do what you can," he said, "and what you can't, you can't."

Tilly picks out the pot holder loop color, and Lana stretches it over the pegs. Sometimes Tilly can be urged to stretch and connect it herself, which, according to the physical therapist who visits for what seems like about three minutes every other month, is supposedly good for Tilly's fine-motor skills, though Lana doubts it.

"Pink again?" Lana says.

"You bet!" Tilly says. Her allegiance to pink is unswervable.

"Whatcha gonna do when we run out of pink?"

When Tilly doesn't reply, Lana looks up to see a panic surfacing on Tilly's face that seems almost brittle, and

Lana remembers Whit's line about everybody worrying too much. "Red's kind of pink when you think about it," Lana says, and just like that, the panic on Tilly's face dissolves.

"You bet," she says. "Red is just a pinker pink!"

Lana has to laugh, because, really, it's more or less true. "Pink squared," she says, and Tilly says, "Pink cubed!"

Garth hasn't moved. He just sits, looking at his Popeye guy, looking down the street one way for maybe five seconds, then looking down the street the other way for another five seconds, then looking again down at Popeye. Garth is skinny in a sickly sort of way. Lana thinks it's because his loneliness is like a tapeworm. His arms poking out of his Spider-Man shirt have no muscles at all, and even when he's looking down the street, he bows his head in a way that makes her wonder if the sun is in his eyes. He begins to twist Popeye's head around and around.

"You okay, Garth-man?" she says.

Garth isn't a talker, but he looks up enough to show that he's heard.

"Where's Popeye?"

Garth lifts him from his lap and rotates the head so that he's looking more or less at Lana. Popeye's definitely on the grimy side. "That sailor man needs a bath," Lana says, which causes Garth to pull Popeye protectively back into his lap. This makes Lana feel a little bit bad, so without thinking she says, "What're you and Popeye doing?"

"'Aiting."

Of course they're waiting. Except today Garth's waiting with particular desperation because it's Carlito's day with his father, which comes once a month, when Whit drives him to the county detention center. Carlito's father is in jail for hitting Carlito and his sister, among other things, so Lana thinks it's more than a little freakish that Carlito even wants to see him, but when she told this once to Whit, he just shrugged and said, "Maybe Carl only remembers the good parts." And then, "Love is a mysterious thing." In any case, Carlito's visiting days always make Garth even more convinced his turn is coming.

"Want to make a pot holder?" Lana asks him.

Garth shakes his head, no, and keeps twisting Popeye's head around and around. When Lana first came here, there was a small round hole in the side of Popeye's mouth, and one morning Whit sat at the kitchen table with a little dowel and some balsa wood. After a while he yelled, "Garth-man, bring Popeye over here!" and when Garth did, Whit slid a perfect little pipe into the hole at the side of Popeye's mouth. Garth beamed, and Whit said, "If Popeye gets lung cancer, we'll sue the dowel maker." A day or two later, Garth lost the new pipe, and Whit said, no problem, he'd make another, but he hasn't done it yet.

Tilly looks up from her plastic bowl of cloth loops and says, "Your mama's not coming, Garthy. You shouldn't sit there like that. No."

Lana knows Garth's waiting like this makes Tilly nervous. Lana knows because the waiting makes her nervous, too. Nervous and sad. How could someone bring her son into somebody else's house and leave him there and never talk to him or write to him or see him again? Why would you do that?

For the same reasons, Lana supposes, that her own mother swallowed methamphetamines and cheap vodka straight from a tall bottle. Maybe it was because her husband died and left her with one kid and zero money. Or maybe it was so she could live her own screwed-up life in her own screwed-up style without a nuisance-type kid getting in her screwed-up way. There are people in the world with zipped-tight hearts, and Lana supposes she should feel sorry for them, given the misery it brings them, but right now she doesn't feel sorry for them. She despises them. Because they're the ones who put the Tillys and the Garths and the Lanas in places like this.

Lana is staring at Garth staring down the street when Tilly hands her a pink loop, and as Lana stretches it over the frame, she has a thought so sudden and pure, she stills her hand so she can look at it undisturbed.

Of course. Of course. Why hadn't she thought of it before?

"I have to do something, Tilly," she says in a distracted voice. "You pick out all the reddish pink loops, okay, and I'll help you finish it later."

Tilly starts to get up, too. "I'm coming with you, Lana."

"No, silly," Lana says. "I need a little privacy."

"You're going to the bathroom?"

Lana nods. She doesn't really need to go to the bathroom, but now she will. She's never lied to Tilly before, and she's not going to start now. Besides, it's as good a place as any for doing the particular drawing she has in mind.

24.

*L*ana slides the black leather box from its place under her bed and carts it down the hallway to the bathroom. She locks the door behind her and after putting the toilet cover down, she sits, opens the flap, slides out the paper, and counts the sheets left.

Eleven.

Plenty, she thinks, and puts ten back.

She smooths her hand across a blank sheet of the old, pink-flecked paper. She takes up her pencil, closes her eyes, and what flows in an easy line from her mind to hand to pencil to page is an average-seeming woman standing on a broad wooden porch, near a door, with her hand raised to the knocker, while, on the other side of the wall, in the interior of the house, a thin boy holding a pipeless Popeye doll cocks his head, about to hear the knock that he never ceased to believe he would one day hear.

When she finishes the drawing, she feels as she always feels—astonished at how good it is and at how little it seems to be her own creation. But there it is, in front of her, a boy with his ear cocked, a mother with her hand raised, a perfect suggestion of fervent hope finally realized.

There, Lana thinks, and she feels the kind of inside-out happiness she felt that day the dust devil swept through her.

A happy ending for Garth.

Lana folds closed the leather cover of the Ladies Drawing Kit.

There's nothing to do now except wait for it to arrive.

25.

*L*ana serves lunch to Garth in his room instead of making him come to the table, adding a sandwich the size of a quarter for Popeye, which Garth doesn't even notice. She and Tilly eat bologna sandwiches with Alfred and, now that she's started Garth on the way to a happy ending, she begins to wonder what she might do for Alfred. She knows from Whit that Alfred's father did a vanishing act and that his mother was ruled incompetent because of suicidal tendencies. "Alfie thinks they're both dead," Whit said, "and in a way, he's right."

Now Lana says, "How long have you lived here, Alfred?"

Alfred chews his sandwich, rocks back and forth a few times. "D-d-don't know. Long time."

"I've been here longer," Tilly says. "I remember when Alfred came. I do."

"You h-h-hit me," Alfred says, and the small turn of his lips looks to Lana like crooked amusement.

"You steal," Tilly says. "You stole my Starburst. I remember. You did."

Alfred still smiles his small, crooked smile. "Th-th-that's right. Sorry."

"Where would you like to live in all the world, Alfred?" Lana asks.

Alfred rocks. His sandwich is gone, and there's a trickle of wet mustard on the pocket of his green golf shirt. Lana knows better than to swipe at it with a napkin. He doesn't like being tidied up.

"H-h-here," he says.

"We already live here," Tilly says. "Silly. With Lana and Whit and Garthy and Carlito."

"And h-h-her," Alfred says without any change of expression, and Lana knows that by this he means Veronica.

A silence follows and a minute or so later, when the doorbell rings, it sends a shock through Lana that's almost electrical.

"Get Garth!" she says at once, because she thinks it's going to be Garth's mother. "Have him answer the door!" Tilly and Alfred just stare at her. "Garth!" Lana yells. "Answer the door! It might be for you!"

Garth comes out of the downstairs bathroom buckling his pants and it isn't lost on Lana that she hasn't heard the toilet flush. He goes to the door, waits for a second, then swings it open.

A small, wiry man in a brown UPS uniform stands before him with a package.

He looks up from his clipboard and says, "Can somebody accept this for Chester . . . Pigeot, who lives next door?" He pronounces Chester's last name "pig-out."

Garth turns a bewildered look toward Lana, who is herself a little bewildered. She believed so completely that the doorbell meant Garth's mother had arrived that she can't quite believe the UPS man is alone. She looks behind him before she signs for Chet's package, and she looks up and down the street as the UPS man walks back to his truck. Nothing. No one.

"It's pronounced 'Pi-*zho*,'" Lana calls out, but the man is already hopping into the driver's seat. Lana closes the door and takes the square box inside. It's from a company in Chicago called Above Average Novelties.

"Me?" Garth says, looking at the package.

"No, Garth," Lana says. "False alarm."

"Let's open it!" Tilly says, and though Lana would love to know what Above Average Novelty Chester Pigeot has plunked down cash for, she knows she can't, and she sets the package on the counter unopened.

26.

A half hour later, outside, in the stale heat, Tilly is scrubbing yellow-brown crud from the Wet-'n'-Woolly plastic wading pool while Lana takes bedsheets off the drying line and wonders about the Ladies Drawing Kit. How it works, she knows, is something that can't be explained, but still, it seems like there ought to be some basic rules. Sometimes what she draws happens fast and sometimes it takes a little while. And what about Veronica's missing arm?—was there a subset of basic erasure rules?

This is a thought that gives Lana another idea, one about the pills Veronica planted in her room.

Tilly's lost in her crud removal, so Lana slips away and, once inside the house, hurries to her room and slides a blank sheet of paper from the leather case. She takes up a pencil, lets her eyes close and open in a long slow blink, and begins to draw. A while later—how long a while Lana has no idea; it feels like seconds—she drops the pencil and looks at what she's drawn: a cutaway of Veronica's purse that shows not just its shape and style but its contents, and in one corner, wedged between hairbrush and tissues, is the bag of pills.

Lana looks at the bag with an odd flush of pleasure, a feeling that grows even more pleasurable when she takes up the pencil again and, this time using its eraser, begins to rub the pills out of the plastic bag, and the sketch, and, she believes, her life.

She feels almost buoyant as she slams out the screen door and into the backyard, where Tilly has strayed from her cleaning project and is sitting in the dirt alongside the garage staring down at something in her hand.

"Look, Lana," she says, holding up a hollowed fist. "Jiminy Cricket!"

"Let him go and it'll be good luck," Lana says, an idea that doesn't seem to appeal to Tilly. She turns her back, so Lana can't see what she does next.

"Be nice," says Lana, and Tilly, with both hands cupped together now, says she's going to go show Jiminy to Garth. Lana starts to say no, she needs to stay here and finish cleaning the plastic pool, but with the first intake of breath, she realizes she's going to sound just like Veronica, so she stops.

"Sure," she says. Then: "But don't put Jiminy in one of your pockets and forget about him!" Last week Lana forgot to go through all of Tilly's pockets and put a lizard through the wash.

Tilly disappears into the house, and as Lana regards the sheets still on the line that need to come down, and the huge wicker basket of wet wash that still needs to go up, not to mention the piles of dirty clothes that still need to be washed, she thinks, *I wish Veronica was back,* and is stunned at what she's just wished.

Lana knows the basic three-wishes plot hinges on people

wasting their wishes, but she has nine pages left, not three, so she's really more like the fisherman and his wife. She needs to be careful with them is all and not get greedy, and even if she uses a wish for each of the Snicks, there will be plenty left for her. Except really anything she wished for herself would be something for her and Whit.

Where is he right now? she wonders. *What does he do while Carlito visits his father at the detention center? Why doesn't he come home and then go back for him instead of hanging around a strange town?*

What she really wishes is that Whit was back.

No, what she really wishes is that Whit was back and he's brought a housekeeper with him.

No, what she really wishes is that Whit was back and he's brought a housekeeper and a cook with him.

No, what she really wishes is that Whit was back and he's brought a housekeeper and a cook and the news that Veronica has run off with an ambulance driver.

Well, well, well, Lana thinks. *Getting greedy comes in a lot of different shapes. You don't have to want to be an empress or the pope or God. Or maybe playing God is exactly what you have to want. Wanting to play God for your own private purposes, whatever they are, might be what getting greedy is. And isn't bringing Garth's mother to the door and getting rid of those pills my way of playing God?*

Lana snaps the wrinkles from a yellow bedsheet and is folding it in half, then half again, lost in her thoughts, when she becomes aware of a presence.

Someone behind her, watching.

Whit, she thinks.

But when Lana turns, it's Chet, and there's a strange

stricken stiffness to his face, like he's been caught at something.

"What were you looking at?" she says.

"Nothing."

"Nothing?"

"I don't know. When you were taking in the dry sheets, it was like you . . ." His voice trails off.

"Like I what?"

He shakes his head. "I don't know. It's just that . . . it was nice to watch."

Lana is not displeased by this, and although she suspects there's more to what he was watching—her shorts are short and her T-shirt's skimpy—she guesses he's not going to say what it was, even if he could.

"So what do you want?" she says.

"Nothing. I was just coming to see if the UPS guy left anything with you for me?"

Lana tightens her gaze. "How'd you know that?"

Chet shrugs. "Mrs. Harbaugh across the street left a message."

Lana has seen Mrs. Harbaugh, has seen how she looks at her and the Snicks. "So Mrs. Hairball saw UPS go to your door, then ours, and she thought you ought to know about it just in case we tried to keep your package for ourselves?"

Chet shrugs. "Mrs. Harbaugh's thoughts are Mrs. Harbaugh's thoughts. They ain't mine." He smiles. "I like the Mrs. Hairball moniker, though. It fits her. She's the kind of gal a town like this coughs up pretty often."

Lana says, "It's yours, free of charge." She doesn't like Mrs. Harbaugh, and she's hoping Chet will use the nickname on one of his podcasts. Which reminds her of something, so as she leads him into the house for his package, she says, "I heard that Chief Chetteroid guy on K-SOD asking questions just like we were asking the other day."

"Who?" Chet says, playing dumb, which Lana ignores.

"Stuff like, 'Which would you rather lose, your right hand or your right eye?'"

"Who's this again?" Chet says blandly.

Lana begins to hand him the package, then, eyeing the address, pulls it back. "Uh-oh. This isn't addressed to you. It's addressed to somebody named *Chester.*"

Chet says, "You're a funny girl, Lana," but he doesn't say it with his usual sarcasm. It's more like he's trying to pay her a compliment, which is something new for him, and it makes Lana a little nervous. She shoves the package his way and says, "So what Above Average Novelty did Chester send away for?"

Chet seems to want to answer, but finally doesn't, not really. "I'll get back to you on that one." He lets his eyes linger on hers.

"Are you okay, Chet?" She has to admit, without the mole and with his little double life, he's become more interesting.

"Yeah, pretty much," he says, and gives it some further thought. "I had Ding Dongs and Dr Pepper for lunch. I don't think I should've done that."

"How many Ding Dongs?"

"Seven or eight. And two Dr Peppers."

Lana grins. "That's some staunch dining, Chester."

Chet laughs, but it's as if there's something going on inside him he doesn't understand, and it has nothing to do with dietary insult. He sighs and starts to go.

"Hey, Chet. One little thing."

"What's that?"

"When Chief Chetteroid was doing his either-ors, he said, 'Which would you rather lose, your mother or your father?' and you know what he said?"

When Chet doesn't answer, Lana says, "He said, 'Both.'"

Chet stares, waiting.

Lana says, "I suppose the chief was going for humor, but if you run into him, you tell him that the guys and gals over at Snick House think it was kind of a low blow."

Chet lowers his eyes, and when he raises them again, he looks abashed. "Okay," he says, "if I see him, I'll tell him."

27.

*T*hat day passes, then another, and Garth's mother still doesn't show. Wednesday, Garth doesn't want to go to the library and clean books because, he tells Mrs. Arnot, "'Other is 'oming day."

"Say again, Honeybear?"

Mrs. Arnot calls everybody Honeybear, except Tilly, who she calls Miz Pinkerdilly or, sometimes, Miz Pinkerdilly Pie.

"Garthy's waiting for his mother," Tilly says glumly before slipping into the backseat of Mrs. Arnot's cranberry Camry. "But her's not coming. No. Her never comes."

"She might, though," Lana puts in quickly, and, strange to say, these are her complete thoughts on the subject. It's been four days and her certainty in the sketch paper has slipped a little. Now, when she thinks of it, she thinks, *Maybe it works, and maybe it doesn't.*

Mrs. Arnot opens her car door and says cheerfully to Garth, "You sit in the front today, Honeybear. It's your turn to ride shotgun. And if somebody comes for you, Lana will call the library. Right, Lana?"

Lana nods. "I'm on it, Garth-man. She comes and I'm here for you."

But Garth's mother doesn't come, not that day and not Thursday, a day when Whit is in Marquette painting a convenience store, or on Friday, when Whit is first at the hospital with Veronica and then back in Marquette, or on Saturday, the day that Veronica is discharged from St. Marie's.

28.

*L*ana is sitting on the floor with Tilly, playing Candy Land, a game easy for Lana to Tilly-rig because Lana controls the cards. She slides cards from the top of the deck (and, when need be, the bottom), and she turns to see if Alfred is still copying headlines from the latest Wal-Mart circular. He is. His handwriting is large and jagged, like graffiti. PRICES LASHED, he writes. It makes Lana want to get him something more profound, like Shakespeare or the Bible, but she knows it's just making the letters that he likes.

The house of pathetic doodlers, Lana thinks.

Garth is outside playing with a tennis ball. He throws it to himself, high in the air, and then usually misses it. He's been eating even less lately, and Lana wonders if somehow, without really saying anything, she got his hopes even higher than before, and nothing happened, so now he has no reason to hope at all. It's depressing. She thought she could do something really good for somebody who'd had something really bad done to him. So what was that? A serious misreading of the facts? Wishful thinking? Delusions of grandeur?

"Double red," Lana says to Tilly, and moves herself past Lord Licorice.

Then she hears the familiar chug of Whit's old diesel, faint, but growing louder, and Lana's heart seems to beat louder, too. Whit's coming and he isn't bringing a cook and a housekeeper. He's bringing Veronica.

The Ice Queen.

Whit comes in first and drops a plastic sack of clothes and Veronica's purse—the blue purse, the one that used to have the plastic bag of pills in it—on the coffee table. He's left the front door open, and Lana turns to see if Veronica will follow him through it. She won't, at least not yet. Veronica is still sitting in Whit's truck, staring forward, a frozen expression on her face, and Lana suddenly knows that as bad as things were without Veronica to help, they'll be worse now.

Whit goes back out. On the coffee table, Veronica's blue purse is within arm's reach.

Do something. Hurry.

"Want a stick of gum?" Lana whispers to Tilly, who looks up from the game board.

"What gum?" she says.

Lana nods toward Veronica's purse, and Tilly grins.

"Shhh, then," Lana says, and, after glancing out the door—Whit has just now gotten Veronica out of the car and onto her feet—she grabs the blue purse, unzips it, and peers in. The bag isn't there, she's sure the bag isn't there, but then, rummaging with her hand, she finds something plastic and fishes it up.

The bag of pills.

So they're still there. They haven't been erased away.

Muffled voices and shuffling footsteps on the walk.

"Easy," Whit is saying, and Veronica keeps groaning and saying "Shit" again and again.

Lana pulls the bag of pills out of the blue purse and freezes. What now? Slide them under a cushion? Shove them down her pants? Heave them into a corner? And then what? Veronica would figure it out and then she'd be not just the girl who stashed drugs in her closet but also the girl who stole them back out of someone's purse. No, no, no. She needs a plan, not something stupid like this.

Frantically she jams them back into the purse, zips it closed, and pushes it back on the coffee table.

"No gum?" Tilly says.

"No gum," Lana says in a tight whisper, and when it seems possible that Tilly might put up a fuss, Lana slips the Queen Frostine card from the bottom of the deck and turns it over for Tilly, who shrieks with ecstatic surprise.

"Good one!" she says, and moves her gingerbread man way past Lana's.

Veronica's appearance, when she enters the room, is shocking. She's sweating, her face is grayish white, and she leans heavily on Whit for support. Hooked over her one arm is a black metal cane. Her left shoulder is wrapped in bandages that disappear under a sleeveless flowered top, and the open sleeve of that arm sticks out slightly, like a mouth saying the letter *O*. The rest of her isn't normal either. Her hair is pulled into a tight, oily ponytail, and without eyeliner or mascara, her eyes, when they dart toward Lana, look surprisingly small and fierce.

"Rest," Veronica gasps, and she and Whit stop in the middle of the room.

Alfred looks up briefly from his lettering. "Hi, R-R-Ronnie," he says, and Veronica, who's been taking in the details of the room, lets her eyes dart to him for a moment, but she doesn't speak, not that Alfred expects her to. He just grins and goes back to his work.

Veronica turns her eyes on Lana and blinks but doesn't speak. She doesn't have to. Her expression says it for her: *What have you been up to?*

"Hi," Lana says, and then forces herself to add, "Welcome home."

Veronica frees her one arm so that she can take the black cane in hand. Without taking her eyes from Lana, she points to a corner of the room and says, "Cobwebs."

F.U., Lana thinks. *F.U. cubed.* She says, "I've had lots to do."

"Yes, I'll bet you have," Veronica says, and for a moment the old ice is back in her eyes, but then she gasps and sighs. "I've got to lie down," she says in a low, miserable voice, the voice of someone who needs others to know of the ordeal she has suffered, is still suffering, and intends to suffer for quite some time. Whit half carries her up the stairs. Lana can hear the thud and scuff of his boots as he moves around the room, tucking Veronica in, she imagines, making her comfortable.

For Lana, the lone bright spot of these circumstances is that she doesn't feel guilty. Erasing Veronica's arm in the sketch didn't cause Veronica's loss of limb. It was just coincidence. Because the facts are all there to see. If the pills are still in Veronica's purse (and they are) and if Garth's mother is still in the great beyond (and she is), then the paper is just paper. If it ever had magical properties, which Lana doubts, it doesn't have them now.

In the strange, altered silence, Tilly loses interest in

Candy Land. She holds the Queen Frostine card in her lap and stares out the window.

"Hungry?" Lana asks. Neither Tilly nor Alfred answers, but it's eleven-thirty, and at noon Carlito will be back from his speech therapy. Besides, Lana has a sudden craving for cheese toast and Chicken and Stars soup. It was her mother's favorite meal when she was off the pills and alcohol enough to think about eating—Chicken and Stars soup with parmesan melted on white bread.

29.

*T*illy slowly stirs two oversized cans of Chicken and Stars in the big copper-bottom saucepan while Lana sprinkles parmesan onto the bread and slides it into the toaster oven.

"Alfred?" she calls. "Thirty seconds to grubville."

Alfred doesn't answer.

"Bubbles!" Tilly says, and Lana knows this means the soup is boiling. She turns the heat down and asks Tilly to stir a little more just to keep her busy. Lana puts out six bowls and place settings, slides four pieces of cheese toast out and four more pieces in, and then calls, "Come and get it!"

As she ladles soup for herself and Tilly, she calls, "Soup's up, Alfred." Then, "Alfred?"

Silence from the living room.

Lana's hand freezes for the long moment it takes for this silence to sink in, then she drops the ladle into the saucepan and rushes into the living room.

Alfred is kneeling beside the sofa, so absorbed in what he's doing that he doesn't notice her. He lifts a black pen out of Veronica's purse and drops it in his tote bag. Then a tube of lip gloss. He unfolds what appears to be a receipt, and he adds that to his tote bag.

"Alfred!" Lana says in a low, tight voice, and his hand jerks out of Veronica's purse.

After the look of shock, his expression dissolves to remorse. "S-s-sorry," he says.

"I know you are, Alfred," Lana says, and puts her hand on his, "but you know you're not allowed to take things from anybody's purse." Lana picks up the purse, looks for the plastic bag of red pills, and can't find them. *Don't panic,* she tells herself. *Don't panic.*

She takes out a cell phone, a pair of sunglasses, and a mashed package of gum. She can hardly breathe. She looks at Alfred. "What else did you take?"

Alfred shakes his head.

"Hand me what you took," Lana says.

Alfred hands her the pen and the receipt.

"Everything!" she says.

He shakes his head, and she says, "Lip gloss, Alfred."

"Okay," Alfred says, rocking back and forth a little.

He hands over his tote bag. Inside it, along with the lip gloss, an ID badge, and two of the special black pens Alfred buys at Wal-Mart, Lana finds an empty plastic bag.

It's hard for Lana to steady herself. She holds the bag in front of Alfred's face. "Did you eat anything out of this?"

Alfred looks away from the bag.

"Alfred!"

He looks off, frozen with fear.

"Okay, Alfred," Lana whispers. "Stick out your tongue. Let me see your tongue."

Alfred shakes his head.

"Please," Lana says. She sticks out her own tongue, and this time Alfred copies her. His tongue is bright synthetic red.

"R-R-Red Hots," he says.

Lana runs up the stairs two at a time and grabs Whit's arm just as he's setting the bedroom door closed behind him.

"Alfred took all the pills," Lana whispers, tugging him toward the stairs.

Whit follows but at a normal pace. "What pills?" he says.

Lana says, "*The* pills! The ones Veronica planted in my room. You left her purse on the table and I forgot to put it away and when I came back in, he'd eaten the pills out of the purse! He thought they were Red Hots."

They reach the living room, where Alfred is still kneeling abjectly by the sofa. Whit puts his hand on Alfred's shoulder and says, "It's okay this time, Alfred. Those were just candy. But you could have hurt yourself. You know that, right?"

Alfred nods.

Lana can't believe what she's just heard. "What're you talking about?" she says. "What do you mean, just *candy*?"

But Whit doesn't answer. He gets Alfred to help him put Veronica's things back into her purse, and then he zips it up and says, "There. We'll put this someplace out of harm's way, okay, Alf-man?"

Alfred nods again, and Whit heads upstairs with the blue purse.

Lana goes into the kitchen and opens a Fresca. She can't stand Fresca, but it's the only soda in the fridge. Tilly, she notices, hasn't left the table during the little crisis and has in fact used Lana's absence to eat everybody else's cheese toast. There are crumbs around her lips and on one cheek. "Everything okay?" Tilly says, still chewing.

Lana nods. "I guess so."

Alfred comes in and begins eating. Lana slides more cheese toast out of the toaster oven and sets it on the table, which she knows will keep Tilly and Alfred occupied. She's leaning against the kitchen counter holding the cold Fresca can against her cheek when Whit walks in. "You all right?"

She waits for him to settle himself close to her. Then, in a low voice and as calmly as she can, she says, "What I saw that day when she accused me was not a bag of Red Hots."

"Well," he says in an amused tone, "maybe Red Hots was what you'd call a misnomer. They were actually more like red placebos."

"Placebos?"

"Pills that look like pills except they don't have anything in them."

"I *know* what placebos are," Lana says with some irritation, but the truth is, she feels like she's chasing behind all this. "How did they get there?"

"How did what get there?"

"The *placebos*," she says through tight teeth.

"Oh." Whit ducks forward and grabs a piece of cheese toast from the table. "Nurse friend of mine switched them out for me." He takes a big bite of the bread.

"Why?"

He swallows, then brushes crumbs from his mouth with the back of his hand. "So if Ronnie ever did get around to sending those pills to the lab, they'd come back negatory."

Lana feels this news enfold her in its embrace. The pills are gone. She will stay. Whit has protected her. She's afraid if she looks at Whit, she might cry, so she again presses the cold Fresca can to her cheek and looks away. "Why?" she says in a faint voice.

"Why what?" he says.

She turns to look at him. "Why did you do that for me?"

He'd been about to take another bite, but now he stops. He straightens up and turns her way and lets his eyes settle into hers. "Oh, I guess you know why," he says, "every bit as well as I do."

For a long moment everything except Lana's heart seems still, and then, from overhead, there is a dim *thunk thunk thunk* and Whit turns his head to listen.

The sound comes again—*thunk thunk thunk*—but this time it's louder and Tilly and Alfred are listening, too.

"What's that?" Lana says.

Whit with a wistful smile says, "That would be the patient upstairs."

"What's she pounding with?"

"Her cane." His smile widens slightly. "The cane is a tool of many uses."

After Whit has departed to see what Veronica wants, Tilly says, "Who's pounding?"

"The Ice Queen," Lana says.

30.

Thunk thunk thunk.

It's always the same. Three thunks. Then, if Whit or Lana doesn't call upstairs to ask what Veronica wants, there will be three more thunks, louder and more insistent. Whit never waits for the second set of thunks; Lana always does. Veronica's been home four days now, and Lana notices Whit is making himself scarce. "Jobs to bid, jobs to do," he says, and off he goes, chugging away from Snick House.

Thunk thunk thunk.

Lana steps out of the kitchen, where she's serving breakfast to the Snicks, and yells, "What do you want?"

"Breakfast," Veronica yells, loud enough so she can be heard and yet weak enough that she'll seem frail. Dr. Gooch, a youngish, unmarried guy, a little goofy-looking with his long neck and big bobbing Adam's apple, has prescribed total bed rest.

"Okay!" Lana yells up.

It's Wednesday. A week before, Lana had proclaimed it Pink Wednesday in Tilly's honor. She'd put strawberry syrup in everybody's milk and red food coloring in the pancakes.

She's done the same thing today, and when she takes the pancakes upstairs, Veronica sits up in bed, picks up a fork with her right hand—her only hand—and then stops. She stares down at the tray. "What's wrong with the pancakes?"

"Nothing," Lana says. "They're regular except I put red food coloring in them to make them pink. Tilly likes it, and so do the others."

"Well, I don't," Veronica says. Then, looking evenly at Lana, "Maybe it's the kind of thing you have to be a little on the mongo side to appreciate. But my disability is physical, not mental, so if you wouldn't mind bringing me some *unpinkened* pancakes . . ."

"The whole batch is that way."

This seems, oddly, to *please* Veronica. Her shoulders drop into a relaxed bow, and a cold smile stretches across her lips. "Then make another batch," she says.

Lana stares at Veronica. Veronica stares at Lana. But there is a difference, and Lana can see it. Veronica is enjoying this. She says, "You know what Whit said the other day when he came into my hospital room? He said he found my new look *disarming*."

It takes Lana a long second to get it, and then—she can't help herself—a quick, nervous laugh slips from her lips.

Veronica nods. "Whit thought it was funny, too, but you tell me, do you think this is funny?" And here, with her one hand, Veronica slides the sleeve off her left shoulder.

Lana doesn't want to look, but before she can avert her eyes, they light on the pale, fleshy protuberance that at its end is conical and pink. It reminds her, strangely, of an extra breast, but nippleless and misshapen, as alien as a third eye on a forehead.

Lana has looked away but now hears a raspy sound and

glances again: Veronica is raking at the fleshy stump's soft pink end with her fingernails, hard, so hard Lana expects the tear of skin and ooze of blood.

"Don't," she hears herself say. And then—she isn't looking anymore; she *can't* look anymore—she actually hears the scratching stop.

Veronica laughs a cold laugh. "You and Dr. Gooch," she says.

A rustling follows, and when Lana looks again, Veronica has covered herself, and a thick silence has filled the room, a waiting silence, because there's more coming, Lana can feel it.

"Things have changed," Veronica says finally, "and I'm not just talking about the itch where my arm used to be." She blinks a long, slow blink. "We need to come to an understanding."

Lana tries to harden her expression, but this merely produces a fresh gleam of cold pleasure in Veronica's eyes. She says, "There's only one reason you're still at this address, and that's because you're the little den mother." Her smile stretches slightly thinner. "Den mother and upstairs maid. And the day you don't handle your duties in a top-notch fashion is the last day you spend under Whit Winters's roof. *Comprende?*"

Outside, the gentle hoo-hooing of a mourning dove, and Lana thinks of gliding away in flight. She imagines a stilted cottage with a thatched roof on a sunny beach.

"Comprende?" Veronica repeats, and Lana is brought back.

"Comprende," she says in a small voice.

"Well, then," Veronica says, and she pushes the tray of offending pancakes in Lana's direction.

Lana, despising herself as much as Veronica, bends forward to pick up the tray. But as she carries it to the door, Veronica speaks again. "Magazines," she says.

Lana turns to see Veronica pointing her black cane toward some magazines stacked on a chair in the corner. Lana sets down the tray and begins to bring the entire stack to Veronica.

"Not all of them!" Veronica says.

Lana looks at her.

"The new *Cosmo*."

Lana finds it near the top and slides it out. Veronica waits until she's nearly to the bed before she says, "And the *Us*."

It turns out there are several copies of *Us* in the stack. "Which one?"

Veronica yawns. "The one with the ten hottest widowers on the cover."

Through the window Lana sees a taxi slowly passing as if looking for an address and she watches until it rolls out of view. Then, in the stack of magazines, she finds a *People* with a cover story of the ten wealthiest widowers. "You mean this?"

Veronica shrugs a yes, and Lana sullenly sets the magazines on the bedside table. Veronica regards them, yawns again, and says, "And a small glass of orange juice while I'm waiting for breakfast."

Lana glares at her.

"*Faith*," Veronica says. "*Unity*." She takes a deep breath as if of alpine air. "They really are words that lift the spirits."

Downstairs, a knocking sound is followed by footsteps.

Veronica glances at the clock. "Oh my God," she says, "it must be John."

"Who?"

"Dr. Gooch. He said he'd drop by this morning. Give me five minutes to get presentable." Then, slipping into a cold smile, she adds, "Offer him some pink pancakes or something."

Lana, leaving with the tray in hand, bumps Veronica's door closed with her hip and has to resist the urge to scream. Scream and throw things.

Which would mean, as Veronica had put it, the end of her time under Whit's roof. Things had changed, all right, and not for the better.

As Lana descends the stairs with the tray, the first thing she sees is Garth's Popeye doll lying on the floor. Then she sees Garth himself, his skinny arms wrapping and unwrapping his chest, his head and feet bobbing, his face tense with rapture. Lana looks beyond him to a middle-aged woman who stands stiffly on the front porch, and the woman casts her dull brown eyes up at Lana.

31.

*G*arth's mother, Mrs. Stoneman, seems as mystified by her presence here as everybody else. She tells Lana that she just decided to come, and something behind the tiredness in her eyes seems to say that now that she's here, she wonders why she is. She'd taken the train from Salt Lake to Cheyenne, she says, and then a bus to Two Rivers, and then a taxi to the house. The house didn't seem familiar to her, but the address was right, so she'd gone ahead and knocked.

Still bobbing, Garth takes Mrs. Stoneman to his room, showing her where he always lines up his action heroes on the sill of his window facing out so they can keep on the lookout for danger, and to the kitchen, where he eats his Cocoa Puffs or pancakes every morning. Each time they run into one of the other Snicks, Garth with a tense, beaming face says, "Is 'y 'om!"

He even takes Mrs. Stoneman upstairs, where Veronica in a weak voice gives the details of what she calls her "personal tragedy" and tells of Dr. Gooch's strict protocol for total bed rest and, letting her eyes shift to Lana standing in the door, thanks her lucky stars that "our Lana has been here to take over as the house major domo." (This is a grade up, Lana notices, from den mother and upstairs maid. She also notices that Veronica, in making herself presentable for Dr. Gooch, has merely changed into a fancier nightgown. What Veronica means to present, Lana guesses, is her blimp-sized bazookas.)

As happy as she is for Garth, Lana cannot stop herself from thinking over and over again, *It works! It works! It works!* This is proof, isn't it?—absolute proof. She erases the pills and now they're gone. She draws Garth's mother coming back and now she's here. She tries not to think about Veronica's red, aching stump. Lana wants to get away to her room, find the paper, and figure out how to make it work for her and Whit. It's better than winning the lottery. It's better than a magic fish or a genie in a bottle.

But Lana can't get away. She's the major domo. She's in charge.

She sets out orange slices, Chips Ahoys, and lemonade at the kitchen table as a special treat for everyone. Garth sits next to his mother while she sips lemonade and doesn't touch the Chips Ahoys. She doesn't talk either. She just sits and looks around.

"Alfred ate a whole toothpaste today," Tilly announces, and then looks at Alfred. "Didn't you?"

Alfred ducks his head and grins.

"And the other day he ate a whole bag of 'Ronica's pills!"

Mrs. Stoneman turns to Lana, who says, "They weren't pills, Tilly. They were Red Hots, right, Alfred?"

Alfred beams.

"But you thought they were pills!" Tilly says. "You told Whit they were pills!"

"But I was wrong," Lana says in a curt voice, and the table falls quiet. She turns to Mrs. Stoneman and says, "I guess you're pretty tired after all the traveling."

Mrs. Stoneman nods. Then she says, "So Mrs. Winters is bedridden?"

"For a while, I guess. Not for long."

"And where's Mr. Winters?"

"He's painting today." Lana feels oddly defensive. "Usually he's home, but today's he's painting. He's painting a three-story Victorian over in Fawnskin, with three colors, yellow, black, and green, except it's more like a sage green." She would keep talking, but she sees Mrs. Stoneman's not listening. Mrs. Stoneman's eyes are crawling around the room, taking in information. She doesn't like this place, Lana can tell, but that's fine. Good, even. It'll just make it easier for her to take Garth and go.

When Tilly distracts Garth by building a leaning tower of orange peels, Lana asks Garth's mother the question she's been dying to ask: "So what made you decide to come back?"

Mrs. Stoneman shakes her head. "I don't know." Garth, giving his chest a happy squeeze, is staring with obvious pleasure at Tilly's budding construction. Mrs. Stoneman regards him for a moment, then her gaze drifts and Lana needs to bring her back.

"But do you remember what day you decided or anything?" Lana says.

Mrs. Stoneman says, "It was just an idea is all. I just kind of woke up with it. What's funny is, I didn't . . ."

Tilly's construction has collapsed and at once Garth says, "'Ee now!" and Alfred starts piling up his own orange peels.

"Do you let them do that?" Mrs. Stoneman says.

Lana shrugs. "It's supposedly good for their fine-motor skills."

"Arguing and clamoring?"

Lana hears the nervousness in her own laugh. "No, the arguing and clamoring aren't good for much of anything, but they're hard to get rid of."

Garth, who's eaten all his own cookies and none of his orange wedges, reaches across his mother to take one of the cookies from her plate, and, in the quickest instant, something flickers in Mrs. Stoneman, and Lana has the feeling that Mrs. Stoneman wants to slap Garth's hand away but keeps herself from it. Again her eyes light hard on the kids at the table, then they become gauzy and drift off, as if she no longer needs to see anything in this house, has seen all there is to see, and is now trying to see all the way back to Salt Lake.

Sudden heavy laughs burst from the table, all directed at Carlito, who's holding an orange wedge in his mouth so that it looks like a giant orange smile. Garth, when he laughs, opens his mouth to expose half-chewed chocolate chip cookie. Again something seems to flicker through Mrs. Stoneman, and again she suppresses it. But a moment or two later, she pries Garth's hand from her last cookie. He stops laughing and looks up.

"You know sugar makes you worse," she says. "I need something out of my bag."

A nasal decongestant, it turns out. While Garth watches, Mrs. Stoneman sprays decongestant first in one nostril, then the other. After she caps the bottle and puts it away, she wraps her hands around the cold, beading lemonade glass, and Garth presses his hands into his armpits as if to trap them. "'Ot eat," he says, shaking his head.

"So you just decided to come back," Lana says.

"Yes," Mrs. Stoneman says, and there is now a clear tone of irritation in her voice. "I just decided."

There's more giggling laughter at the table, and now Tilly and Alfred are wearing giant smiles made with cookie halves, and Garth, laughing his thick laugh, abruptly grabs the Chips Ahoy, and in the instant he starts to position it on his face, his mother turns rigid.

"Stop that right now!" she barks, and as the whole table turns quiet, Garth puts down the cookie and seems to shrink down into himself.

"'Orry," he says in his mangled voice, and it reminds Lana of Tilly saying she was a big mistake, and Lana sees suddenly and all at once how all of the Snicks have been made to know they are big mistakes and that what small portions of love or affection or even tolerance might come their way will come at the pleasure of people like Mrs. Stoneman, or Veronica, or her own mother.

"Don't be sorry," Mrs. Stoneman says, her voice still hard, "just be good."

Garth looks like a scraggly dog who's just been hit and might be hit again. Without a word, he slips from the table and leaves the kitchen, probably to get Popeye, Lana thinks.

In the silence that follows, Mrs. Stoneman becomes self-conscious. "Please," she says in a tight voice, "just go on about your business. Whatever it is you do. Just go ahead and do it." She turns to Lana with a helpless look. "In Salt Lake City, I do the bookkeeping for a restaurant called Mack's. I take the bus, two transfers each way. I eat lunch at my desk so I can leave early enough to catch the four twenty-five. I have a room with a hot plate and its own bathroom and cable TV." Mrs. Stoneman makes a small unhappy smile. "I like that room. I like that job. I like that life. How . . . ," she begins, but she doesn't finish. She collapses back into her thoughts.

In the quiet, from the other room, Garth's feet shuffle toward them. He stops at the kitchen door. He looks limp again, and he's holding Popeye in one hand and twisting Popeye's head around and around with the other.

It's quiet for a few seconds and then, again, the sounds carry down from overhead: *thunk thunk thunk*.

32.

*W*hen Lana has mixed up the fresh pancakes (without any offer of help from Mrs. Stoneman), she delivers them to Veronica and explains the situation. Mrs. Stoneman is tired and is having some kind of allergic reaction to the pollens here and wants to get a motel room, but she doesn't want to spend money on a taxi and Whit's gone, so there's nobody to take her.

Veronica seems not to hear. She hands Lana her orange juice and says, "Sip this."

"What?"

"Sip it."

"Why?"

"Yours is not to reason why."

Lana sips it. "It's fine."

"Good. Now try a bite of this." She extends a forkful of pancake.

Lana already has it in her mouth when she realizes what Veronica's doing. She swallows and says, "Doesn't seem poisoned to me."

Veronica doesn't respond to this, but she does begin to eat. "Here's my question," she says while she chews.

"Does Garth's mother think she can just walk in here and whisk him away, because if she does . . ."

But Lana interrupts. "I don't think she thinks any- thing," she says. "I don't even think she's sure why she's here."

This interests Veronica. "Then why did she come?"

Because I drew her here, Lana thinks. "I have no idea," she says.

Veronica chews, swallows, sips. "Okay. How about asking your little boy chum to take Mrs. Stoneman to the motel. He can drive her in my car." The Monte Carlo, which was finally back from the auto shop.

"If you're talking about Chet, he's not my *boy chum* or whatever goofy thing you just called him."

Veronica shrugs this off. "He's got his license, doesn't he?"

Lana has no idea. All she knows is that K.C. has let Chet drive his LeSabre once or twice. "Yeah," she says.

Veronica leans from her bed, uses the crook of the black cane to hook the strap of her purse, and pulls it toward her. Her hand disappears into the purse. "A shame about Alfred stealing those pills," Veronica says casually, and lets her gaze slide toward Lana. "But the nice thing about pills is they're replaceable." A moment later, she hands Lana the keys. "Tell your little boy chum, no new scratches."

Lana ignores this and asks where he should take her.

"I don't know much about motels," Veronica says, "but my recommendation is the Best Western on High- way 20."

33.

"Not much of a recommendation," Chet says when Lana hands him the keys. "The only other motel is the Wagon Wheel, and it's a different kind of motel."

Lana asks what "different" means.

"Well, it was an old five-unit apartment building before they converted it, and what motel customers of a certain type like is that you can park your car in a garage, close the garage door behind you, and go right into your room without prying eyes knowing you or your vehicle is there"—he wags his eyebrows—"if you get my drift."

She does. "I thought it was a big trucker place."

"Is. That's the other clientele." He rattles the keys. "Is Mrs. Stoneybrook going to tip me?"

"It's Mrs. Stoneman, and I doubt it very much."

Chet is nodding. "Though I don't see what would keep me from doing a little joyriding on the way back."

"That's some staunch thinking," Lana says, which, to her surprise, seems to embarrass Chet. Something's changed in Chet. Something's definitely changed. Maybe he has a girlfriend or something. She thinks of asking, but she's afraid that'll embarrass him, too.

"So do you have a driver's license?" she says.

"The question is, *Do I have a driver's license?* And the answer is, Yes, I do."

Lana thinks she sees the loophole he's wormed through. "Okay. You have a driver's license, but is it yours?"

"No, it's not."

Lana laughs. "All righty, then. What I'm going to remember here is the 'Yes, I do.'"

"Glad we could do business," Chet says, and adds an easy smile.

Something occurs to Lana, something she's been waiting to ask. "So tell me, Chester," she says to Chet, "what Above Average Novelty came in the Above Average Novelty box?"

Chet's face immediately and intensely colors.

"Ha!" Lana says. "It's something embarrassing. Tell, tell, tell."

Chet's discomfort doesn't abate. "The truth is, it wasn't for me."

This time Lana actually laughs. "That is the lamest of the lame," she hoots. "That is the mother of all lameness. *It wasn't for you.* Who was it for, then?"

Chet looks down. His forehead is pink and glazed with sweat.

"Speak, Chester," she says, with real fun in her voice, but something happens then to save Chet.

Behind them, a screen door creaks open and bangs closed. They both turn to look. Across the lawn, Mrs. Stoneman is standing alone on the Winterses' front porch holding her bag in one hand, waiting.

34.

"She's coming back," Tilly says. "She's not leaving."

Garth sits hunched on the ottoman in the front room, clutching his Popeye doll, twisting the Popeye head. Garth's eyes look frantic.

"Tilly's right," Lana says. "Everything's okay. Everything's all right."

But the truth is, nothing feels okay or all right. She wonders what's gone wrong with the sketch, what she put in or left out that wasn't right. She wants to put her arm around Garth or hold his hand, but she knows she can't. "How about an Otter Pop?" she says, and Tilly says, "Yes!" but it's as if Garth doesn't even hear.

Lana shepherds him into the kitchen, but when she lays a turquoise Otter Pop in front of him, he doesn't look at it.

"C'mon, Garth-man," she says. "It's turquoise. Your personal fave."

He just keeps twisting Popeye's head around and around, and Tilly, almost done with her red Otter Pop, says, "Can I have Garth's?"

A minute or so later, Veronica thump-thump-thumps, and Lana goes up. "Dishes," Veronica says, and nods at the tray of dirty breakfast dishes. "And this."

She presents Lana with a long list of grocery items. "Buy the generic in the biggest sizes, and take the Snicks to help you carry," she says.

As Lana carries the tray off, Veronica says, "And go by the drugstore and pick up the prescription Dr. Gooch is calling in for me."

Lana stares at her. "And still be back by Thursday?"

Today is Wednesday.

Veronica in her iciest tone says, "Very droll."

On the way downstairs, Lana detours to her room, lays the breakfast tray on her bed, and slides out the Ladies Drawing Kit. She finds her drawing of the woman on one side of the door about to knock and the boy with his Pop-eye doll on the other side of the door waiting. It's skillful and seems complete and yet something is wrong with it. That much Lana knows. Something's wrong. But what? The faces, maybe. Garth and his mother look apprehensive. They don't look happy enough.

Downstairs something crashes. From the next room, Veronica yells, "What was that?" and from the bottom of the stairs, Tilly yells, "Lana!"

Quickly Lana grabs the pencil and, without waiting for the calm feeling to come over her, she sketches smiles onto the faces of Garth and his mother, but she knows at once it won't work. She has the feeling you can't change anxious faces to happy ones. Even with the smiles drawn in, they don't look that happy.

"Lana!" Tilly bawls again, and this time Lana answers.

"Coming," she yells.

35.

A half hour later, after cleaning up the pieces of a pudding bowl (broken by the Snicks while eating the pancake batter out of it with their fingers), Lana, Carlito, Tilly, Alfred, and Garth set out in single file for the market, a long twenty-minute walk. Taking the Snicks someplace on foot, Whit once told Lana, is like herding a pack of cats.

The main store in Two Rivers is Rodeo Meats. It always makes Lana think she's buying the rejects from the Dawes County Rodeo—roping calves whose legs got broken, broncs too old to buck, Brahma bulls too easy to ride. The aisles are narrow and short. It's not like shopping at one of the big supermarkets in Lincoln or Rapid City, where the inside light is brighter than the sun and you can fit three shopping carts side by side and there are thousands of things to choose from. At first Rodeo Meats seemed dumpy and puny to Lana, but now she thinks it's almost perfect. The Snicks only like the most basic foods is one reason, and another is that the Snicks tend to drift off and the one thing you can't do in a place as small as Rodeo Meats is lose a person.

Today, as usual, Carlito touches things as they go along: bags of pasta, boxes of cookies, cans of soup. Alfred makes polite comments. "That's cute," he says of a little plastic bag of jacks. Garth carries Popeye and walks with his head down and his feet pointed outward in a kind of a shuffle. Tilly says, "I'm smart, Lana. I'm helpful. I can shop. Yes."

Lana's given Alfred the list because he's the only one who can read. "F-f-f-frankfurters," he says.

When Lana makes a list, she organizes it according to their route through the store, but Veronica's list has them going every which way. She's reading over Alfred's shoulder, looking for something canned, when Tilly grabs three big cans of generic chicken noodle soup. "Soup!" Tilly says, and, amazingly, Lana finds it on the list.

"Thumbs-up, Tilly," Lana says, trying to herd them to the back of the store, to the meat counter. Ground beef's on the list, and she tries to turn Carlito and the cart at the same time. The only way to keep Carlito with you in a store is to keep one of his hands on the handle of the shopping cart, as if he's helping you drive. Finally they reach the glass case of red meat.

"Hi," Lana says to the butcher behind the counter, a man with huge eyebrows who is checking out each of the Snicks like he's never seen them before. "Are you new?" Lana asks.

"As opposed to old?" the man says, but there's no fun in his voice. He's staring at Carlito, whose mouth hangs open, and at Garth, who is moaning quietly. The butcher keeps staring at them, something you might expect from a five-year-old, not a fifty-something. Besides the bushy eyebrows, the man also has stray hairs sprouting from his nose and ears.

"Five pounds of hamburger," Lana says, and this at

least pries the man's eyes from Carlito and Garth. He's staring now at Lana. "Say again?"

She repeats her order, and when the butcher begins to grab the ground meat from the browning part of the loaf, she points to the fresher stuff and says, "From the front if you wouldn't mind too much."

The butcher glares at Lana, but he takes it from the front. Lana knows that this hairy-eared butcher thinks old browning beef is just about right for the Snicks, and she also knows that if Whit were here, he'd introduce each of the Snicks to the butcher, maybe tell him what each of the Snicks is good at, turn it all into a festive little event that leaves everybody feeling just a little better about themselves, even the hairy-eared butcher, who, at the moment, is sullenly taping the hamburger into brown paper. Lana glances at her list and asks Tilly if she can go get the ketchup.

"You bet!" Tilly says, "I can shop, Lana, yes," and sets off for the wrong side of the store.

"Other way, Tilly," Lana says, running after her and gently turning her toward the condiments.

Alfred is standing still, holding his grimy old tote bag. "I n-n-need to go to the bathroom, Lana," he says.

"Okay," Lana says. But Tilly hasn't come back yet. "Tilly?" she calls, loud but not too loud.

To her relief, Tilly comes back grinning and holding the ketchup. It's the fourteen-ouncer, the tiniest bottle the store sells. They need the forty-eight-ounce Western Family at least, and the sixty-four would be better.

"Excellent, Tilly!" she says. "Go see if they have a bigger one, too, okay? I'm going to take the guys to the bathroom."

Alfred doesn't really need help, but Lana stays nearby because it's an employee bathroom and way back in the stockroom, where the others could get into trouble.

One minute, two minutes, three minutes pass.

The stockroom is cool, at least. Garth has stopped moaning, but he keeps his eyes down and twists the head of his Popeye around and around. Carlito runs his hand over each stack of plastic-wrapped boxes, then moves to a row of watermelons, which he touches as if baptizing a baby.

"You okay in there, Alfred?" Lana asks.

"Yes," Alfred calls back. "I'm w-w-wiping myself."

Just a little too much information, Lana thinks.

By the time she's made sure Alfred has washed his hands and Carlito has blessed all the watermelons, Lana's begun to worry about Tilly, and, sure enough, when they come back out of the stockroom, she's not in the ketchup aisle. She's in the cereal aisle, sitting on a produce crate, eating Cap'n Crunch from a box she's opened. "Where were you guys?" she says.

Lana checks her watch. She's now been in Rodeo Meats for thirty-five minutes and they've only gotten half their list. "Okay," she says. "Listen up. If you all follow me in a single line until I finish, and if you don't fight or stop, and if we're done in ten minutes, I'll buy powdered doughnuts for the walk home."

The Snicks are quiet for a moment, then Tilly says, "Lots of *if*s," and Garth says, "'Awk-lit," which Lana knows means he wants chocolate doughnuts instead of powdered.

"We're wasting time," Lana says, and begins arranging

the Snicks one after another, each holding the shirttail in front, except for Garth, who will only touch the front of the cart that Lana pushes, so that before long they're moving through Rodeo Meats like a slow-motion conga line, Lana tossing in items whenever she finds them. It takes them fifteen minutes to finish, but Lana buys doughnuts anyway, the variety pack, and leads the conga line to the checkout stand.

When they stop, Carlito breaks formation, walks up to Lana, and reaches out to bless her shoulder. Lana pats his hand and smiles at the checker, a big woman named Francine who's always been friendly to Lana.

"Just shoot me," Lana says.

The checker laughs. "Honey, you won't know real misery till you try marriage on for size."

Alfred's picked up a *National Enquirer* next to the candy display and in his thick voice reads the headline: *DWARF PARENTS BEAR GIANT BABY*. He pronounces *dwarf* as "dorf" and *baby* as "babby." When he starts to read the next headline, Lana gently takes it from his hand and puts it back in the rack.

"How's Veronica doing?" Francine the checker asks.

"She's good," Lana says.

"She cried today," Tilly says. "She's had a personal tragedy. She's handicapped now. That's why she's sad."

Francine wears a green apron with a tag on it that says *Hi! I'm Francine,* and it goes through Lana's mind that name tags might be a good idea for the Snicks to wear when Mrs. Stoneman comes back, so she can start putting names with faces.

Francine rings up the hamburger and says, "I didn't know Veronica was that bad."

"She's getting better," Lana says hurriedly. "She's under a doctor's care, taking it easy."

Francine looks up from the register. "Dr. Gooch, right?"

"I'm not real sure," Lana says. "I haven't personally seen him." The one thing Lana knows about small towns is you don't pass out any information you don't have to.

"And she lost her driver's license, I heard," Francine says.

Lana forces a laugh and says Francine knows more about it than she does.

As Francine rings things up, Lana considers pocketing some of the change, enough to redeem her two-dollar bill from Miss Hekkity's, but what would be the use? Veronica will check the receipt and count the change down to the penny.

The doors open behind Lana, and Francine flicks a glance that way before she starts with the bagging. She's halfway through when Carlito goes behind the checkout stand to bless her shoulder. She seems used to it and lets him reach out and touch. "Okay, doll," she says. "Thanks for the blessing."

A sound behind them, a snickering sound, and when Lana glances back, she sees Trina and Spink leaning against the magazine stand, staring at Lana and the others, grinning with the kind of malicious keenness they might direct at a circus sideshow.

Lana turns quickly back around. It feels suddenly hot here toward the front of the store. Her legs are sticking together.

Francine turns to Alfred while Lana is counting money from her wallet. "And how are you, young fella? Did you get everything on your list?"

Lana can feel the eyes of Trina and Spink swarming all over them, as clammy as the heat.

"Yeah," Alfred says, thickly but without stuttering.

"No Baby Ruth bar today? Aren't you the king of the Baby Ruths?"

"I d-d-don't like 'em anymore," Alfred says. "They make my poop not come out." He gestures behind him to demonstrate, as if she might not otherwise know what he's talking about, and at once they are pelted with the hard derisive laughter of Trina and Spink.

Francine shoots a glance toward the magazines and then turns to Alfred in a nice unruffled way. "Then don't you buy them, sugar."

"I w-w-won't," Alfred says, "I'd rather p-poop," and this sends Spink and Trina into another dimension of hard, raucous laughter, their bodies rocking, beating their thighs, gasping for air.

Lana, face reddening, hands over the money and waits for the change, but Francine is looking tensely away from her. She's staring at Trina.

"G'wan, git out of here," she says. Which, if anything, seems to heighten the amusement of Trina and Spink. They stand grinning back at Francine. "I mean it now," Francine says. "I'll call Griff Terwilliger over here and I mean right now!"

Griff Terwilliger, Lana knows, is the local sheriff and not an especially terrifying figure.

Still, Trina and Spink stumble out the door laughing, and Lana watches them disappear. By taking four bags herself and giving one to each of the Snicks, she's able to move all the groceries out the glass doors. The drugstore's a half block off, and Lana wants to re-form the conga line, but she sees that Trina and Spink have joined up with K.C. and another kid she's never seen before, and they're leaning against the post office, in the shade, across the street, waiting.

36.

Fly away home, Lana thinks.

Like the ladybug rhyme about the house on fire. But she has to get Veronica's prescription.

"Okay, behind me, single file, no stopping," she says, and begins to lead the line of Snicks through the glaring sun toward Helton's Drugs. She can feel the eyes of Trina's group on them, but Lana looks straight ahead, like a horse with blinders.

"Hey, is that Foster?" It's K.C.'s voice, loud, pretending to talk to the others.

"I do believe," Spink says, "it's Foster and her spaz cadets." Then slowly, loudly, with perfect enunciation: "The wisdom of the mothers who have abandoned these humatoids cannot be overstated."

Lana hopes the Snicks can't understand what Spink is saying, but she can feel them slowing behind her, and she turns to take Carlito's arm and press him forward. "Straight line," she says. "No stopping."

Across the street, Spink gives the boy she's never seen before a friendly shove, which for a moment moves the boy out into the sun. He's short-legged and rumpish, with a big upper body and flowing blond hair. He reminds Lana of a Shetland pony.

"Make way for ducklings!" K.C. yells, and then revises: "Make way for ugly ducklings!"

It's Tilly who stops first, and then the rest have stopped, too. Tilly stares with theatrical petulance across the street and Alfred without emotion says, "Th-th-they're mean," and hugs his grocery bag to his chest.

"C'mon, c'mon," Lana says, and the line again begins fitfully to move.

Spink says, "Spaz cadets on parade!" and K.C. lets fly with a wolf whistle.

Tilly stops, plants her white sneakers, and points her finger at Trina and the group. She's wearing multi-pocketed pink clam diggers and a pink floral blouse, something somebody's great-aunt would wear on a bus trip. "You can't call us spazzes," she says. "No, you can't. I learned that in school. You go home and sit in your room. You go right now."

Which is of course exactly the kind of entertainment K.C.'s group has come to see, and their laughter and hoots are loud and flinty. Trina is leaning against the brick wall. She puts one hand nonchalantly in the pocket of her tight denim skirt, and when the laughter dies, she says, "I won't be going to my room just yet, spazter child, but when I do, I won't be heading back to a home chockful of spazter kids who are just as weird as your spazter self."

"Come on, Tilly," Lana says. "Don't talk to them."

Lana leads the Snicks forward and pulls open the pharmacy door, props it against her shoe, and herds them into the air-conditioned drugstore, grateful for the little tinkling bell, the sudden coolness, the smell of soaps and antiseptics

165

and mint chewing gum. She's just told the clerk that she's there to pick up Veronica Winters's prescription when one of the Snicks says something Lana can't understand. She turns. "What?"

"'Ito gone," Garth says, and he gestures toward the street.

Through the tinted glass, Lana sees Carlito crossing the street toward Trina's group. There aren't many cars in Two Rivers, but she's scared for him just the same. Lana rushes to the door, but Carlito is already across the street, like a boy doing an impression of Dr. Frankenstein's monster. He moves openmouthed toward Trina, arm outstretched.

Lana knows what he's going to do. He's going to bless Trina.

"Carlito!" Lana shouts from the pharmacy sidewalk, wondering whether to run forward or stay with the other three. The outside air is sticky hot and smells of cinnamon gum and her own sweat. Carlito reaches out to Trina. He's going for her shoulder, Lana knows, but Trina flinches back and his hand grazes her breast.

"Hey!" Trina says. "This freaking spazter groped me!"

K.C. shoves Carlito backward.

"Get back, mutant!" K.C. yells. Carlito is tall and solid, so the shove hasn't moved him much.

"Stay here with them," Lana turns to tell Tilly, and she tries to get across the street fast enough to take Carlito's hand, but K.C. isn't finished. The fact that Carlito is still standing, that his mouth is still open, seems to incense K.C., and he steps forward and gives another hard shove. This time Carlito is standing so close to the curb that he falls backward into the street and his head cracks against the pavement.

Francine must have been watching, because she comes running out from Rodeo Meats as fast as a fat woman can. "I'm going to call the cops on you, K.C. Miller," she screams. "You leave them kids alone."

"He tried to molest me!" Trina shouts back.

"I'm calling Terwilliger!" Francine yells. "I'm calling him right now!" And she goes back inside as if to show she means what she says.

Tilly, Garth, and Alfred have drifted out of the pharmacy, and when Lana turns around, she sees that they're all in the street, and the girl from Helton's Drugs has followed them to the door, where she stands staring.

"Get in the car," K.C. tells Trina. "Let's go."

The emerald green Buick LeSabre glints in the sun in front of the market, and Lana is disgusted that she ever wished to ride in its front seat. As K.C. leads Trina by the arm past the group, Tilly says, "You're a bully, yes, you are. I saw it. You pushed."

When K.C. turns his handsome head Tilly's way, his lips curl back from his teeth and he says something in a low, snarly voice that is so profane Lana can hardly believe she's heard it.

"Suck me dry," he says.

Tilly seems stricken.

"What?" Lana yells at K.C. "What did you just say?"

But K.C. has recovered himself, and, turning to Spink, fakes a laugh and says, "What about it, Spinko, don't we have a policy about talking to Fosters?" and Spink says, "Indeed we do." The Shetland pony boy gives this a big, knowing laugh, like this is an old joke he's already in on.

Tilly's face is contorted—she's trying not to cry. A middle-aged woman standing outside the post office looks on in what appears to be fright, a small bundle of envelopes in her hand. Beyond her, the sky is furred with strips of humid clouds. The asphalt of Main Street is hot enough to heat up the bottom of Lana's tennis shoes as she crouches beside Carlito, who's holding the back of his head. His elbow oozes crimson blood. The LeSabre squeals away down Main Street. When Lana glances again toward the post office, the woman with the envelopes has disappeared.

Lana's hands are sticky with blood, and Carlito has begun crying, blubbering, actually, a childlike weeping that makes his cheeks, nose, and chin wet. Otherwise it's eerily quiet, with Garth and Tilly and Alfred all standing a little back, staring.

Lana hears a single car approaching on the street, and when she turns, she sees it's Veronica's white Monte Carlo, and it stops mid-block. But it's not Veronica who gets out.

It's Chet.

"Hey, padre," he says, kneeling right down by Carlito, who has added a whimper to his weeping. "How're you doing?"

Carlito shakes his head miserably.

Chet's wearing an old burgundy button-down shirt open over a ribbed T-shirt. He takes off the button-down and uses it to start soaking up the blood.

"You'll get that dirty, Chet," Tilly says, and Chet without looking up from his work says, "It was already red, Tilly." Which, Lana can see, is only in the loosest sense true, because the reds of the blood and the shirt are different. When Chet has cleared away most of the blood, he begins to daub the dirt, blood, and mucus from Carlito's cheeks, and Carlito's crying begins to slacken. Chet cleans the cut on Carlito's elbow—the cut isn't big—and Chet, to Lana's surprise, pulls a Band-Aid out of his wallet and presses it over the cut.

"Better?" Lana says.

Carlito nods. When he breathes out, a mucousy bubble forms from one nostril; when he breathes back in, it disappears. He lets Chet and Lana help him up, and they guide him to the backseat of Veronica's car with the other Snicks following. As Chet and Lana gather up the plastic sacks of groceries and set them into the trunk, the girl from the drugstore brings out a small paper bag and hands it to Lana. "It's the prescription," she says. "Mr. Helton says you can just pay for it next time."

"So what happened?" Chet says once they're on their way, with Lana scooched next to Chet, Garth beside her but not touching her, and the other three in back.

"What didn't?" Lana says. "The final straw was Carlito trying to bless Trina. She moved and he touched her boob or something. She screamed bloody murder and K.C., her big freaking hero, beat up on poor Carlito for her."

Chet is quiet for a few seconds and then he says, "Some people just don't deserve to be blessed."

Lana thinks about telling him what K.C. said to Tilly, but the words are too horrible to say out loud. So she says, "There was somebody I've never seen before with K.C. and them. A buff kid with a big head and long blond hair. He reminded me of a Shetland pony."

This gets a good laugh from Chet. "That's some guy they call Lido, a big steroid freak. He wants to go to L.A.

and be in porno movies." Chet makes a wry grin. "And to think some people just want to be president or go to medical school."

As they turn off Main Street, a sheriff's car turns onto it, traveling at a leisurely pace. Griff Terwilliger, behind the wheel, doesn't even flick their packed Monte Carlo a glance. He's working a toothpick in his mouth, fussily, like there's something back there in the molars that's really giving him trouble.

"Guess that'd be your Crime Scene Investigative Unit," Lana says, which gets another laugh from Chet. She likes sitting next to him. With his smooth tanned arms flowing out of his white sleeveless T-shirt, he reminds her of one of those young farmhands or work-project guys she sometimes sees in old photograph albums. *Winsome* pops into her head, and she nearly says, "In that shirt you look winsome," but what would Chet do with a compliment like that? Probably just be embarrassed.

Garth is holding his Popeye up at window level so they can both stare out, his body pressed close to the door to avoid Lana's legs and arms, so Lana decides to risk a question about Mrs. Stoneman. "So how'd it go with . . . your last passenger?"

"Fine. She sprang for my lunch, actually."

This is news. "She gave you money for lunch?"

He shakes his head. "No, she took me to lunch. We went to the Fryin' Pan." He grins. "Had me a patty melt."

"Did she talk?"

"Not much. Some, though."

"What about?"

Chet shrugs. "The house, mostly."

Lana lowers her voice even further. "And the person the passenger came to see?"

"Not so much, to be honest."

The house, though. "What about the house?"

"Just Whit and Veronica and the other kids and stuff like that. She was interested in what had happened to Veronica."

A faint alarm sounds within Lana. "You didn't tell her that Veronica had been drinking, did you?"

Chet doesn't answer, and Lana says it again. "Did you?"

"I think she already knew it," he says in a small voice. And then, defensively, "Besides, if you didn't want anybody to know it, why'd you tell me?"

They drive a block or so in silence. In the backseat, Tilly says, "You're wet," to Carlito. "Not supposed to wet yourself. It smells bad."

It does smell bad, even with all the windows down. Lana is staring past Garth out the window trying not to smell, trying not to think, when Chet says, "Oh God."

Lana turns.

A car has drawn up beside them, K.C.'s LeSabre, and sticking out of the rear window nearest them is a large set of white bare buttocks. Trina is riding shotgun, and her shrieking laughter seems to stretch her face in all directions. Beyond her, K.C.'s face is red and fierce and he yells something that Lana can't understand.

"Speed up," she says, but when Chet speeds up, the LeSabre speeds up, and when Chet slows down, so does the LeSabre. Lana feels a mix of revulsion and fear—the bare buttocks are like a huge eyeless face staring an eyeless stare. Alfred and Tilly are laughing, Carlito is crying again, and Garth doesn't make a sound. In the other car, K.C., red-faced, screams unintelligible insults and Trina is hysterical with laughter. Fingers appear on the sides of the bare buttocks and begin to pull them apart to expose what lies between.

Chet's face goes suddenly to stone. He slams on the brakes, K.C. does the same, and for a long moment nothing happens—the cars, idling, stand side by side. Then, all at once, Chet jumps out, plants himself, leans back, and kicks the offending bare buttocks back into the car. And he's not done. He moves toward Trina, whose face for a moment is frozen with fear, and then she yells, "Go! Go!" and the LeSabre squeals, fishtails, and speeds away.

When Chet gets back into the car and starts driving, Lana looks at him with disbelief. "Wow," she says. "I've never known anyone before who actually kicked butt."

A chuckle slips from Chet. Already he's beginning to look normal again.

"So what was that?" Lana says.

He shrugs. "Dunno. Something just got into me."

Lana looks at him. She likes what he's just done but doesn't want to be sappy about it. So she simply repeats his words: "Something just got into you."

Chet keeps his eyes forward and keeps driving. "It was stupid, though," he says. "If K.C. and Spink and that Lido guy had gotten out, I'd be the new grease spot on the road."

"We'd've helped," Lana says, then considers it. "Tried anyway."

A short block passes in silence. Then Lana says, "So what happened? I thought those guys were your friends."

"Yeah, well," Chet says, and his eyes slide away. "Things change, that's all."

There's more to this, Lana can feel it, but with Chet, it's almost always like this. There's almost always more to it. A few seconds later, he says, "The problem now is, they won't be happy till they even this up. I kicked Lido's butt and now they'll need to kick mine." He gives Lana a small unhappy smile and then looks forward. "It'll be a pummeling."

A few seconds go by, then Lana says, "How do you know that was the pony boy's butt?"

Chet shrugs. "K.C. and Trina were up front, and Spink's got a skinny little butt."

Another short silence. They pass two boys playing catch with a football from one yard to another over a cyclone fence.

"F-f-football," Alfred says from the backseat, and Lana says, "That's right, Alfie. Football." After another second or two, she turns to Chet and says, "If you could have one wish, what would it be?"

Something in Chet's eyes gives way, and for a moment an odd, ardent expression forms, an expression Lana has seen before, mostly on girls gone gaga over some guy. But then it's gone, and Chet says, "Guess I'd wish not to get pummeled by K.C. and those guys."

Lana studies him for a long moment. "You got a girlfriend now, don't you?"

Chet keeps staring forward, then he turns his head toward her. "What makes you think that?"

Lana laughs. "Girls just know these things," she says. He's not denying it, which is as good as saying it's true, but still, she wants confirmation. "So am I right?"

He smiles. "Kinda."

She laughs again. "Kinda. What does that mean, that you've got her hooked but not netted?"

Chet turns the Monte Carlo onto their street. "It means the subject is closed," he says.

As they ride the last block to the house, a thought sneaks up on Lana, and after all the Snicks are out of the car and walking into the house and Chet is about to park the car in the garage, she leans back into the window and says, "Well, you won't tell me anything about the girl, but I can tell you one thing about her."

Chet looks at her. "Yeah? And what's that?"

Lana grins. "That she's lucky."

37.

*A*s soon as Lana returns to the house and gets Carlito cleaned up and the food put away, she puts on a video for the Snicks and sneaks up to her room. She takes out the drawing kit. She knows exactly what she wants to do. She doesn't count pages. She takes the pencil in hand and closes her eyes and lets the calm come over her. Then she begins to draw.

A large wooden crate appears, and within the crate four bodies with four heads are soon poking out between the slats, Trina's head, and K.C.'s, and Spink's, and the big head and long flowing hair of the pony boy they call Lido. In another few seconds, the crate lies on a flatbed car, one of a long line of railcars that pass across the flat plains under a bare sky. On the side of the crate is a shipping label, on which in neat letters, as a final gesture, Lana's pencil writes the single word *Elsewhere*.

After laying her pencil down, Lana feels the same sense of exhaustion she always feels after doing a sketch and the same sense of appreciating the skill of what's been drawn without quite feeling that she herself has drawn it. But it's there, and it's done, and with any luck, it'll save Chet and at the same time deal a little justice to K.C. and the others. A twofer.

She sits thinking for a moment of Chet. His mother ran off with a guy when he was in sixth grade, Lana knows that much, and his father was too depressed to do much but go to work and come home again, and if anybody had really ever been nice to Chet, she hadn't seen it, and yet Chet knew exactly how to be nice to Carlito, knew exactly how to take care of him. And now Chet was gaga for some girl.

Lana turns to a fresh sheet of sketch paper. A warm feeling has spread through her in the manner of liquid or light. Chet is deserving, something good should come his way, and she wants to help him have it. She takes up her charcoal pencil. Chet appears on the page, in silhouette, and in his hand is a silhouette heart and from the side of the page two hands reach in to receive it.

Lana puts down her pencil. What she sees in front of her is simpler than the other drawings, sketchier, but it seems complete. She doesn't know who the girl is, but she's there, whoever she is, just beyond the edge of the paper.

Thump thump thump.

From this short distance, Lana can feel the reverberation of the thumps through the walls and floorboards, and they send through her own body three short shocks of the kind of humiliation that turns almost at once to anger.

"Okay!" she yells, but before sliding the drawing kit back under the bed, she quickly counts the remaining sheets.

Seven.

Plenty, she thinks.

Seven should be plenty.

38.

"Where were you?" Veronica says when Lana comes in.

It's Veronica's usual accusatory tone, but something feels different about the room, something Lana can't put her finger on.

"I was at the market," she says. "And Helton's."

Lana presents the small bag containing the prescription, along with the Rodeo Meats receipt and change, all of which Veronica takes without thanks. "I mean just now," she says. "Where were you just now?"

"In my room, if that's okay with you."

"Doing what?"

"I'd prefer not to say."

Veronica thinned her lips. "I'd prefer you did."

Lana stares sullenly ahead.

"Speak," Veronica says.

Lana shrugs. "Okay, then. I was taking advantage of myself."

Veronica's eyes go narrow and cold. And then slowly relax. "And who were you thinking about during this little exercise?"

It takes a moment for this to sink in. "You're sick, Veronica. Truly sick."

A quick snickering expulsion of air from Veronica's nose. She seems amused. "Disabled, actually," she says. With one hand, she opens the stapled Helton's bag and slides out a boxed tube of ointment and reads its prescriptive label. After rolling back the empty sleeve to expose her pink protuberant stump, she holds the tube in her teeth to unscrew the cap and then uses her teeth to squeeze ointment from the tube onto her one hand. She begins rubbing it onto the stump's pink nub.

Lana looks around the room. Nothing's out of place, nothing's different, and yet it seems changed. Less light, maybe. The sheers are all drawn. And then something occurs to her.

"Has somebody been here?" she says, and turns to see—or thinks she sees—a funny expression cross Veronica's face.

"Dr. Gooch came to check on me," she says, and resumes rubbing ointment onto her stump. "He thinks my case is remarkable, how I've coped with my personal tragedy, how quickly I've adapted. He's thinking of writing a paper about me." An odd look of pride takes hold of her face and she stops applying the ointment. "Dr. Gooch calls my resilience exceptional."

Lana bets Dr. Gooch thinks the boobs busting out of Veronica's nightgown are pretty exceptional, too. She turns to go, can't wait to get out of here. "Anything else?" she says.

"Yes. A small plate of melba toast, celery stalks, and green olives and a medium glass of grape juice. Two ice cubes."

Lana gives Veronica her most sullen stare. "Any particular shape of ice cube?"

Veronica throws her head back and lets out a gay laugh. "I don't have many blessings to count," she says, "but it is nice that the upstairs maid has such a rich sense of humor. I thank you for that."

F.U., Lana thinks. "You're welcome," she says, and on her way out kicks the door closed behind her.

39.

usk is the time of day Lana feels least at home. It's something about the sunlight, the way it changes colors on the walls. It always makes her feel she's looking for something she only has a few more minutes to find.

She goes out to the porch, sits on the swing, and rocks ever so slightly back and forth. She wonders why, just beneath the surface, she feels so wistful and sad. Yes, Veronica is horrible, but Veronica only has Veronica. Lana has Whit and the kit with its seven blank pages like seven wishes waiting to be made.

Except Whit isn't here, and the wishes seem to have minds of their own—they head off in directions she can't guess at. Lana touches her ear and wishes she had her two-dollar bill back, but she's pretty sure that if she uses one of the pages to draw it back behind her ear, it will happen, if it happens at all, in a way she doesn't expect and might not like.

Where is Whit anyhow?

Why can't he just paint till five and come home?

From inside the house, the Snicks suddenly whoop and laugh. They're watching a video because Lana's too tired to organize board games or anything else. Lana has had it. She's absolutely had it. She did an early supper of tuna, noodles, and peas because it was easy to make and easy to clean up, and then she let the Snicks fight for a while over which video before she chose for them, a cartoon Robin Hood that, she knew, would keep them in their seats and out of her hair for an hour or two. She served Veronica her dinner and after two extra trips for first butter and then parmesan cheese, she was done, and she came here, to the porch, to be alone and to think.

And, to be honest, to wait for Whit.

To see him and greet him and let him make her feel better than she feels right now.

The crickets have started and across the street Mrs. Harbaugh steps down from her porch, gives a look Lana's way, then uses her garden hose to tug a green sprinkler to a dry spot in the yard.

No activity at Chet's house, not a light, not a sound. But she has to smile. For a few seconds there today, Chet was like one of those superheroes who goes around like a nerdy citizen and then when peril presents itself takes off his shirt and assumes his super-role. And then he'd come back into his old nerdy-citizen self, and she'd had to help Carlito shower and change and wash his peed-upon clothes, and while she'd wiped down the backseat of Veronica's car, a memory came to her of herself as a little girl. She'd wet herself and her mother hadn't known why Lana was crying, so she picked Lana up. Probably Lana was five. Her mother smelled of squashed, spoiled fruit, which was really the smell of wine that had moved through her mother's blood for so long in those days that it had begun to seep out through her pores, and when she held Lana to her, she must have felt the wetness of Lana's urine soaking through her own clothes. She couldn't put Lana down fast enough and her face was a mask of disgust. "Go take a bath," she'd told Lana. "You've gotten me all dirty."

Their bathtub was pink that year, and the water that came out of the tap smelled of rust.

A faint thrum, growing closer. A diesel, Lana thinks, and then she sees it: Whit's green pickup.

He doesn't glance her way as he turns up the dirt driveway, so she darts from the porch and jumps onto the rear bumper and rides with the truck into the garage. When the truck stops, she lifts her head over the tailgate and peers forward. Up in the cab, Whit smooths his hair and collar.

When he gets out and begins to pass by her, Lana in a quiet voice says, "Boo."

It gives Whit a start, but it's a brief one, and he falls into happy laughter and steps forward and, slipping his hands into her armpits, actually lifts her into the air, twirling her in a circle, which floods her with feelings of giddy, childlike pleasure. As he sets her down, her breasts slide against his chest, and that's a pleasure, too, but neither giddy nor childlike.

"Where've you been?" she says, and with a mild shock realizes these are the same words Veronica greeted her with when she came back this afternoon.

"Painting," Whit says. "Bringing home the bacon."

"Yeah? So where's the bacon?"

"Careful what you ask to see, little girl," he says, and follows it with a laugh that's looser than his normal laugh, slacker, wider, rowdier, a laughter most at home, Lana guesses, in a barroom, which is where she's betting he's recently been. She leans back an inch or two, which reins him in a little. There's something not right about him, Lana can feel it, just like she could feel there was something not right about Veronica's room when she returned to it this afternoon, and this is like that—it's something Lana can't quite put her finger on.

"So how're things at Snick House?" Whit says.

"Okay," Lana says.

"Hey, it's Whit you're talking to. I can handle an honest answer."

Lana's eyes and voice both drop. "Horrible."

"Horrible how?" he says, and in the next two minutes it all spills from Lana in a great rush, all the day's little trials with the Snicks, and what happened with Garth's mom, and what K.C. Miller did to Carlito in the street, and even what K.C. said to poor Tilly.

Whit listens, but in a slightly detached way, without questions, as if this is a parade of sad events that ought to be watched from a distance if it had to be watched at all. "Ahh," he says when she is done. He falls quiet for a second or two. Then, "I'm sorry," he says. "I'm sorry for everything." He takes a deep breath, so deep it seems to swallow back sad thoughts.

"So how was your day?" she says.

He looks off for a moment. There are last long shafts of light that cut through the cracks in the side of the garage, and dust motes float in that yellow glow. And then he's looking back at Lana.

"Honestly?" he says.

"Honestly."

He keeps his eyes on hers. "My day was a piece of shit, just like almost all my days are, and the only thing that kept me thinking anything close to hopeful was the thought of coming home to this house and seeing your face."

This person standing in front of her, laying himself bare to her, is, Lana believes, the secret person who's been locked inside the old Whit Winters, the secret person Lana saw that day in his room, wanting to get out. It is the secret person she is in love with.

Later, when Lana thinks back to it, she can't really say for how long they had stood silently staring at each other in the last light of the day, and she can't really say who kissed whom. It wasn't one or the other, it was more a gravitational pull that moved them each equally toward the other, and then each was pulling the other close, and what started at the lips spread through their bodies, and when finally the kiss was over, Whit Winters looked gravely at her and said, "Well, that's about as carnal as two people standing up with all their clothes on can be."

Lana had been kissed before, but never by someone she liked. She wanted the light-headed happiness to go on and on, to keep feeling its exhilaration, but Whit glanced toward the house and sighed a slow sigh and, just like that, the real Whit slipped back inside his body. He gave the nape of her neck a soft, whispery kiss, and then he said, "Guess we'd better go back in."

And they did. But when they left the garage and began crossing the lawn to the back porch, Lana glanced up toward the roof of the house and saw for a fleeting instant Veronica standing in the window staring down at them before the curtains pulled closed.

40.

That night, Lana can't sleep.

Tilly can, of course, and does, the gentle singsong pattern of her snoring interrupted only when she repositions herself in her bed. But Lana is too agitated for sleep; the pleasure in recalling her moments that day with Whit is too keen to let go of. There are two kinds of pleasure for her in these recollections. When she thinks of Whit telling her of the hope it gives him to think of coming home and seeing her face, that's one kind of pleasure, and when she thinks of her lips and body pressed hard against his, it's another, and there's a strange need within her to alternate from one to the other, because each makes the other more intense.

It's too much finally, and she gets up and goes to the bathroom to take a shower, to wash away the confusion. She closes the bathroom door behind her without locking it, and only a minute or so after the water pipes shudder and the hot water begins to flow, she hears the door creak open.

"What are you doing?"

It's Veronica, and Lana, standing behind the solid shower curtain, freezes.

The curtain slides back, and there stands Veronica, solid amid the cloudy vapors of the room. This time her voice is lower, colder, tighter. "What in God's name are you doing?"

Lana has covered herself below the waist with one hand and above the waist with a crossed arm, and her speech is similarly defensive. "Taking a shower," she says.

"You know the rules," Veronica says. "No showers after ten."

"I forgot that rule," Lana says, which is the truth, not that it matters.

Before Veronica turns to leave, she gives Lana a long, icy stare. "You forgot that rule," she says, "and some others besides."

Finally Veronica breaks her gaze, and Lana glimpses what she's wearing—a long white nightgown, almost totally sheer—and Lana realizes that what, just now, she couldn't avoid seeing, Whit, too, could not avoid seeing. And why not? He is her husband.

Whit is Veronica's husband.

Veronica is Whit's wife.

An hour later, Lana has come to understand that, for keeping you from sleep, the only thing worse than romantic giddiness is gnawing guilt.

You forgot that rule and some others besides.

Lana is sixteen.

Whit is thirty-one.

And married.

These are the hard facts, and at 3:35 a.m., wanting to escape them, Lana slips on the earphones of her iPod.

41.

*C*het begins that day's podcast with what he calls the Mailbag Segment. "We get very few letters," he says in his heavy, Chief Chetteroid voice, "but those we do get don't say much." Pause. "Okay, let's reach into the ol' canvas mailbag and see what bites us."

There is the exaggerated rustling of paper.

"Dear Big Chief Chetteroid, you have sprinkled wisdom over the waters of the Two Rivers. Your people will sing your song before the fires of many winters. P.S. My suggestion for the Oddball Olympics is a naked-woman box-elder-bug-eating contest." A pause. "There it is, Chetteroids and Chetteristas, proof positive that the K-SOD listenership is AT LEAST TWO STANDARD DEVIATIONS FROM NORMAL."

Again the rattle of paper, then: *"Dear Chet in your Chetness. Love your show, et cetera, et cetera, fabulously witty, et cetera, et cetera, but when I go to my rhyming dictionary software and punch in* Chetteroid, *nothing comes up but hemorrhoid."*

Long silence, then the sounds of paper being rumpled, followed by chewing sounds and finally a loud gulp. "Sometime Big Chief Chetteroid need eatum venomous letter even though eatum venomous letter give Chief Chetteroid great gas."

Lana, sitting up in bed in the predawn hours with the man she shouldn't love sleeping one wall away with his wife, can manage a smile at Chief Chetteroid, but not a laugh.

Still, a smile is better than nothing.

After a long pause, Chet does a segment on the Oddball Olympics—he has in fact scheduled what he calls a tractor-styling event for that week, with "all interested members of the K-SOD Nation to congregate at nine a.m. Friday at the Highway 20 rest stop just east of town."

Lana has seen this rest stop. It consists of a dirt turnout, a rickety picnic bench, and a single shade tree.

"Bleachers will be provided, as well as an official Oddball guide to this Oddball event. All Sodbusters invited, as well as their second, third, and fourth cousins."

A short silence, then the sudden sound of a loud buzzer, and Chet says, "Hell's bells. It's the formidable Miz Buzzbottom telling us it's time for a . . . *CHANGE O' TOPICS*. There goes Buzzbottom now waddling up to the Change-o-Topic Spin-o-Meter. She grunts, she spins, she hopes no one wins! Round and round it goes and where it stops . . . well, actually we do know. It . . . stops . . . on . . . *Conversations with the Long-leggedy Neighbor Girl*. Good luck, I say, because today, in just such a conversation, the Long-leggedy Neighbor Girl said to the Chetness, 'Did you know that spinach is nothing more than a potherb of the goosefoot family?' and the Chetness said, 'No, I did not know this fact if it is one, but I am not surprised,' and the Long-leggedy Neighbor Girl, WHO IS NOT A SEQUENTIAL THINKER, said,

'What one wish would you make if one and only one wish was granted you?'"

Pause. "A good question, one I'd suggest that every Hemorrhoid and Hemorrista ask her- or himself. It is not easy and can in fact be borderline paralyzing. Because for the one wish you do make, there will be dozens, hundreds, gazillions you don't."

There's a long stretch of dead space, then Chet begins to talk about his mother taking him to the wishing well at Pioneer Park and telling him that William the Wish Reader lived at the bottom of the well, just waiting for wishes to read and make come true, so Chet would write his wish down and fold the paper tight and drop it in, and his mother did, too—all of which is interesting to Lana because Chet hardly ever mentions his mother. All Lana knows is that she ran off.

"Horse," Chet says, breaking one of his characteristic silences. "That's what I wrote down every time, except maybe once or twice I might've put *pony*." Pause. "That wish is still technically outstanding, by the way. I'm still listening for that friendly nicker at the kitchen window."

Pause. "After talking to the Neighbor Girl today, I took a little field trip down to Pioneer Park to take a firsthand look at the wishing well, and let me tell you, Sodbusters, it wasn't pretty. The bucket's gone, the crank handle's gone, and the well . . . well, the well is filled with Dorito bags. I mean, WHAT IS IT WITH THESE DORITO EATERS?"

Another pause. "I found a *custodial engineer*. Borrowed a rake. I'm going to clean that wishing well out, clean up William the Wish Reader's personal habitat. It takes a little while, raking those Dorito bags up the side of a wishing well, and the custodial engineer watches the whole time. 'Whew!' I say when I'm done. 'That's a job.' The custodial engineer nods but doesn't speak. 'How do you do it?' I say, and he says, 'I just throw a match down there and burn it all.' I say, 'I guess that would be easier.' And you know what he says? He says, 'Yes, it would.'" Pause. "I'm telling you, 'Roids and 'Ristas, that custodial engineer down at Pioneer Park is a dry one."

Pause. "Okay, let's stay focused. You have one wish. I will pass on the advice of my mother. 'Don't wish for a thing,' she would say. 'Wish for a condition.' She gave good health, happiness, and being less stupid as examples." Pause. "I myself went with a one-word wish this afternoon, two consonants, two vowels, starting with the twelfth letter of the alphabet. Wrote it down, dropped it in, and can only hope that our flame-throwing custodial engineer hasn't turned William the Wish Reader into Crispy Bill."

A few minutes later, Chet signs off—"This is kay-ess-oh-dee. Keep those cards and letters coming. And please don't call again"—followed by his signature theme song.

Lana sets her earphones on the bedside table and walks down the hall to the window that gives onto Chet's house. It's dark out still, but Lana hears three different roosters beginning their crowing. Across the yard, Chet's room is dark, but a downstairs light is on and the figure of Chet's father moves from counter to counter in the kitchen, Chet's father, who works in a machine shop in the next town and who Lana's hardly ever seen because he leaves for work so early and comes home so late.

Lana starts counting letters on her fingers and when she gets to twelve, she's on *l*. Four letters, two vowels, beginning with *l*. *L-o-v-e*, she thinks. It had to be love Chet was wishing for. A little sappy for his Chetness, frankly, but she can't help but smile. He's been turned to mush by some girl. She wonders who, but she doesn't wonder long. She yawns. It's almost dawn, and her thoughts are finally willing to release her body to sleep.

42.

A bouncing ball and giddy shouts.

Lana's eyes blink open. It's hot in the bedroom, her skin is glazed with sweat, and Tilly's Cinderella clock says 10:13. Lana bolts up and goes to the window. Down below, on the uneven concrete in front of the garage, Whit is playing basketball with all the Snicks, passing the ball, dribbling the ball, making them all laugh.

Lana washes her face, dresses, hurries down. Sticky plates and used forks are all over the table, the waffle iron is out, and cracked eggshells sit openmouthed on the counter.

Lana's annoyed, thinking what she's going to say when she gets outside, but once she gets to the back door, she stops. Carlito and Tilly and Alfred all shout for the ball, and Whit, like some close cousin of Spider-Man, snatches the careening ball and passes it to one or the other of the Snicks, who shoots or passes and then grins with pleasure. Whit keeps up a streetwise patter and it occurs to Lana that Whit talks to the Snicks like they're not handicapped and he acts like they're not handicapped, and suddenly they don't seem so handicapped. *Maybe only men can do it*, she thinks. *Women feel too much pity.*

Whit seems different, too. It's the Inside Whit released for a few minutes, out in the dappled sunshine of a cracked basketball court, set free from his own life. As she watches, he lobs the ball to Carlito, who heaves the ball toward the backboard. It tips the front of the hoop, bounces off the backboard, and, to everyone's surprise, drops down through the net.

"Bandito scores!" Whit yells. "Bandito scores, and the Maniacs take the lead!"

Among the Snicks, there are whoops, grins, and bobbing heads. Tilly yells, "Ban-dito, he's our man!"

When Lana walks out and catches Whit's eye, he sets the ball down and tells his team to take five. He walks over smiling. He looks almost as happy as he did after their long, stand-up, close-hold kiss. "Well," he says, "if it isn't sleeping beauty."

"Couldn't sleep last night," she says. "And then finally I guess I did. Who made breakfast?"

"Yours truly. Banana waffles." He's still smiling. He's like an overflowing vessel of happiness.

"What about your housepainting?"

"Got the crew going by phone."

Lana glances at the Snicks. "And your team seems to be winning."

Whit goes into coach mode. "This is no ordinary team," he says. "What they lack in skill, they make up for in heart."

Lana is quiet. It seems like the perfect way to say something she's known but hasn't found the words to say.

"How come you couldn't sleep?" he says.

"Just thinking. I couldn't stop thinking."

"About what?"

About you and me and you and Veronica, she thinks. "I don't know. Everything, I guess."

He leans slightly closer. He's been sweating, but she likes his smell. He says, "Well, I spent a little time thinking about a particular kiss that I believe you also had a part in."

Lana feels color rise in her cheeks, but when he smooths his hand along her bare arm, she turns cold from a mix of fear and guilt. She pulls her arm quickly away and glances at the upstairs window.

Whit keeps smiling. "She's gone. Off with Dr. Gooch to get her physical therapy lined up."

"He took her himself?"

"Yep. He thinks she's an extraordinary case."

Whit seems oddly proud of this, and Lana wonders if he ought to know that just before Dr. Gooch's visit yesterday, Veronica cleared the house and put on an X-rated nightgown, but before she can say anything, Whit says, "This Gooch fella's a genius when it comes to insurance. He got all our deductible paid for us, and he's got a plasma TV and state-of-the-art DVR coming to the house today or tomorrow and it's not costing us a penny; it goes down as rehab expense or something. So I can't complain about Dr. Gooch taking an interest."

Something has changed in Whit while he's been speaking these words, something that at first Lana can't identify, and then she can. The Inside Whit is gone, swallowed up again by his life.

"Well," he says. "If you don't mind taking over, I better get over to the job site."

Lana nods. A plug's been pulled; she feels suddenly empty. "The Victorian over in Fawnskin?"

He nods. He's searching his pockets for keys.

"How long're you going to be on that house?" she says.

He pulls the keys from a pocket. "A while yet. It's a big ol' thing, and the widow who owns it is going with five different colors and"—he winks—"she keeps changing her mind which five they're going to be. The crew gets a little antsy, but you know what I tell them? I say, 'Fellas, this ain't a house, it's a cash cow!'"

Lana gives a little courtesy laugh. "I'd like to see that house sometime," she says, and a funny expression passes across his face for just an instant and then is gone, replaced by his everyday grin.

"When it's finished, I'll take you for a ride so you can see it." Mischief shines in his eyes. "Just you and me. We'll make an occasion of it."

Lana can again feel the color rising in her cheeks and he laughs and heads off toward his truck. As he passes the Snicks he says, "Teamwork, Maniacs, and remember, how you practice is how you'll play."

As Lana settles into her duties, she does what she always does: she takes a head count, but she's short one, and she quickly realizes who it is. She runs over and stops Whit as he's backing out the driveway.

"Where's Garth?"

Whit nods toward a trio of lilacs in the corner of the yard. Garth is sitting on a piece of cardboard in the center of the three shrubs. Several superhero figurines are positioned around him.

Lana looks back to Whit. "And his mother hasn't shown yet?"

Whit shrugs. "She called. She's feeling punk, but she said she'd be here as soon as she could."

43.

"Hi, Garth-man," Lana says, peering into Garth's little room among the lilacs. He hears her, she knows, but he doesn't look up at her. He just keeps looking out through a gap in the shrubs. He's wearing his Incredible Hulk T-shirt that's a little too small for him—the sleeves ride up on his skinny white arms.

"Can I come in?" she says.

He doesn't look up or speak, but he does move his Popeye doll so there's room for Lana to sit on the cardboard.

"This is nice," she says once she's seated, and it *is* nice. The density of the lilac shrubs makes it private and their shade makes it cool. It reminds Lana of a closet where she used to hide from her mother and a particularly mean boyfriend. While she hid she would play house, making rooms and furniture out of shoes and scarves and, as she remembers it now, putting the baby in her slipper crib for a nap. "You worried about your mother coming?" Lana says.

Garth's jaw thrusts slightly forward, a signal he could cry.

"She's coming, Garth. She's right here in town. She could be on her way right now. She's probably just having trouble with her allergies."

Garth doesn't say anything, but he looks slightly less likely to cry.

"If she's not here by lunchtime, I'll call and find out how she's feeling," Lana says.

Garth stares into the gap between the lilacs, and Lana realizes that, through this gap, he has a clear view of the street.

"Want to play house?" Lana suddenly asks. Garth doesn't respond, but she starts anyway, snapping twigs from dead branches, laying out rooms, arranging tables and beds.

"This is the living room," she says, "and this is the kitchen," and pretty soon Garth is breaking twigs, too. "'Opeye's 'oom," he says, pointing to a marked area in the dirt, and then, lining out a triangular room with three twigs, "'Ider-Man's 'oom."

Lana and Garth play this game for Lana doesn't know how long, adding rooms and then furniture to the rooms and then stick people to use the furniture. It's quiet in the little lilac room, and they are busy. It's as if they've entered a perfect and wordless world.

"Anybody home?"

Lana turns and sees Chet grinning down. Her skin begins to burn. She expects him to make fun of her, ask something like who's the mommy and who's the daddy, but he doesn't. He just stares quietly in for a few seconds and then says, "Sanctuary."

"What?"

"Sanctuary. That's what your little place looks like there. A place where you can be safe. Where no law enforcement can follow."

"I'd say that's taking it pretty far," Lana says, but the

truth is, she likes Chet's way of looking at it. Garth, moving one of his stick figures through the dirt, says, "'Opeye 'o to 'ath'oom."

Lana gives a little laugh and says, "Make sure he washes his hands afterward."

A few seconds pass, and Chet says, "Did you hear about K.C. and Trina?"

She cocks her head. "Hear what?"

"They got busted. Spink and Lido, too. First-degree burglary. They're in some sort of place for underage housebreakers."

"Wow," Lana says. "That was fast." She'd only sketched them on the Elsewhere train the day before.

Chet looks at her. "What was fast?"

Lana fumbles for an answer. "Well, yesterday they were kind of on top of the world, and now . . ." He's staring at her and his expression is quizzical. She decides to shift the focus. "So how'd they get caught?"

A quick laugh escapes from Chet. "That Lido guy was supposed to do our former job—hang out and watch for the cops—but he got excited and wanted to go in. A neighbor saw what was going on and tipped the folks at the sheriff's office." He smiles. "Griff Terwilliger's actually catching a lawbreaker is pretty big news."

After a second or two, Lana says, "So what happened with you and K.C. and Trina and them anyhow?"

His eyes slide away. "I told you. Things change."

Just then, Garth sees something through his gap in the hedge. He steps through the lilacs and begins to walk slowly toward the house. Lana suspects his mother has just shown up.

"Do you see your mom?" Lana calls, but Garth doesn't

turn. He just keeps walking. She notices he's left behind his figurines. "You want Popeye?" she calls, but Garth doesn't answer that either.

Chet, she notices, is grinning. "Guess Garth didn't want you to cry if he took all the toys and went home."

"Hey, I'm not the one who goes public with a wish for L-O-V-E, *love.*"

A blank look from Chet. "What're you talking about?"

"The Chetness writing out his big wish. Two vowels, two consonants, beginning with the twelfth letter of the alphabet."

"Oh," he says, and then his look slowly turns serious. He says, "Maybe the Chetness, whoever he is, had another word in mind."

"Such as?"

The seriousness is still there for a moment and then it is gone, and he says, *"Like."*

Like instead of *love?* It would be just like the Chetness to do something minimum like that, but it's oddly disappointing. "Maybe," she says. "But it's not exactly reaching for the stars."

Chet's silent for a few seconds and then something decisive seems to come into his expression, but when he opens his mouth to speak, someone else's voice carries across the yard.

"Lana?"

It's Tilly, calling from the back stoop, but Lana keeps looking up at Chet. "What?" she says. "What were you going to say?"

Chet looks at her and shakes his head. "Nothing," he says.

"Lana!" Tilly yells, louder now, and after a last look at

Chet, Lana stands and looks out over the lilacs. She feels like a giant poking through the roof. "Over here!" she calls.

Tilly turns her way. "Somebody's come!" she yells.

"Who?"

Tilly throws out her arms as a show of wonderment. "Somebody new!"

44.

$\mathcal{T}$he woman standing in the kitchen with a clipboard is of blocky proportions, short and wide, and her black hair is cut in the style of the comic-strip Prince Valiant, so it crosses Lana's mind that this is a new Snick, but when the woman turns toward Lana, Lana sees she couldn't have been more wrong. This is somebody official, and she's all business. She wears the expression of a cop at a crime scene. "Are you Lana?" she says.

Lana nods and looks around. The woman seems to be alone. "Who are you?" Lana says.

"Inspector Stiller from Protective Services." She presents a laminated badge identifying herself as such. "I just need to ask you a few questions."

Lana's head is swimming. Inspector Stiller? Protective Services? Why is this woman here? And why isn't Veronica or Whit here to handle it? "Sure," she says. "I can try to answer your questions."

The woman snaps on a small tape recorder, takes up her pencil, and looks at the form on her clipboard. "Full name?" she says, and, just like that, they have begun. After a few preliminary questions, Inspector Stiller says, "Where at this moment to your knowledge is Veronica Winters?"

"She's doing her physical therapy treatments."

"When will she be back?"

"Anytime now."

"When precisely did she tell you she would be back?"

Lana wants to lie but doesn't know in what direction she ought to be sending the inspector. "I'm not sure," she says.

Inspector Stiller scribbles for a few seconds, then, "Where at this moment to your knowledge is Lucian Winters?"

"Painting a house."

"Where?"

"In Fawnskin."

"When will he return?"

"Tonight after work."

More scribbling, then, "Who is in charge of the foster facility at this moment?"

"I guess I am."

The woman looks up from her clipboard. Her eyes light for a moment on Lana, then drift to the mess in the room.

Lana says, "It's usually neater than this. It's just that I overslept. I couldn't sleep all night, then around dawn I fell asleep and . . ." Her voice trails away. Each new thing she says makes matters worse. "I should've set my alarm," she says.

The woman is writing again, her hand flowing across the page. It reminds Lana of drawing on her sketch paper, and she has the bad feeling that this woman's scribbling has its own power to change things.

"Why are you here?" Lana says, but the blocky woman doesn't look up from her writing.

"Did somebody complain about us?"

The woman keeps writing.

"Was it Mrs. Harbaugh across the street?"

The inspector stills her pen. She raises her eyes to Lana. "There's been a complaint, yes, but the agency never discusses the source of a complaint." Her eyes drift past Lana. "Now, if I can just take a quick look at all the rooms," she says, and without waiting for permission, she heads for the living room.

It's strange following the woman around because it makes the house seem different—it's as if Lana can now see it only as Inspector Stiller sees it. Everything in disorder. Nothing clean. When Inspector Stiller stops in the living room, Lana follows her gaze to a smear of strawberry jam on the glass-topped coffee table and then to several nibbled bread crusts on the carpet. The blocky woman stops for a moment to make a note of it and stops again when she spies a thick network of cobwebs in a corner of the ceiling. After visiting the downstairs bathroom, Inspector Stiller says, "Somebody should flush that toilet."

While this inspection is going on, Carlito and Tilly follow a little behind Lana, and Lana notices that Garth has retrieved his Popeye from the lilac room and now sits with it near the front door, waiting for his mother. That leaves Alfred unaccounted for, Alfred who will put almost anything into his mouth, who needs supervision more than anybody, but Lana can't let on to Inspector Stiller that anyone's missing, and she can't ask Tilly where he is, because she'll blurt out whatever she does or doesn't know on the spot. When the woman goes into the pantry, Lana peers out the window into the backyard. No Alfred.

"That's it downstairs, correct?" the woman says when she comes out of the pantry.

Lana nods, and she follows the woman up the stairs, Tilly sticking close behind. Alfred will just have to wait.

Lana has left the upstairs bathroom a mess, of course, and the bedroom that Carlito, Garth, and Alfred share is even worse.

Inspector Stiller doesn't spend much time in the boys' room, but when she gets to Veronica and Whit's room, she becomes much more attentive. She observes the piles of clothes and moves slowly from point to point in the room.

Lana goes to the window in which she'd seen Veronica staring down at her and Whit. She looks out as Veronica had looked out and is relieved to see that, from this viewpoint, she couldn't have seen into the garage, where they'd stood kissing.

When she turns back, Inspector Stiller is bending close to the stacks of magazines piled on top of Veronica's bedside table.

"Mrs. Winters spends a lot of time in her room?" the woman asks, and while Lana is composing an answer, Tilly says, "Yes, her does. Her watches TV, you bet."

Inspector Stiller looks at Tilly and nods.

"It's just during her recuperation," Lana says. "Actually, the doctor thinks she's coming back really fast."

The woman doesn't even look at Lana when she says this. She goes back to the stack of magazines, bending close to them. A few seconds later, she sets her clipboard down on the bed, pries up most of the stack, and pulls free one of the magazines on the bottom. Lana sees there's a buff bare-chested guy on the cover, but she can't read the name of the magazine. Inspector Stiller slides it under her notepad on the clipboard and makes some kind of note on her report.

The inspector's gaze settles on the various jars and bottles of creams and emollients on the tray beside the bed. She sets her clipboard down again and begins scrutinizing each bottle and jar. One by one, she reads the label, unscrews the lid, and takes a look or a sniff. When she gets to the large glass bottle of T.L.C. Primera, she quickly unscrews the lid, holds it to her nose, then holds it to her nose again. Lana can see the recognition in her eyes, and when, a moment later, she shifts her gaze directly to Lana, Lana feels her cheeks pinken and realizes she's feeling just like she used to feel when a social worker would come to her house when she still lived with her mother, and even though she hated what her mother did with the alcohol and the pills, she knew that whatever the social worker was going to recommend would be worse.

After Veronica's room, Inspector Stiller merely pokes her head into Lana's room, which is in as much disorder as all the others. "Yours?" Inspector Stiller says to Lana after peering into the room.

Lana nods and, glancing in, sees the room as the woman has seen it: twisted sheets, strewn earphones, iPod, books, papers, candy wrappers, encrusted plates, dirty glasses, birds' nests along the windowsills. And there's something else, too—one of her photograph albums is poking out from beneath the bed.

Inspector Stiller heads downstairs. She's carrying the T.L.C. Primera bottle as well as the magazine. At the door, she hands Lana a piece of paper. "This is a receipt for the bottle and the magazine, which I'm taking for evidentiary purposes."

Lana nods again.

Inspector Stiller looks evenly at Lana. "I suppose the

bottle is Mrs. Winters's. As for the magazine with the naked men in it, I don't know if that belongs to Mrs. Winters or Mr. Winters."

At these words, Lana's body goes rigid. "That's not Whit's," she says with sudden vehemence.

"Whit's?" Inspector Stiller says. "I thought his name was Lucian," and as the woman says this, her eyes seem to dilate to take something in, and Lana knows, knows for a fact, that Inspector Stiller has uncapped the lid, taken a whiff, and recognized within Lana the scent of forbidden fruit.

"Everyone calls him Whit," Lana says, and tries to keep the sulk out of her voice.

Very calmly Inspector Stiller says, "You mentioned you couldn't sleep last night. Any particular reason for that?"

Lana begins to compose an answer, but Inspector Stiller, watching and realizing, probably, that Lana's composing an answer, holds up a hand. "It's okay," she says, and a faint smile seems to appear on her lips. "I'm pretty good at filling in the blanks."

A hole to crawl into. That's all Lana wants.

"I'm leaving," the inspector says finally. She sidesteps Garth, who's sitting on the floor near the door. But from the bottom of the front porch steps, Inspector Stiller casts one last look back at Lana. "By the way, where would"— she flips to a page on her clipboard—"Alfred Mobilio be right now?"

This time Lana doesn't try to compose an answer. She opens her mouth and hears herself say, "He's with Mrs. Arnot. His job coach."

Inspector Stiller takes this in. "When are they due to return?"

"About an hour," Lana says, surprised at the size and

quickness of her lie. "Mrs. Arnot always does her job and then some," she adds, suddenly afraid the inspector will call and check.

There are a few moments of complete stillness before the inspector says, "I see." She jots something on her clipboard and, after giving Lana a smile that seems now not only small but cruel, she walks to her car.

45.

"Alfred?" Lana calls when the car has pulled away. "Can you hear me, Alfred?"

Tilly and Carlito stop and listen when Lana stops and listens. They follow her up and down the street, a few houses in each direction, calling out Alfred's name as they go. When Lana sees Mrs. Harbaugh across the street staring at them with a jutting chin, she yells, "What're you looking at, Hairball?" and without a word Mrs. Harbaugh moves back into the deeper shadows of her porch.

They are looking for Alfred, but behind the looking is a waiting. Waiting for what happens next with Protective Services, because something's going to happen, that much Lana knows. This, she thinks, is how people would feel if they knew they were about to have a terrible earthquake or hurricane or fire, but it just hasn't happened yet. Someone complained about the Winters house, and Inspector Stiller had gotten the goods on them, and now the disaster is heading their way. It's just a question of when it will hit and what the damage will be. But Snick House is over; Lana's sure of it. Whit and Veronica will lose their license. She'll be separated from Whit and she'll be separated from Tilly and Garth and Carlito and Alfred.

She needs to do something.

She needs to *draw* something.

But what?

What do you draw to keep things from burning up or falling apart or blowing away?

"Alfred!"

She and Tilly and Carlito stop, and listen, and move on.

Lana gets the flashlight from the storeroom and they check the attic, then the basement. They check the backyard and the alley in each direction. Then they check the garage. Inside, no one answers when they call, but they hear a scritching sound.

"Mouse," Tilly says, and it's true, it does sound like a mouse, except the sound doesn't stop when they call Alfred's name. They creep toward the sound, Lana scanning the dark corners with the beam of the flashlight. The *scritch scritch* gets louder as they approach a row of rusty gray file cabinets—a repainting project Whit's never quite gotten to—and there, behind the wall of cabinets, sitting on a pile of old boat cushions and staring up into the beam of the flashlight, is Alfred. Positioned across his knees is the Ladies Drawing Kit.

"Alfred!" Lana screams, and this freezes everybody for an instant, and then Alfred puts down the pencil and starts saying, "S-s-sorry, s-s-sorry, s-s-sorry."

Lana grabs the kit from him and holds it under the light. There they are: the thick pink-flecked sheets of old paper, and he's been writing on them. Lana feels the terrible sensation of tumbling into free fall. On the first page, Alfred has written: BIE SAINGS ON MENWEAR. RDE TAG FRIDAY COEM SEE. There's more but she doesn't read it. Two whole pages are filled up like that. The next one says MISS TEEN AMERICA TESXA. MISS TEEN AMERCIA ARZIONA. Five teens and five states in big block letters. There's one that seems to be a recipe for CHOCLAT CKOOIES and one about Christmas centerpieces. The last is just one line: BCKKK OFF VRONICA.

Back off, Veronica. Lana has seen this kind of note before. Alfred wrote one to Carlito once and one to Mrs. Arnot when she wanted him to try working at the D.Q.

The paper is wasted.

Alfred is hitting himself in the face, not too hard, but hard enough so Lana knows he's upset, and yet Lana feels a hardness take hold of her, the same hardness she saw in her mother when Lana would pour her mother's booze down the sink or flush her drugs down the toilet, the hardness that made her mean.

"Stop hitting yourself, Goddamn it!" she shouts at Alfred, but he doesn't stop, he starts crying and hits himself harder. Tilly's crying now, too, and Carlito.

Lana wonders why she doesn't feel sorry for them, but she doesn't. "Stop it!" she hears herself yell again. "Stop it right now!" and Alfred's sobbing deepens until Tilly does something surprising. She walks up to Lana and pushes her in the chest and through her own sobbing says fiercely, "*You* stop it! *You* stop it, Lana!"

And when Lana does stop it and looks into Tilly's squinched, fierce, weepy face, all her normal feelings come flooding back, and she drops the used papers and goes over to Alfred and puts her arms around him and feels his warm tears on her neck and hears her words flow in an easy, soothing stream. "It's okay, Alfred, the paper doesn't matter, I'm not mad, Alfred, it's okay, it's okay, it's okay."

Later, when Alfred is calm again and they are all walk-ing back into the house for the Otter Pops Lana has promised them, she flips the drawing kit open.

There is one blank sheet left.

Only one.

46.

*W*hile the others are eating their Otter Pops (there is no quarreling, for once, over flavors), Lana hides the drawing kit on the top shelf of her closet, and after she's done this, her hopeful spirits slowly begin to build again. Inspector Stiller found the house in bad shape, but maybe this will somehow be a good thing for her and Whit. Alfred wasted six pages, but she still has one left, and she's always sensed that the last one would be the most important one anyway.

When she gets downstairs, she organizes a big housewide, room-to-room cleanup campaign so things'll be spick-and-span in case the state sends anybody else out today. She even gets Garth to pitch in by promising to call for his mother as soon as they're done. It goes slow—the Snicks are easily distracted—and matters aren't helped when, about a half hour in, Chet shows up with a jar full of smallish black and red bugs.

"What're those?"

"Box elder bugs," he says.

Lana remembers the Oddball Olympics. "You going to get your new girlfriend to take off all her clothes and eat one?"

This seems to amuse Chet. "I'd enjoy that," he says.

"Which—her taking off her clothes or her eating a bug?"

"Both," he says, and Lana has to laugh.

Tilly, who's been staring into the jar, says, "Let them go!"

Chet looks at them. "Yeah, I probably will, but I might keep a couple as pets. They're harmless; I looked them up. They eat tree leaves and stuff. They won't bite you. The article I read said they have *slender, sucking mouthparts.*"

Lana says, "I wouldn't want to keep as a pet something with slender, sucking mouthparts."

Chet stares into the jar. "They stick together, though. In the winter I've seen them in huge masses on sunny sides of rocks and stuff."

Tilly says, "That's good," and Chet nods. "Yeah, it is."

Lana says, "You going to eat one, just to see how the event might go?"

Chet regards the bugs for a long moment and says, "No, I don't think I will." Then, to Tilly and the others, "Shall we set my beetles free?"

The Snicks are keen on the idea, though the beetle-freeing is a little disappointing in that the bugs don't go when the lid is lifted off. They have to be shaken out. Only Chet's thumping the bottom of the jar with the heel of his hand gets the last few to fly.

Lana asks Chet if he wants to help with the gala Snick House room-to-room cleanup, and, to her surprise, he accepts. Better yet, he works hard and fast, and before long, things look more or less presentable. Chet's hair is damp with sweat and Lana pulls her shirt at the collar to let in air.

"Was there a reward at the end of this quest?" Chet says, and Lana says, "How about salami sandwiches?"

"With iced tea?" Chet says.

While they eat, Lana gives Chet the details of Inspector Stiller's visit. "Anyway," she says, "I think they're going to close down Snick House."

Chet has stopped chewing during this last observation but resumes now. "Well, that would make my dad happy."

Lana asks what that means.

"He's just never liked having . . . this facility next door. Says it drives down the property values." He smiles wanly and shakes his head. "That's just who my father is."

"Well," Lana says, "maybe if there's a God, he'll devise just the right punishment for your father."

Chet grins. "Maybe."

Garth, who's eaten only one central bite from each half of his sandwich, rises and goes back to his waiting post by the front door. Chet says he's going, too.

"Where to?"

An odd look crosses Chet's face. "I've just got to do a couple of things," he says.

Lana guesses he's going to see his new girlfriend or at least try to, an idea that, to her surprise, makes her less happy than she knows it should. She does her best, though. She nods and smiles and says, "Good luck with those errands, Chesterfield."

She's never called him Chester before, let alone Chesterfield, but after it comes out, she kind of likes it, and Chet doesn't seem to mind. On his way out, he says, "Later, Garth-man," but Garth doesn't even look up from his Popeye doll.

Lana washes down the last of her sandwich with tea

and heads for the house phone. She dials the Best Western and the clerk answers on the second ring.

"Are there phones in the rooms?" Lana asks, and the clerk says, "Yes, ma'am. Also color TVs and vibrating recliner chairs."

"Well, could you connect me to Mrs. Stoneman's room?"

"Mrs. Stoneman," the clerk repeats. Then, "I don't see a Mrs. Stoneman."

A faint alarm sounds within Lana. "She stayed there last night."

"Checking," the clerk says. A few seconds pass. "That's right, she was here last night, but she checked out this morning at ten-thirty. I remember she used the pool and then a short time later she left."

"Mrs. Stoneman?" Lana says.

"That's right. Mrs. Stoneman. Is there anything else I can help you with?"

"No," Lana says. "No, there's not."

47.

*L*ana doesn't speak to Garth about his mother's leaving. She doesn't have to. She knows Garth knows. And she knows Garth knew. Probably from the moment his mother snapped at him yesterday. Certainly when she didn't appear after breakfast today.

Garth sits now by the front door, his thin legs stretched in front of him, his back braced by an old upholstered chair, all of his action figures stationed on the wood floor around him except Popeye, who Garth holds with one hand and strokes with the other.

Lana slides down onto the floor beside him, close but not too close. She picks up the Spider-Man doll and realizes how much he resembles the buff guy on the front of Veronica's magazine except Spider-Man has his tight costume painted on. "Know why I like Popeye best?" she says.

Garth doesn't answer.

Because he looks like a normal person, she starts to say, but stops herself. "Because he looks just like you and me," she says.

Garth stops smoothing his hand along the length of Popeye's back. His face twists into a look of terrible anguish. "'Ot 'umming," he says. "'Ot 'umming for me."

It takes Lana a second to supply the right consonants, and by the time she gets "not coming for me," Garth has started to cry.

"She might, Garth, your mother might come back," Lana says, but she hears how puny and untrue the words sound even as she speaks them.

"'Ot!" he says with awful vehemence. "'Ot 'umming ever!"

Lana starts to disagree, to offer hope where there isn't hope, but she can't. She just can't.

She eases closer to Garth. She's almost holding her breath as she extends her arm beyond him and carefully lowers her hand until it barely touches his shoulder and then, as she slowly lets the full weight of her arm settle across the breadth of his thin shoulders, he screams and pulls back from her. He trembles and holds himself and seems so incredibly slight, as if there is nothing to him except skin stretched over hollow bones.

"It's okay," she says, trying to soothe him with her voice. "It's okay, Garth, you've got us."

And it's true, for the moment, it's literally true. Tilly and Alfred and Carlito materialize from nowhere, and Carlito leans forward to bless Garth's shoulder, which Garth allows, to Lana's surprise, and then Tilly and Alfred and Carlito are standing around them in a circle of oddness and fondness and need, and Garth stops crying. If Lana has ever felt more certain of anything, she can't remember when it might've been.

"You've got us," she says again. "You've got me."

48.

*M*id-afternoon, Veronica returns home. Her face has a radiant quality—it almost glows. Lana, unobserved, watches her from the kitchen, and Veronica starts slightly when Lana says, "How'd the physical therapy go?"

After Veronica realizes that it's Lana, her surprise fades. "Oh, it's you," she says, hardly glancing Lana's way, which is fine by Lana because she's in her bathing suit, a thick, horrible two-piece that she only put on because nobody but the Snicks were around. Veronica picks through the small pile of mail that had been neatly stacked on the kitchen table. If she's noticed how clean the house is, she doesn't mention it.

Lana glances out the window to the backyard, where the Snicks are sitting in the plastic wading pool they've cleaned and filled, or at least all of the Snicks except Garth. He's gone back into his lilac room.

When she turns back, Veronica has left the mail scattered on the table and is heading for the stairs.

Lana steps out of the kitchen. "So was it tough?" she says.

Veronica looks back. "Was what tough?"

"The physical therapy," Lana says. "With Dr. Gooch."

"Oh," Veronica says. "Yes, it was. It was very demanding." And then Veronica's eyes go regal and cold and sly. "But I took a surprising amount of pleasure in it." She sends her gaze beyond Lana. "Unfortunately, I'm a long way from finished. Dr. Gooch says we will definitely need to schedule some extra sessions."

As Veronica lets this settle in, her gaze drifts down to Lana's swimsuit. "Well, aren't you the long, skinny thing," she says. She smiles her cool smile. "But the bikini is all wrong for you. You should try a high-cut one-piece to distract from the fact that you are for all practical purposes boobless."

Snick House is waiting for the wrecking ball and I'm getting fashion tips from the Sleaze Queen. That's what Lana thinks. "Faith," she says. "Unity."

"And the same to you," Veronica says pleasantly, and begins again up the stairs.

"An inspector was here today from Protective Services."

Veronica turns. "What did he want?"

"It was a woman. She seemed interested in your whereabouts. Somebody filed a complaint."

"About what?"

Lana shrugs. "Who knows? She went through your room, though. She took a bottle that said T.L.C. Primera on it. Also a magazine with naked men in it."

Veronica is surprisingly calm. She comes to some quick conclusion about what has happened, and the conclusion, whatever it is, doesn't disturb her. "It's just as well," she says. "Dr. Gooch doesn't like the fact that I have to deal with the added trials of running a foster home when I should be dedicating myself to my complete recovery."

As if running Snick House has been much of a trial to her recently, Lana thinks, but she doesn't want to argue. Besides, that isn't what concerns her. "You don't care that it might be the end of Snick House?"

Veronica gives this a frosty laugh. "I've spent years praying that I wouldn't need to run this place, but we always needed the money. And now . . ."

"And now you don't?"

Satisfaction slips into Veronica's expression. "Dr. Gooch is very committed to my full and complete recovery."

"Are you going to marry him?" Lana asks.

A laugh explodes from Veronica. "Marry him? God, no. He's just become . . . an ally. An ally in the day-to-day battles of life. Besides, as I think you're aware, I am already married."

Lana stares at her and wonders if she's looking at a new kind of cannibal, one who uses everybody up, who eats people from the inside. She wonders if it's too late to erase all of Veronica. Make her disappear.

Veronica is smiling. "You've got attitude, Lana, but you're so *young*. You have a child's eyes. You haven't begun to see how actual adults really get by. You think I'm evil, I can see it in your eyes, but what I do is no different than what your beloved Whit does. He has his allies, too, the people he gets to do what he needs done."

Veronica lets this idea hang in the air. Lana wishes she could run from it and never hear what's coming next, but she knows she will, and she stands where she is.

"You, for example, are one of his allies," Veronica says. "You take care of the house for him and"—she smiles coolly—"you take care of me for him."

Lana starts to disagree but isn't sure of her footing. She doesn't want to admit she does anything in particular for Whit.

"And that nurse at the hospital that replaced your pills with placebos," Veronica says. "That was another of his allies." She takes a deep breath. "And now of course he has the widow."

Confusion floods Lana. "What widow? What're you talking about?"

"The widow Mullins. The widow whose house Whit has been painting."

"What about it?"

Veronica pretends to be bored, but Lana can tell how much she's enjoying this. "Have you ever noticed how when he comes home, he never has paint on his clothes or on his arms or under his fingernails?"

Lana hasn't noticed, as a matter of fact, but now that she thinks about it, she doesn't remember paint on him.

Veronica says, "And have you ever noticed how he doesn't smell of turpentine?"

Lana wants to object, but she can't. One of her mother's boyfriends had been a painter, and he always smelled like paint thinner, even on weekends when he wasn't painting. But Whit never smelled like anything other than himself, or lime shaving cream, or sometimes smoke and gin.

"The widow Mullins is rich and she's old," Veronica says, "but she's not so old she doesn't like a little . . . *company*."

"Are you saying . . . ," Lana says, but she doesn't even know how to complete the sentence.

"I'm saying that one thing Whit and I have always

understood is that allies come in all shapes and sizes." Her smile is sly and wintry. "It's how we got into the foster business."

Lana shakes her head violently. "But Whit likes us."

"It's true," Veronica says. "He does. But without the check from the state each month, he would like you less." She smiles. "Quite a bit less, actually."

Lana stands dazed. She feels vulnerable. She wishes she had something to put on over her swimsuit.

"You see?" Veronica says. "You're surprised. In fact, you're mortified. That's because of your child eyes. When you're a little more mature, you'll see things differently, and, believe me, you'll have allies, too, lots of them, probably more than Whit and me combined."

"I won't!" Lana says, and even as she says the words, she hears how young her voice sounds.

Veronica seems to hear it, too, because she feels no need to rebut it. She starts again to go upstairs but again stops for another word.

"Oh, and just so you know, that magazine with the cute, stark-naked men in it? I didn't bring that home. Whit did. He likes me to go through it and decide which one I'd like to . . . canoodle with"—Veronica actually winks—"if I wasn't married to him." She smiles. "It's surprising how it ratchets up the evening's high jinks."

Lana tries to hold herself very still. She feels actually, physically ill.

"Ah," Veronica says. "You're appalled. And yet, someday, you won't be."

Veronica takes the stairs then up to her room. By the time her door closes, Lana still has not moved. What has come into her mind are the words Veronica's friend Louise had used to describe Veronica's going out to find Whit the night of the car wreck: *The tender little secrets between a wife and her husband.*

Louise had made it seem like these were the kind of secrets Lana couldn't understand now but one day would, but she was wrong about that, Lana thinks, she was completely wrong. Lana will never understand secrets like these.

Lana takes a beach towel from the back of a kitchen chair and wraps it all the way around herself, feeling the thin cotton fabric tighten over her shoulders, elbows, and wrists. She stands there like that for at least a minute before Tilly's voice calls her into the backyard.

"Found a marble!" Tilly shouts, and waves the small object in her hand. She's wearing a pink two-piece that makes her look oddly toddler-like, and her knees are muddy. "It's a green one," she says, beaming, "but I'm calling it Pinky!"

"Makes sense to me," Lana says, but without her usual irony. The truth is, at the moment, calling a green marble Pinky makes as much sense to Lana as anything else in the world.

Part Three

49.

One slight change for the better.

Veronica hasn't thumped her cane today. Probably she knows Lana will no longer respond and doesn't want to give Lana the pleasure of proving it, but no matter what the reason, it's one slight change for the better.

Around three, Veronica comes down and makes herself some toast and soup. (Lana watches her struggle one-handedly with the can opener for a few seconds before opening it for her.) Veronica then sits at the table eating and reading *Us* magazine without a glance at anyone or anything around her.

When she's finished, she leaves her dishes on the table and says she's not to be disturbed, she's taking a nap. "Dr. Gooch says I need a one-to-two-hour nap every afternoon."

After she's beyond earshot, Lana says in a low voice to Tilly, "Dr. Gooch is probably practicing without a license."

Once it's quiet upstairs, Lana goes to the house phone and dials Hallie's number. She gets a secretary who says, "I think Miss Simpson's in a meeting. Let me check."

Lana knows what *Miss Simpson's in a meeting* means. It means Hallie's trying to get some work done or is taking a break or is just in a really bad mood, but whatever the reason, she doesn't want to be disturbed and, since she's Hallie, she isn't going to be.

Which makes it all the more amazing when Hallie comes on the line and says, "Hello, Lana. How are things?"

"Something bad's happening here, Hallie. I think the state's going to close this place down or something." She starts to tell her about Inspector Stilller, but Hallie gently interrupts.

"I heard about it this morning. There has been a serious complaint."

"Was it the woman across the street? Mrs. Harbaugh?"

"It was a family member."

Lana is confused. "What do you mean, family member?"

"Someone from one of the clients' families. Someone from the immediate family."

The answer comes to Lana with startling certainty. "Was it Garth's mom? A Mrs. Stoneman? Was it her?"

Hallie says she has already said too much.

So it was her. It was Garth's mom. Lana can hardly believe it.

"Now what?" Lana says. "What will happen to us?"

Hallie explains that the department will quickly come to some disposition with regard to the complaint and investigation. "They could close the place, they could order another inspector out, or they could do nothing."

"What do you think they'll do?"

A second or two passes before Hallie speaks. "I don't know, Lana. But I'm pretty sure they'll do something."

"Could they put us all someplace together?"

Over the telephone line, with more than five hundred miles between her and Hallie, Lana can almost feel the kindness of Hallie's soft laugh. "Oh, sweet Lana," she says. "You are such a dreamer."

"But could they?" Lana says.

"This is the state, Lana. We're already standing room only. There's no way we're going to find five seats together in one row." She is quiet a moment, and then she says, "A couple of months ago you wanted me to transfer you away from these kids. Now you want the whole bunch of you to stay together? What happened?"

"I don't know," Lana says. This is the absolute truth. She doesn't know what happened. All she knows is that something has.

"Is there another element here, Lana? Someone you're attached to?"

"Maybe."

"Who?"

"I don't know." This is the truth, too. It's Whit, of course, but it's not just Whit. Tilly and Garth and the other Snicks need her, and the Inside Whit needs her, and this has changed everything for Lana, the fact of people needing her. "Look, Hallie, could you try to get another inspection, tell them that the first inspector came at a bad time and kind of had a chip on her shoulder?"

Hallie takes a deep enough sigh that it's audible over the phone lines. "I'll try, Lana. But no promises."

"And if there's another inspector coming, could you give us a little heads-up?"

"I'll pretend I didn't hear that," Hallie says, but Lana knows that she did hear it and that she'll give the heads-up if there's some discreet way she can do it.

Fifteen minutes later, Mrs. Arnot stops by to take the Snicks to the library, but Tilly says Lana needs her, *you bet,* so Tilly stays. Lana tries to talk Tilly into taking a nap so Lana can nap herself, and Tilly does lie down on the carpet, but she can't stop talking and squirming, so they decide finally to take snacks to Tilly's rock place, a big bunch of boulders under a pine tree at the outskirts of the town cemetery.

Lana stretches out on the big rock in the shade and is nearly drowsing when Tilly says, "Is everything going to be okay?"

Lana blinks open her eyes. "Why do you ask that, Tilly?"

Tilly shakes her head without speaking. On a platter-sized, flat-topped rock, she's making a loose, rounded pyramid of smaller rocks.

Lana looks at her and says, "If you could have one wish, Tilly, what would it be?"

"For everything to be okay," Tilly says without even thinking about it.

Beyond the cemetery, along the flat horizon, a dark truck moves east to west, right to left, so far away Lana can't hear it. It could be anybody's truck. It could be Whit's truck. Lana eases her eyes closed. She wants to talk to Whit, she wants to talk to him in the worst way, but she doesn't want to think about him and what Veronica called his allies. It's quiet except for the slight rattle of cottonwood leaves in the breeze and the dim click of rocks as Tilly builds her little pyramid, but then that stops, and Lana feels Tilly moving close, and after a moment or two, Tilly touches one of her stubby fingers softly to Lana's eyelids and then smooths it slowly over the contours of Lana's cheeks and forehead, chin, and nose.

"Pretty face," Tilly says, and Lana clicks open her eyes and looks up at Tilly.

"Yours too. You have a pretty face, too," she says, and she means it, which is why, she supposes, Tilly seems to believe it.

Whit hasn't gotten home yet when Lana and Tilly return to the house, but some men are inside hauling a plasma TV upstairs. It looks really heavy. The men stagger, grunt, and stop every few feet, and these are beefy men. Veronica stands above them wearing house slippers and a short robe. "I don't know how you lift that big old thing," she says in a cooing voice.

It makes Lana want to puke, but Tilly is fascinated and wanders upstairs. A few minutes later, Veronica drops the cooing and yells, "Come get Tilly, Lana! She's in the way!"

Lana doesn't have to get Tilly. Tilly leaves on her own when she hears this.

It's almost dusk. The sun slants through the window, and when it catches the motes of dust floating in the air, it reminds Lana of the minutes in the garage before she closed her eyes and let Whit kiss her. Those minutes felt like seconds, but today's minutes feel like hours. Whenever Lana looks at the clock, she wonders if it has stopped and needs a new battery, but it doesn't. When she goes over and puts her ear close to it, she can hear its dull rhythmic clicking.

She and Tilly play two rounds of Candy Land, then Lana browns meat for spaghetti, and Carlito, Alfred, and Garth return and the beefy TV guys leave and supper's over and most of the Snicks are watching a show and Lana and Tilly are standing at the kitchen sink rinsing dishes when Whit's truck finally turns up the driveway and pulls into the garage. Lana hears him whistling "Some Enchanted Evening" as he crosses the yard.

"Well, there are two fetching individuals," he says to Lana and Tilly when he comes in, a remark that pleases Tilly more than Lana.

"I just put the spaghetti in the refrigerator," Lana says.

He slides behind her and, careful that Tilly can't see, gives the nape of Lana's neck a quick grazing kiss. When she shrugs him off, he says, "Tilly, did you put Lana in the refrigerator by mistake?"

Tilly laughs at the thought but says she did not, no, sir.

Whit starts eating the spaghetti straight from the pot while leaning against the refrigerator. Lana supposes he'll finish it all, then put the pot on the counter to be washed. By her.

His little ally.

Who sees with the eyes of a child.

She wipes her hands on a towel and turns around. "How'd the painting go today?" she says.

"Not bad," he says, chewing. "Better than yesterday anyhow."

Lana nods. "And yet there's no paint on you."

Whit chuckles and keeps eating. "I'm a clean individual. It's a personal trademark of mine. You know what I always say? Nothing shouts *no prospects* louder than a painted-up painter."

"But how do you do that? Paint without getting paint on you?"

Whit tips the pot to get the last of the spaghetti. "Well, for starters, I wear coveralls and a separate pair of paint boots, all of which I can remove at the end of the painting day."

He must see her looking at his hands because he says, "Then I clean up my hands real good."

"But you don't smell like turpentine."

Whit makes a snorting laugh. "Turpentine? Nobody uses turpentine. They don't even use paint thinner. Everything's latex now, water-based, cleans up with water." He winks. "And water, you may have noticed, is odor-free."

He drops the fork into the pot and, slipping by Lana, goes to the sink and washes the pot himself, which is just one more strange aspect of this conversation. The explanation he's given her about coveralls and latex paint was convincing, and now he's washing his own pot and fork, and drying them, too, carefully, with a tea towel until the aluminum shines. As he sets the pot into its proper place in the cupboard, he says, "So how was it today with Ronnie?"

When Lana doesn't immediately answer, Tilly says, "Her got a big giant TV!"

Whit turns from Tilly to Lana. "Yeah?"

Lana nods, and Whit's face breaks into a beaming smile.

"I told you that Gooch guy was a genius for gaming those insurance boys," he says, and before Lana can say anything else or even mention Inspector Stiller's visit, he hurries upstairs.

Lana hopes Whit will suggest everybody come up to watch a movie on the enormous TV, but he doesn't. He closes the door to their bedroom and doesn't come back out for the rest of the night.

50.

That night Lana falls asleep listening to Chet's podcast—Chet spends a lot of time reminding the Sodbusters about the Oddball Olympics event scheduled the next day on Highway 20. Lana sleeps a deep dreamless sleep, and when she gets downstairs the next morning, Garth is sitting by the front door, Tilly is eating Trix, and Carlito and Alfred are still sleeping. Whit's already gone. His half-filled coffee cup stands on the kitchen counter, and Lana can see that his truck's not in the garage. She looks around for a note, but there isn't one. From upstairs the shrieks and applause of some kind of audience-participation show carry down from Veronica's plasma TV.

Lana doesn't know how many more breakfasts there will be together, so she makes pancakes and spreads baked apples over them, a dish that everybody likes and is Garth's personal favorite. She calls them together at the kitchen table and while she's pouring milk in glasses, she has an idea. She sits and has everybody be quiet and close their eyes.

"Thank you for this food," she says, "and thank you for this day, and thank you for the company of Alfred and Garth and Carlito and Tilly." She stops. She doesn't know what to say or do next. She's had her eyes closed, but now she opens them and looks up. All of the others are just staring at her.

To everybody's relief, Tilly says, "A-men! Let's eat!" and they all dig in.

Garth didn't eat yesterday, but today he eats fast, as if somebody's going to take it from him. "More?" Lana says when he's done, and he nods, yes.

After breakfast, Lana cleans up the kitchen, gets Tilly to sweep the porch, and sends Alfred up to make beds in case another inspector comes. "And flush the toilet, okay?" she shouts, just in case. She calls Mrs. Arnot then to make sure she's coming for the boys *and* Tilly this time.

When Mrs. Arnot says she'll be there in two shakes of a lamb's tail, Lana goes upstairs to talk to Veronica, but as she approaches, she falls quiet. The door is cracked open, and she can see Veronica standing in front of the mirror. She isn't wearing anything flirty, so she isn't getting ready for Dr. Gooch. She's just wearing slacks and a cotton top, a good, normal-seeming look for her, the kind of outfit she used to put on just before Whit came home. Veronica stares at the mirror and turns one way, then the other, and starts to cross her arms, but she no longer has two arms to cross. The awkwardness of it, and of her pinned-up sleeve, collapses something in her face, breaks it down, tears everything away, and what's left, Lana can see, is fear, pure, childlike, naked fear.

Then Veronica's eyes flick toward Lana, and the coldness snaps back.

"What're you looking at?" she says.

"Nothing. I just came to . . ."

"Came to what?"

Lana takes a deep breath. "Came to tell you that breakfast's done, the house is picked up, Mrs. Arnot's coming for the Snicks, and I have to run an errand, so you're in charge."

"Oh, no, you're not," Veronica says, but Lana's already on the stairs and heading down. "Where're you going?" Veronica calls, but her voice isn't all anger now—there's an imploring element, too. "When will you be back?"

For the first time since coming to the Winterses' house, Lana feels almost sorry for Veronica.

"As soon as I can," she calls back.

Lana has braided her hair and threads the braid now through a green DeKalb cap with a flying corncob on the front, one of Whit's vast collection of caps. There is a bicycle in the garage, an old Schwinn with ten gears, of which, it turns out, only four actually work, but those are enough. Lana pedals six or seven blocks and then turns east onto Highway 20, toward the rest stop where Chet has scheduled his Oddball Olympics event, tractor-styling or something like that.

It's only a little after nine, the heat is already searing, and the highway, which seems flat in a car, turns out to have a surprising number of gradual climbs. There aren't many cars, but there's no shoulder on the highway, and when a car does overtake her, it screams by. The big rigs are worse—each one creates a whooshing wake of air that nearly knocks her over. It's far to the rest stop, very far, so far that she's begun to think she's missed it or gone the wrong way, when finally she crests a rolling ridge and sees it: a cottonwood tree and, beneath it, a small set of wooden bleachers.

On the approaching downhill, Lana straightens her

back and, coasting, lets the cooling wind flow into her shirt and over her face. The brakes squeal as she eases to a stop near the bleachers.

No one else is here.

In the dirt she can see some footprints and some deep scrapes from the bleachers being pulled into the shade of the cottonwood. She wonders if she has the wrong day.

"Hello?" she says. "Chet?"

The only sounds are the clicks of cicadas, the stir of cottonwood leaves, and the faint drone of a distant tractor. It smells good, though—beyond the tall, dry weeds, the dirt at the fringes of the near field has been freshly turned.

"Hello?" Lana yells again.

Nothing.

Lana's instinct is to leave, just write a little note and leave, but it occurs to her that if Tilly were with her, Tilly would want to stay and collect leaves and rocks and, if it was her lucky day, feathers and bones. Lana wishes she'd brought water and maybe a snack. That would be the other thing Tilly would've wanted—a little picnic. Lana rests the bicycle against the tree and climbs toward the top of the bleachers. She leans back and stretches her legs over the next seat. She stares off, trying to imagine what kind of event Chet might've imagined taking place here. She can't, though. But it begins to seem interesting to her that someone has put bleachers in a place like this, where there is nothing for a spectator to look at.

Except there is, in a way. There is the half-cultivated field and beyond that a long stretch of green pasture with three massive buttes rising up behind. There are the dense, gray-tinged shapes of clustered clouds with a fancy name Lana doesn't know. And there is the chorus of cicadas and the hum of the electrical line and the rumble of a passing tractor trailer on the highway. It all creates the same sense of wonder she used to feel during field trips to museums when she would look into those dioramas, except now she feels like she's inside it. It has a calming effect on her—it causes a pleasant loosening of her perspective. It's as if her whole being has been decongested. She likes simply sitting here breathing in, breathing out.

Lana cradles the back of her head into her knitted hands. She closes her eyes. She wishes Tilly were here, and Whit, and her father as he looked in photographs and dreams, and maybe her mother on one of her good days. She wishes Garth and Carlito and Alfred were here. She expels a deep breath, and another, and has just dipped into the first hallucinations of sleep when she hears the sound of dry breaking weeds. For a moment the sound is part of her dream, and then it is not. She wills her eyes closed for a long moment, squinching them into a wishing mode, then she blinks them open.

It's Chet, standing at the base of the bleachers.

She'd hoped, fantastically, that it was Whit walking toward the bleachers, but when it's Chet instead, she's surprised to find she's not particularly disappointed.

"Hi," she says.

He's carrying a blue backpack, and his smile is sheepish. "You came," he says.

Lana grins and looks around at the empty bleachers. "Not a big crowd by most standards."

Chet says, "What it lacks in size, it makes up in quality."

"Well, well," Lana says. "Big Chief Chetteroid gives the Neighbor Girl a little compliment."

Chet shrugs, and she says, "So do you think people got the day confused?"

"No, I think the problem is nobody listens to K-SOD, not that they should, really." He smiles. "I think it speaks well of the K-SOD audience that it doesn't actually listen to me."

Lana says, "You're kind of funny."

"Is that kind of good?"

"Yeah," Lana says, grinning, "it kind of is."

Chet opens his backpack and starts pulling out food. Within a minute Lana's washing down a bologna sandwich with lukewarm Mr. Pibb. When she's done, she says, "That was the best bad sandwich and warm drink I've ever had."

Chet says, "It's not often you're slammed and complimented in the same sentence."

"No, I mean it," Lana says. "It hit the spot." It's quiet for a few seconds. "I like it here." She looks off. "What I realized a while ago is that from these bleachers, you can't see a single man-made structure."

Chet follows her gaze. "I guess you're not counting the fences," he says.

A green tractor that had disappeared from view now turns a corner and, running parallel to the fence line, heads their way.

"Okay, let's get ready," Chet says, and Lana says, "Get ready for what?"

Chet doesn't answer. He just pulls two heavy cards out of his pack and hands one to Lana. They're the kind of adjustable black-and-white scorecards Lana has seen in televised ice-skating and gymnastics events. You can flip the numbers to determine a score of one to ten, with added tenths.

"What am I doing with this?" she says.

"Scoring the guy on the tractor."

"On the basis of what, exactly?"

"Style," he says. "Don't you remember anything? This is the tractor-*styling* event. Look for attitude, grace, and whether or not he's picking his nose."

The drone of the tractor is louder now, and Lana watches it approach. It's not one of the newer, closed-cab, air-conditioned tractors. The driver sits out in the elements, shaded only by a canvas umbrella. He is a stout, middle-aged man in jeans, a long-sleeved shirt, a cowboy hat, and dark glasses, which glint as he regards them in passing. Lana watches him another few seconds, then flips her cards to a 6.1. She holds hers up only when Chet does.

The man on the tractor stares solemnly at them. It's clear he has no idea in the world what they're doing.

"I think he's disappointed in his score," Chet says.

After he's gone, she turns to see what Chet gave him. A 3.4.

"I would've given him something in the twos," Chet says, "except for the dark glasses. I liked those glasses." He looks at Lana's 6.1 score and says, "I should've known it. Next thing I know, you'll be chanting U-S-A!"

He puts down his scorecard and pulls two Laffy Taffys out of his backpack. "Dessert?" he says.

The taffy is soft and yummy, and Lana's whole body feels like a lazy day as she sits here in the shade listening to the cicadas and looking out at the buttes.

Chet, she realizes, has been staring at her, and he says, "It was nice of you to come." He waits a second. "I'm kind of glad now that nobody else did."

"How come you were hiding, then?"

He shrugs. "Embarrassed. I'm actually pretty embarrassable."

"Not so much on your show, though."

Chet considers it. "Yeah, well. That's me being somebody else."

A truck passes on the highway, then it's quiet again. Lana says, "So what happened between you and K.C. and them?"

Chet's answer is another question. "Have you ever heard of something called the Truth Room?"

Lana admits she never has. "Why?"

"I just wondered if it was something other people had heard of or whether it was just something my mother made up."

"What do you mean?"

"Well, according to my mother, there is this room called the Truth Room and when you enter it, you have to tell the truth, and if you can't, you shouldn't go in. It was how she'd get me to tell her things. She would say in a really soft voice, 'Do you want to go into the Truth Room?'"

Lana and Chet are both quiet for a few seconds. There is a whisking sound in the dry weeds. A field mouse, probably. Then Lana says, "Why do you bring it up?"

"Well, when you asked what you asked, if you had been my mother, you would've asked me if I wanted to go into the Truth Room."

Lana thinks about it a few seconds. "Do you?"

"I might, if you'd go in, too."

Lana thinks it over some more. "That seems like a pretty big *if*."

Chet waits a second or two before saying, "So?"

"How do you get back out of the Truth Room?" Lana says.

Chet grins. "Simple. You just say, 'I'm opening the door and leaving now.' "

Lana considers it. She stretches her Laffy Taffy until a piece breaks free. She puts it into her mouth and chews it until there's nothing left. She swallows the sweet juice. She breathes freely in and breathes freely out. "Okay," she says.

"Okay, what?" Chet says.

Lana grins. "The Truth Room," she says. "I'm going in."

51.

*T*o decide who goes first, Lana picks a number between one and ten and asks Chet to guess whether the number is odd or even. The number is four, and he guesses odd.

"How do you know I didn't cheat you?" she says, and he says, "I just do." Then he says, "That was your first question, by the way."

"How many do I get?"

"Five," he says, "and you just used your second. That leaves three."

Lana stares out toward the buttes. She's lost sight of the green tractor and can barely hear its dim drone. "Okay," she says. "Three questions."

Chet looks a little nervous.

"First question," Lana says. "What happened between you and K.C. and Trina and them?"

Chet looks off. When he speaks, it's in a monotone, a dull recitation of facts. "I told them I thought we should change our policy with you so we could talk to you and let you ride up front."

Lana doesn't know the protocol in the Truth Room. She wants to say, Wow, you did that?—but she thinks she's supposed to act more like a school psychiatrist and just listen in a neutral, almost zombie-like way, so she says what one school psychiatrist always used to say to her.

"And?"

A sour smile. "They thought about it for maybe two seconds and announced that they now had a policy with me. 'What do you mean?' I said, and Trina looked at K.C. and said, 'Who's he talking to? He doesn't think we can talk to him, does he?'"

Lana says, "I think I'm just supposed to listen and not comment, but what you did was really nice, and . . ."

"You know what?" Chet says, looking now at Lana. "It was a relief, really. I didn't miss them at all. I expected to, but I didn't." He's clearly finished with the subject. "Okay, what's question two?"

It takes Lana a second to remember. "Oh. What came for you from the Above Average Novelties Company of Chicago, Illinois?"

Chet doesn't answer. A full minute passes and he still doesn't answer.

"Hey," Lana says, "are we in or out of the Truth Room?"

Chet expels a heavy breath. Then, "I thought it was something for me—these scorecards, actually—but it was something for my father."

"And?"

"It was a new item for his collection."

"Your dad has a collection?"

Chet nods, and Lana thinks of Mr. Pigeot and wonders what kind of things he might collect. "What are we talking here?" she says. "Indian artifacts? Frontier tools? Shot glasses with sports logos embossed on the side?"

Chet looks a little morose. "Ceramic vases with flowers on the side. Roseville, it's called."

A laugh bursts from Lana. "Why wouldn't you want to tell me that your dad has a vase collection?"

"Yeah, well, it's not *his* collection, really."

This is too good. "They're yours?"

Chet seems actually shocked. "God, no," he says. "My dad gets them in case my mom comes back. She used to want nice things we couldn't afford. She bought a Roseville vase once—she wanted to start a collection—but he made her take it back."

"So she left him?"

"I guess it was other things, too. She didn't like it here. I used to beg her to tell me what wish she left with William the Wish Reader, but she never would. But you know, the other day, when I got all the Dorito bags out of the well at Pioneer Park?—that wasn't the first time I did that. When I was ten or so, I went back with a rake and pulled up the wishes that were down there. The only ones were hers and mine. Mine all said *Horse,* naturally." He looks off. "Hers all said *Deliverance.*" He turns to Lana and makes an unhappy smile. "Her deliverance came in the form of a man from Ashland, Oregon, whose car broke down on Highway 20, so he had to wait in town almost a week to get it repaired. My mother met him when he'd gone to Pioneer Park and attracted a small group of onlookers while he practiced yoga on the grass. The others just gawked, but my mother asked him to teach her. That's what we heard later, anyhow."

The drone of the green tractor has grown slightly louder. In silhouette, it moves its slow course in the distance, east to west.

"Okay, time's running out," Chet says. "My turn."

Lana had one more question, but she can't remember what it is, so she takes a deep breath, closes her eyes, and says, "Fire away."

"How do you feel about Whit Winters?"

Lana's eyes blink open. "How come you're asking that?"

Chet smiles. "You seem to have forgotten where you are."

Lana remembers that she can open the imaginary door and leave the Truth Room anytime she wants, but it doesn't seem right, not after Chet answered her questions. "Okay. At first I wanted him to adopt me and be my father. And then I wanted him to . . . divorce Veronica." She looks off. "I know that's wrong, but there's something about the way he can make you feel and about the way he can make the Snicks feel. Like they're the real thing, and the K.C.'s and Trinas are the mongos and 'tards."

"Well, you can't argue with that," Chet says, but his tone is subdued.

"The problem is, I'm not sure who Whit is," Lana says. "I thought I knew, but now I don't." There's a lot more she could say, about how good and how bad Whit can be, how there seem really to be two Whits, the Outside Whit who everybody sees and the Inside Whit who only she sees, but Chet has fallen quiet and seems to have heard all he wants to hear on the subject, which makes Lana feel a little funny.

Lana says, "I remember my third question. Can I still ask it?"

Chet shrugs.

"What was the wish you wrote down and dropped in the well?"

At first Chet is merely looking at her, but then—Lana's not sure when or how this change occurs—he seems to be looking into her. She feels a mix of fear and excitement. The drone of the green tractor is growing louder. Chet opens his mouth and says, "C-r-r-reak."

"What was that?" Lana says.

"The sound of Chet stepping out of the Truth Room."

"C'mon, Chesterfield," Lana says in a pleading voice.

The tractor rises from the swale and heads their way.

Chet picks up his scorecard and hands Lana hers. "Ready, judges and judgettes?" he says.

As Lana looks off toward the approaching tractor, she can hardly believe her eyes. The stocky, middle-aged farmer has taken down the canvas umbrella so he can stand up on his tractor. He plants one foot on the tractor seat and the other on its steering wheel. When he gets fully in front of them, he takes off his cowboy hat and uses it to exaggeratedly fan himself, as if his act is so red-hot he has to cool himself off.

Lana laughs out loud, and so does Chet. Then they both put up scores of 10, and the farmer immediately sets his hat on his head, lowers himself back into his seat, and drives woodenly on.

"Okay," Lana says. "That was the most unexpected thing I think I've ever seen, except maybe you kicking that guy's butt the other day." She grins at Chet. "I'm ready to sign on. What do I have to do to become an official Chetterista?"

"I don't think you have to do anything," Chet says. "You can just say you are one."

Lana feels a strange mix of fear and excitement building within her. She wants to say something, something important, but she isn't sure what, and then out of the blue she hears herself say, "I think I ought to have to kiss you once."

He seems as surprised by her words as she is. "You don't have to do that," he says.

"I want to, though," Lana says. She tries to make her grin frisky. "Where shall I kiss you?"

Chet's whole face pinkens. "Wherever you want, I guess."

"Well, close your eyes," she says.

He does.

She considers his forehead, his nose, even his ears, but she chooses his lips and makes it a quick one, but not so quick she doesn't notice how pleasantly soft are the lips of Chester Pigeot.

52.

On the return trip to town, Chet rides the bike and Lana sits on the handlebars. She doesn't like it, sitting up there with not much to hang on to and no good place for her feet, and at first she hates how completely out of control she feels, but Chet is a steady rider. He keeps an even pace and doesn't wobble on the climbs or let the bike pick up too much speed on the downhills. Still, when finally they turn the corner and pull up in front of Snick House, Lana's happy to jump off. She glances toward the house—everything seems normal, and there are no strange cars parked out front—then she turns to bid Chet good-bye.

"Thanks."

"No problem."

"No, I mean it, Chesterfield. Thanks for everything. Especially for sticking up for me with K.C. and them."

Chet seems slightly embarrassed. He shrugs and heads back for his place. Lana waits for Chet to disappear into his house, takes another quick glance behind her, then sets off on the bike.

She has one quick errand to run.

Just one.

53.

S̸nip snip snip.

When Lana finds the gardener at Pioneer Park, he's pruning a red-leafed hedge at one end of the cinder-block restrooms. He's piled clippings onto a big square of burlap, his rake leans against the hedge, and his clippers go *snip snip snip.*

"Could I borrow your rake for a minute?" Lana says.

The man stops clipping and looks down from his stepladder. "What for?"

"I dropped something down that well over there and I want to get it back out."

The man isn't a white man, but Lana doesn't know where he might've come from. To her, he looks kind of Chinese and kind of Mexican. He looks off toward the well, then back at Lana. "You want me to get it for you?"

"I can do it myself."

The man nods. He's thinking it over. "You'll bring the rake back?"

"Yep."

"Take it, then," he says.

There is all sorts of litter in the well, including a Dorito bag, several Burger King wrappers, and a pair of boy's gym shorts. There are also two balled-up sheets of paper, which Lana smooths flat. One is a flyer for someone willing to paint address numbers on your curb. The other one is just a single word, and the word is *Lana*. The handwriting is Chet's.

Lana flushes. *Lana*, not *Love*.

It's flattering, being somebody's wish, but beyond that, Lana isn't sure what she feels. She stands staring at her name, trying to figure it out. She's looked at her name thousands of times, so many times in fact that looking at it usually doesn't mean a thing, but this is different. Here is her name, written on this sheet of paper because a boy named Chet has seen in her something more than anyone else has seen. She doesn't feel suddenly, reciprocally smitten with Chet, but she does feel a pleasant warmth, a slow, unfolding fondness for him that goes with the way she felt when she kissed him. It was a guilt-free kiss, for one thing, and that gave it a feel she liked. Liked a lot, in fact.

Lana looks up, suddenly aware of something missing. It's the *snip snip snip* of the hedge clippers. It's stopped. The gardener is looking at her, but now, when he sees her looking back at him, he goes back to his cutting. He's still cutting when she comes back with the rake.

"Find what you were looking for?" he says.

The sheet of paper with her name written on it is in her back pocket. "I did," she says. "And thanks for the rake. I threw away all the trash that was in there, too."

"Good." The gardener looks off toward the well. "The city wants to fill in the well. It is a liability issue, they say. They asked me to come to a meeting one evening to give my good opinion. They said they hoped I would point out that the well is a maintenance problem and also a health problem because once somebody threw a bag of dead kittens in there. I told them I would give my good opinion if they wanted it. I went to the meeting and stood up when my name was announced. I said, 'Mr. Mayor and Common Council, my good opinion is that sometimes people make wishes in the well, and if you fill in the well, they won't do that anymore." The gardener gives a small nod. "That's all I said."

"And?" Lana says.

"And what?" the gardener says.

"What did they decide to do?"

The gardener shrugs. "I don't know. I went home. I have television shows I don't like to miss." He takes another long look at the well. "But it's been seven years since the meeting, so maybe the well will stay."

"Seven years?"

The gardener nods. "Seven or eight."

She decides that, without question, this is the gardener Chief Chetteroid described as dry. It's quiet in the park, and the quiet stretches into a kind of calmness. Without thinking about it, Lana says, "What would you wish if you had one wish?"

The gardener's eyes blink slowly closed and open. "I'm not a wishing man," he says, and then his lips stretch into something close to a smile. "But if I was a wishing man and had only one wish to wish, I would go with *being less stupid*."

Lana can hardly believe her ears. "You listen to K-SOD?" she says.

The gardener seems to nod. He seems to say, "Now and then."

And then he is cutting again. *Snip snip snip.*

54.

*G*overnment plates.

This is what alarms Lana as she pedals toward the gray Plymouth parked in the shade of a cottonwood a few doors down from Snick House. The car has government plates. She slows as she passes the Plymouth by. The windows are down, and a man sits dozing in the front seat.

Seconds later, Mrs. Arnot's Camry pulls into the driveway, and Tilly, Carlito, Garth, and Alfred spill out. Lana greets them and glances toward the gray Plymouth. The man is awake now, sitting forward, watching.

"In, in, in," Lana says, herding Tilly and the boys toward the house. She doesn't know why she's scared, she just knows she is. Inside, the phone is ringing. As she heads toward it, Lana picks up the note that Veronica has left her, along with a wad of eleven one-dollar bills.

> I'm at physical therapy. Not sure when back.
> Am sure you can handle it.
> V.
> P.S. The money's for pizza.

Well, there's some high-grade fostering for you, Lana thinks. *Veronica goes off with Gooch and doesn't come home by the time the Snicks are back.* Lana pockets the eleven dollars, drops the note on the floor, and picks up the phone. Her hello is sharp.

"Lana?"

It's Hallie, and Lana asks the first question that pops into her mind. "Is something wrong?"

"Lana, listen. They're coming for all of you. You need to keep the others calm. You can't let them be alarmed."

But Lana already is alarmed. "Coming when?"

"Today," Hallie says. "Any minute."

"Where are they taking us?"

"To a group home."

Group homes are bad, Lana knows, but at least they'd all be together. "And that's where we'd stay?"

"No, Lana. They'll just stage you there until they find places for everybody."

"Different places?"

"Lana, sweetness, I told you they wouldn't . . ."

Lana puts the phone down. Through the window, she sees the inflatable swimming pool with water still in it, she sees Garth's little lilac room with its cardboard floor, and she sees Veronica's car in the garage. She opens the spice cabinet and reaches to the far back for the cumin box. The keys are still there.

"Tilly!" she shouts. "Go next door and get Chet quick."

"How come quick?" Tilly says.

"Tornado," Lana says. "There's a tornado coming."

Tilly runs out the back door.

"Garth! Alfred! Carlito!" Lana yells. "Grab your tornado packs! We gotta go!"

They start to move, then stop. She's scaring them. "It's okay; the tornado's not going to hurt us. We just have to get in the car and go now."

She goes to the window seat, lifts the lid, and grabs their backpacks. "Here," she shouts. "They're right here! Take them out to the car!"

Garth and Alfred just stare, but big Carlito moves forward and takes three of the packs. As he goes outside, Garth and Alfred follow. Lana grabs two more packs and goes upstairs for the things she can't afford to forget.

She finds the Ladies Drawing Kit, and she drags a box out from under the bed and pulls off the lid. She pulls the picture of her father from the black corners that hold it inside the souvenir album from the Hoover Dam.

She tucks the photo into her shirt pocket and glances out the window. The gray Plymouth is still down there, but now it's been joined by a gray van, and three adults are huddled nearby, talking and glancing toward Snick House. Lana's heart is pounding and she's breathing through her mouth.

Chet's waiting on the back porch when she comes down hugging the packs and kit to her chest.

"Tornado?" he says. He seems amused until he sees she's not.

"It's a kind of a tornado," she says in a gasping voice. "It's the state. They're shutting down Snick House and sending all of us every which way." She's moving toward the garage as she speaks. "We've gotta go," she says, tossing him the keys, "and you have to drive."

55.

*C*het does a three-point turnaround in the backyard so he doesn't have to take the long dirt driveway in reverse. He accelerates down the drive, spraying rocks and dust behind, fishtailing as he veers sharply right when the Monte Carlo hits asphalt.

The state people, two women and a man, all carrying folders in their hands, are halfway up the front walk when the Monte Carlo tears past. They turn and stand frozen for a second, though when Lana looks back through the rear window they've begun to move again, the man and one woman running a few steps in the direction of the squealing car and the other woman mounting the steps of the house.

"You think they'll follow us?" Lana says to Chet.

Chet says, "Why? Because five minors are out in a car driven by someone without a license?"

Lana stares at him. "You're right," she says, deadpan. "They won't."

She turns to Alfred, Tilly, and Carlito, giddy in the backseat. Garth is up front with her and Chet, pressing himself nervously against the car door. "Hope somebody's chasing us," Alfred says.

"Nobody's chasing us," Lana says.

"Where's the tornado?" Tilly says.

"Behind us," Lana says. "The tornado's behind us. We left in the nick of time."

Tilly and the boys all smile.

Chet has brought the car to a stop at an intersection. "Since I'm driving, maybe I should know where we're going," he says.

"Fawnskin," she says.

"What's there?"

"A house Whit and his crew are painting five different colors."

Though when they get to Fawnskin and they find the house belonging to the widow Mullins, there are only two colors, the white the house used to be and the pale yellow it was now becoming, if anybody ever painted it. At the moment, nobody is, though. Whit's truck is parked in the driveway, and a boy wearing earphones and paint clothes sits on a five-gallon paint can under a tree.

When Lana comes up to the boy, she has to shout to penetrate whatever it is he's listening to. He opens his eyes and looks at her uncertainly for a second or two before slipping off his earphones.

"You painting this house?" Lana says.

He nods. "I'm on my break right now. I'm going back to it in about three minutes."

"Where's the rest of the crew?"

The boy seems confused. Lana guesses he goes through most of the day confused. "I'm it," he says. "Except for Mr. Winters."

"Where's he?"

"He's with Mrs. Mullins running errands."

"You mean like picking out paint?"

The boy nods. "Yeah, either that or something else."

"They run errands a lot?" Lana says, and she wonders if her eyes are growing up, just like Veronica said they would.

"Quite a bit, yeah," the boy says. His cheeks and chin are smooth, but he has a cluster of swelling pimples on his forehead.

"So he doesn't help with the actual painting very much?"

The boy gives this a little thought. "Not so much, no. Mrs. Mullins has a lot of inside projects for him, too."

"And you believe that?"

The boy seems even more confused. "Believe what?" he says.

Lana looks back toward the Monte Carlo. Everybody has gotten out, and Tilly is squatting in the dirt studying something she's found there. It could be anything—a stick, a beetle, a smelly pod. The painter boy has opened the lid of a five-gallon paint can and is stirring easily with a long stick. It looks like buttermilk. She says, "When Mr. Winters comes back from his errands, tell him Lana and the Snicks came by to see his five-color house."

The boy stops his stirring. "Lana and the who?"

"The Snicks. Lana and the Snicks. Tell him we came by to see his five-color house. Tell him we were disappointed."

The boy nods, but he's distracted by something behind her, and Lana follows his gaze to Chet, who's climbing an elder tree while the Snicks stand at its base looking up, watching his progress.

"What's he doing?" the painter boy asks.

Lana shrugs and walks over to the tree to find out.

"Returning an egg to its nest," Chet says when Lana asks what he's up to.

Lana sees something brown on one of the upper branches. When Chet gets near it, he eases a tiny pale blue egg from his shirt pocket and sets it into the nest.

Tilly says, "All back now!" and begins to clap while Alfred and Carlito stand by beaming. Even Garth seems pleased. Carlito steadies himself against the tree so Chet can step onto one of his big shoulders before springing onto the soft dirt.

"Okay, back in the car," Lana says, and the others follow. Chet starts the car but doesn't put it into gear. He's waiting on instructions. They sit there in the driveway, listening to the engine tick, and Lana wonders what to do next.

"Where're we going?" Tilly asks, and when Lana doesn't answer, Chet asks it, too. "Where to now?"

Everyone turns toward Lana and their eyes seem to push her up against a wall. She doesn't know where to go next. She doesn't know what to say and she doesn't know what to do. She reaches to touch her two-dollar bill, and when it isn't there, she fights off the impulse to cry. "Okay," she says. "Just a second."

She closes her eyes.

She inhales, exhales. Inhales, exhales.

Then, suddenly, an idea slides into her mind.

She turns to Chet. "How much gas you got?" she says.

Chet checks the gas gauge. "Half a tank," he says.

"Remember the town you and K.C. and those guys found when you were chasing the dust devil that day?"

Chet inclines his head. "The historic town of Hereford."

"Yeah, that one," Lana says. "Do you know how to get there?"

"Maybe," Chet says. "But why would we want to?"

Lana doesn't know. She has no idea. So she says, "I've got my reasons."

56.

*A*s they're leaving Fawnskin, a black-and-white cruiser approaches from the opposite direction, and Lana sees the deputy behind the wheel glance at the Monte Carlo and glance again.

When she looks back, the cruiser has pulled over, and then, perhaps five seconds later, it wheels into a quick U-turn.

"Police," Lana says in a tight whisper to Chet, who immediately takes a hard right into an alley and then turns into an empty garage, slams the car to a stop, and jumps out to pull the garage door closed. They hear the crunch of gravel as the cruiser passes by. Lana pushes the garage door up and peers down the alley just as the cruiser turns off in another direction.

"Okay!" she yells, and Chet reverses out of the garage. Lana jumps in, the Monte Carlo weaves out of the neighborhood, and they're soon flying down the highway. Lana watches the speedometer climb to almost eighty.

"Easy, Chester," she says. She's been keeping an eye on the road behind them. "I think we're fine."

"Is the tornado still after us?" Tilly says, and when Lana says, "No, I don't think so," Tilly seems disappointed.

A few miles pass, then Lana turns to Chet. "I think I failed to mention that you drive a mean getaway car, Chesterfield."

Chet nods. "I *was* pretty good, wasn't I?" Then: "I should do Career Counseling Day. I could sit in a booth under a sign that says *Driving Getaway.*"

This is reasonably funny, but Lana can't quite bring herself to laugh. She feels tense. Tense and a little scared. Leaving Two Rivers is something she understands, but she has no real idea why they're heading off toward Hereford. She could just be making things worse. To the rest of the world, what she's doing might look a lot like kidnapping and grand theft auto.

The Monte Carlo hums along. Garth settles his head against the car door and closes his eyes. "It's kind of funny," Chet says, breaking the silence in the car. "I'm being chased toward the town I was only recently run out of."

"What do you mean *chased*?" Lana says. She swivels in her seat but sees no one following them.

"I don't know," Chet says. "I just have that old-fashioned *chased* feeling."

Lana does, too. She guesses probably everybody does when they're doing something that might not be right, which is what they're doing right now. She glances at Chet. "You worried about getting busted by that old German restaurant guy?—the one you and K.C. and them stiffed?"

"Naw," Chet says, and gives Lana a quick grin. "I think the only one of us old Friedrich could actually ID is Trina, and he probably wouldn't ID her if she didn't have plenty of cleavage on parade."

"When would that be?" Lana asks, and gets more of a laugh from Chet than she really believes necessary.

A few seconds later, Chet abruptly brakes and takes a hard right onto a dirt road. Garth jerks awake, the Popeye doll slipping from his hand. Lana hands it back to him, and Garth clutches it close and stares ahead.

From the backseat, Tilly says, "I love a bumpy road!" then lowers her window, all at once filling the car with sound, dust, and wind. It reminds Lana of the dust devil that first came to her and Tilly as they sat that Saturday morning on the front porch and of the pleasant emptiness that came with it. But the other Snicks hate it and are screaming at Tilly to close the window, which she finally does.

"Nobody's fun." She scowls and stares out at the others from an elaborate sulk. Carlito grins at her. Alfred roots in his tornado pack and pulls out a package of smooth red licorice ropes. Garth sets his Popeye into his lap, closes his eyes, and again snugs himself against the hard car door.

Before them, the dirt road splits fenced fields as far as the eye can see.

Lana turns uncertainly to Chet. "So this is the road to Hereford?"

He squints and considers. "Maybe," he says.

Lana folds her hands on the pebbly leather of the Ladies Drawing Kit that sits in her lap. At least she's got the last sheet of paper, if she just knew what to do with it, if she just knew how to draw a happy ending. A pretty big *if*, really. Because a mistake with the last wish would be the worst kind of mistake, the kind that could make you think you just weren't smart enough or good enough to make a pure true wish and never would be.

Lana closes her eyes and an image comes into her mind: the other two drawing kits, the ones she saw that day in Miss Hekkity's shop.

Her eyes snap open.

What if they're still there?—and what if they have powers, too? Then she could buy the other kits and she and the Snicks would have all the wishes they'd ever need. She wouldn't have to worry about making the last wish good.

For the next mile or so, Lana tells herself that gathering another batch of wishes must be the reason for bringing the Snicks to Hereford, but it doesn't really feel like it.

The real reason is something else, something she doesn't understand.

She looks down at the black leather case, thinking of the last wish it might or might not contain, and suddenly she just wants to get it over with. She wants just to remove the last page and pick up the pencil and close her eyes and see what lines her hand might draw, and then that would be that, done deal, end of story.

But the moment Lana begins to untie the case, she stops short.

Thoroughly and with perfect clarity, she knows she can't draw the last wish riding in the car. She can't draw the last wish anywhere, except in the town that it came from.

The last wish needs to be drawn in Hereford.

That's the reason she's going there.

Whether it's a good reason, Lana can't say. She only knows she trusts in it completely. Completely and possibly foolishly.

Just like she trusted in Whit.

The Whit who wasn't.

This is the general vicinity of Lana's thoughts when Chet for no apparent reason says, "There."

"What?" Lana says, and then she sees it, too.

There, at a T in the road, is the sign that says *Hereford 11.2 miles,* with an arrow pointing east.

57.

Without the distractions of the annual picnic, Hereford looks like a different town. Almost normal. Two stout women wearing shorts and knee pads weed the irises encircling the commemorative cow statue at the entrance to town, and on Main Street, a young woman pushes a double stroller up the sidewalk. A short, gray-haired man, dapper in a blue suit, carries a parcel toward the post office, and a boy pedals by on a bike with a baseball glove hung over the handlebars. It reminds Lana of a scene in a movie that's meant to show that everything is hunky-dory, just before it isn't anymore.

Chet parks the Monte Carlo in the shade across from Miss Hekkity's building, and Lana slides the Ladies Drawing Kit under the seat. As she gets out, two men inside a nearby insurance office look up from their standing conversation to stare at the unfamiliar car and at her.

It's hot, even in the shade.

Lana glances down the street for any cars that might've followed them into town—there are none—then she looks across the street at the wooden stairs leading up to Miss Hekkity's shop.

"This'll just take a second," she says to Chet, then she

looks into the car at the others. "Can you all just stay quiet in the car until I get back?"

The Snicks look back at her blankly. Lana knows that the second she leaves, they'll do what they want to do, which could be anything.

"Leave it to me," Chet says. "Chet's in charge."

Lana is frankly doubtful of this fact, but she doesn't have any other choice. She crosses the street—she can feel the heat of the asphalt through her shoes—and hurries up the stairs, but before she gets to the landing, she sees a sign on the door that says CLOSED. Above it is a small version of the shop slogan: WHAT YOU DESIRE, MISS HEKKITY PROVIDES.

Lana feels thwarted, then angry. The sun burns into her back. *What I desire,* she thinks, *is that you have your shop open during normal business hours.*

She cups her hands around her eyes and leans forward to peer through the glass. The lights are off and the shop is dim. Inside, nothing moves. Lana knocks three times, each time louder, but nobody answers, nothing changes inside the shop. She looks around. She checks the street and she checks the windows of nearby buildings. Nobody's looking, or at least nobody she can see.

She tries the door handle.

It clicks and gives.

With a nudge of her hand, the door swings open.

Lana feels a drop of sweat break from her armpit and course down her ribs.

She takes one last look around and ducks into the shop.

It's cool inside and dark, but Lana finds the string that switches on the overhead lamp. She thought she'd look for the drawing kits first, but she doesn't. She goes straight to the cash register and starts pushing keys until a bell rings and the cash drawer slides open. She lifts the upper drawer and there, beneath it, is the two-dollar bill.

Exactly where, that day, Miss Hekkity had put it.

Lana smoothes the bill over her hand for a second or two, and as she does this, her body begins to relax. Her heartbeat slows. She rolls the two-dollar bill tight, secures it with a rubber band she finds on the counter, and tucks the bill behind her ear. She touches it there and feels better. Good, in fact.

She breathes in and breathes out.

There's money in the top drawer of the cash register, quite a bit of it, enough that a few twenties might not be missed, and if she and the Snicks are going to keep moving, they could use a few twenties—but Lana doesn't take any. Instead she peels off two one-dollar bills from her folded pizza money and slides them under the cash drawer.

There. Even steven.

She supposes it should bother her that she's buying back her two-dollar bill with Veronica's money, but it doesn't much. She figures her gig as upstairs maid earned her at least a couple of bucks.

Now, the drawing kits.

Lana walks down the aisle to the pile of antique petticoats and chemises she'd seen before. She sets aside the pile of clothes, and there are the two drawing kits, just as before. But this is strange: there's none of the excitement she felt that day when she'd picked up the first sketch paper.

She takes the two drawing kits to a chair near the overhead light, and as she opens first one and then the other, Lana has the growing sense that something's wrong. The cases are the same, and the paper and pencils seem the same, but something is different. Wrong. She can feel it.

Still, she should try them. She opens a case, takes out one sheet and a pencil, and stares off. Start with something simple, she thinks. Outside, it's a hot glary day. She'll draw clouds to cool it.

But as she begins to draw, there is no automatic feeling running through her fingers, there is no smooth living line. In fact, what Lana begins to draw barely resembles a cloud, and she can't bear to look at it. She quickly tries the second kit. Worse. The results are even worse.

So there won't be a new supply of wishes anytime soon.

There is just the one wish, the last sheet of beautiful, pink-flecked paper, her one last chance for drawing a happy ending, a fact that sends a small shock of fear through Lana's body. Maybe she should go down to the car and draw the last wish right now, but she doesn't know what to draw. She isn't ready. She needs to wait until she's ready.

Lana is buttoning the kits when she's aroused by the sudden sound of music from outside. It's somebody's rock music, played loud, so that all Lana can really hear is its steady throbbing bass. *Which sounds like what?* she thinks, but she doesn't know.

She goes to the window and looks down. The music is coming from the Monte Carlo. Three older people stand huddled across the street staring at the car and at the Snicks, who are going in different directions. Garth and Alfred are halfway down the block with Chet chasing after them. Carlito has just stooped to bless a large black dog, who seems to hope that the blessing will lead to petting. When it doesn't, the dog trots off. Carlito rises, spots the cluster of three old people, and moves their way to bless them, too. Tilly is the only one who has stayed in the car, but she's the one who's turned the music up high, so high that the windows of Miss Hekkity's shop vibrate slightly with the throb of the bass. *Which sounds like what?* Lana thinks again, and this time she knows. It sounds like the giant heart of the world.

If a giant heart is what the world has.

A big *if,* Lana has to admit. Maybe the biggest one of all.

Down on the street, the three old people watch Carlito approaching them with real alarm. He is huge, he walks as if made of wooden parts, and he is heading toward them. As one, they step back until they hit the wall behind them. If they weren't so old, they'd run for it.

Lana wonders what it means that she isn't alarmed by this unfolding spectacle.

A young girl in a cowboy hat approaches the Monte Carlo and bends in to talk to Tilly in the backseat, then the cowgirl leans far into the car to turn the volume down, but not off. Tilly leaves it that way. She's hunched over something in the backseat, intently doing something. What it is, Lana has no idea. Not yet.

Lana has the sense that time is slowing down, stretching out.

Her gaze drifts over the commercial buildings on Main Street to the green roof of the tall Victorian she'd noticed the first time she visited here. Then a crow perched so still it seemed part of the roof's ornamental openwork slowly rises and draws Lana's gaze east.

There, far off, moving left to right through the flat fields, is a cloud of dust.

A car, probably, or maybe a dust devil.

In the display case beside Lana stands a pair of old brass binoculars, painted black, with leather grips. She picks them up and reads the tag: *French Horse Racing Binoculars, c. 1895, $42.* Lana trains them on the dust cloud, and as she slowly brings them into focus, she sees that at the leading edge of the dust is a car, and not just any car.

It is a police car.

And then Lana thinks of Tilly. She thinks of Tilly and wonders what she's doing down there in the backseat of the car, but for only a moment, because then Lana *knows* what Tilly is doing, knows it in her every bone.

She lowers the binoculars and stares down at the Monte Carlo. Through the rear window Tilly can be seen in the backseat, hunched over something and doing something to it. Lana brings the antique binoculars to her eyes, finds Tilly, and brings her into focus.

She finds a pencil in Tilly's hand and below her hand the pink-flecked edge of the last sheet of paper.

Tilly is drawing the last wish.

And far away, but not as far as before, the cloud of dust that carries with it the police car is moving their way.

There is time. They could do something. Chet could

make a show of driving off, create a distraction while she and the others hide someplace in town. Or they could hide the Monte Carlo and themselves in somebody's empty garage.

Lana slips the picture of her father from her shirt pocket and tilts it to the light. He stands with his line of fish, grinning back at her.

A siren. She can hear it now. The police car is coming with its siren growing louder.

We don't run and we don't hide, Lana suddenly thinks, her father's words, but they feel like her own now, and it's not just what she thinks, it's who she is. *I don't run and I don't hide.*

The sound of the siren is close and piercing.

The red spool bed stands under the one large overhead light. Lana walks over to it and sits on its edge, as if under a spotlight. She puts the photograph of her father back into her pocket. She touches the rolled bill over her ear. She feels for the piece of paper in her back pocket, Chet's wish, the one that says *Lana.*

They're all there, all of her talismans, safe and sound.

She breathes in and breathes out.

She feels the same calm elation she felt the day the dust devil came onto the porch and went right through her and took away all the bothersome thoughts and left behind a tranquil emptiness that made her feel hopeful about things.

And then she is grinning. She has no idea what Tilly might have done or might still be doing with the last page of sketch paper, but she's glad, deep-down glad, that the pencil is in Tilly's hand, because Lana has the sudden certain idea that finding the right wish might be a lot like finding the right rock or stick or feather, and nobody is better at that than Tilly.

The sirens, close by and shrill, abruptly stop.

It's still and quiet for what seems like a long while before Lana hears heavy, hurried footsteps on the wooden stairs.

Then the door to Miss Hekkity's shop bursts open.

58.

*T*wo men in sheriff's uniforms rush a few feet into the dim room, spread their positions, and stop. Each holds a flashlight in one hand and a gun in the other.

"I'm right here," Lana says, and at once one of the men crouches and trains his gun on her. Lana, strangely, is not afraid. She is in fact a little indignant. "What're you *doing*?" she says, and the man yells, "Hands to your sides, fully extended!"

The other man, older than the first, says, "Jesus, Ronald, take it easy, it's a girl," and the other deputy says, "You don't think girls kill people?" but he does relax a little.

Lana stands, and the older man says, "You okay, miss?"

Lana casts a glance at the young deputy. "I am as long as he doesn't start shooting up the place," which gets a small smile from the older man.

"Why don't you go ahead and holster it, Ronald," he says, and after a second or two, Ronald does. Ronald looks about nineteen. There's a lot of red in his face—he's tense and tightly wound, a type Lana saw more than once in the long line of her mother's boyfriends. The older deputy works at a lower pitch and is clearly in charge. He looks at the younger one and says, "Go down and radio the sheriff that everything's secured and we don't need any backup."

The younger one seems reluctant to go. The redness in his face is fading, but as it recedes, his self-pride rises. They've caught somebody, and he doesn't want to miss a minute of it. "Shouldn't we cuff her?" he says.

"No, Ronald, we shouldn't," the older deputy says. "But what you should do is what I asked you to do, which is to go downstairs and radio Sheriff Burns that everything's under control here."

"What about those retards down there?" the young deputy says.

The older deputy takes a deep breath, and Lana wonders if he doesn't spend a lot of his day trying to keep himself from strangling the young deputy. In a restrained voice he says, "That's fine, Ronald. Let the sheriff know we found the kids, too. That they're all safe and accounted for."

Ronald starts to say something else, but the older deputy cuts him dead with a look, and Ronald turns to go.

"And get hold of Miss Hekkity," the older deputy says. "She's the lady who owns this place."

Once Ronald is out the door, the older deputy looks around the room for a few seconds, then turns to Lana. "Kind of a funny location for a stickup," he observes dryly.

"I didn't steal anything," Lana says. "I was looking for something and when I found it, I paid for it."

The older deputy's eyes are fixed on Lana's. "And yet the cash register is open," he says.

"Yeah, that's where the two-dollar bill was that used to be mine," Lana says, and points to the bill rolled over her ear.

The older deputy's eyes go from the bill to the cash register and back to Lana. "You were looking for a two-dollar bill that used to be yours." He says the sentence slowly, as if that might help reveal its meaning.

Behind him, the door opens, and they both turn to see Miss Hekkity walking toward them. The older deputy nods. "Hello, Julia."

"Hello, Carl," Miss Hekkity says, but she's already looking past the deputy toward Lana. She's wearing slacks and a light cardigan and the same red shoes as before, and she looks cheerful, as if she's walked into a surprise party. "What's the occasion?"

The deputy fills her in briefly, right up to the two-dollar bill. Miss Hekkity listens, and nods, and more than once peers at Lana through her glasses. Again Lana is surprised at the woman's slightness, the luminous blueness of her eyes, the way she looks like a girl whose skin alone has aged.

"So that's where we are at the moment," the deputy says when he's finished.

Miss Hekkity doesn't say anything. She laces her fingers together in front of her chest and seems to be thinking. Lana expects her to ask if anything's missing, but when she finally speaks, she says, "Who're those other kids down on the street?"

The older deputy is about to speak, but Lana says quickly, "Those are friends of mine. But they don't have anything to do with this. They don't even know why I wanted to come here."

The woman lifts her chin slightly. "And why *did* you want to come?" Not sharp or accusing, but actually curious.

"I'm not sure," Lana says. "I guess because I had the money to buy back my two-dollar bill."

There is a brief silence, then the deputy says, "You'd better check out your money drawer, Julia."

The shopkeeper goes over, gives the open cash register the quickest glance, and says, "Everything's here."

The deputy shrugs. "It's still breaking and entering, if you're interested in that."

"I'm not," Miss Hekkity says in a firm voice. "I'm not in the slightest." Then, her expression softening: "But that isn't to say I don't appreciate your looking after things here, Carl."

The older deputy takes this in, then nods toward the door. "Let me just have a word with you, Julia," he says, and the two of them go out to the landing and stand talking in low voices for a minute or two. Once they both look down toward the street and the deputy points at something.

The Snicks, Lana thinks. They're talking about the Snicks, and her, and probably the car that could be considered stolen. Lana walks over to the window and looks down. Chet has rounded up Alfred and Garth and is standing near the Monte Carlo talking to them and Tilly, who is out of the car now. The sketch paper is nowhere to be seen.

A few seconds later, Miss Hekkity reenters the shop alone. Lana can hear the boots of the older deputy as he descends the stairs.

Lana says, "I put two dollars under the tray in your cash register. To replace the two-dollar bill. So we'd be even steven."

"Even steven," Miss Hekkity says in a low voice, almost to herself. She regards Lana for a few moments, then gazes down through the shop's front window. The two policemen are across the street, talking to a farmer wearing a seed hat. Carlito has spotted them and is walking toward them in his stiff, openmouthed manner. The young policeman shrinks back a little, but the farmer and older policeman seem relaxed. Carlito touches the policeman on the shoulder, then the farmer, then the younger policeman.

"What in the world is he doing?" Miss Hekkity says.

"That's Carlito. He's a shoulder toucher. The girl down there—her name is Tilly—she says it's Carlito's way of blessing people."

Miss Hekkity nods and keeps watching. The older policeman leads Carlito back to the car and addresses Chet. It looks like a friendly conversation, but it goes on a while, and then Chet takes something from his pocket and hands it to the older deputy.

The car keys is Lana's bet.

Chet and the deputy both glance up at Miss Hekkity's shop, then the deputy points down the street while Chet nods and looks off in the designated direction.

"I imagine Carl's telling them where the park is," Miss Hekkity says. "It's not big, but it has a gazebo and nice shade trees."

Chet writes something on a piece of paper that he slips under the Monte Carlo's windshield wiper, then he leads the others off in the direction of the park, single file, a short parade that a few of the people on the street stop to watch. Lana knows that probably all of them are looking forward to never seeing them again.

Miss Hekkity says, "A little while ago you said those people down there are your friends."

"That's right."

Miss Hekkity turns to look at Lana. "They aren't more than your friends?" Her voice is soothing, coaxing, but she seems to want a real answer, not just something that will sound good.

Lana tries to compare the Snicks to her friends, but the truth is, she only has one friend, and that's Chet. She says, "They're more than my friends in some ways, less in others."

Miss Hekkity takes this in. "But something's gone wrong with your more or less friends?"

Inside Lana, some of her composure gives way. "*Everything,* actually." She glances down toward the street. "They don't really get it yet, but their whole world's coming apart at the seams. The state's going to send all of them every which way and I sort of . . . drew it on them. I just can't . . ." Her voice trails off.

"Let that happen?" the woman says.

Lana nods.

Miss Hekkity pulls in a deep breath, then slowly releases it. She slides two chairs from a nearby table and positions them by the window. They sit down. The air smells faintly of eucalyptus. Probably liniment oil, Lana thinks.

"What's the worst thing about taking care of your friends?"

To Lana's surprise, this is the question Miss Hekkity chooses to ask.

Bathroom problems, Lana thinks, then, *Never being able to leave them alone.* And *How people see them in public.* But then to her own surprise she says, "Nothing. There is no worst thing."

A silence stretches out.

Miss Hekkity says, "The last time you were here, I

mentioned that I took care of a nephew nobody wanted. He was over forty years old by then, but he was still like a child in his head. Like your friends out there."

Lana remembers the nephew's name and says it out loud. "Quinn."

Miss Hekkity nods and stares off with her luminous blue eyes. "When he was small and came visiting, I used to make him happy by pretending to draw illustrations on his back for the stories I was telling him. He loved adventure and he loved beef stew and he loved the color red, so most of the stories were about a Quinn-like character going through a deep and scary forest full of traps and trolls and wolves until he finally found a snug little cottage with a red door. On his back I would scratch out the thatched roof and the red door with black strap hinges and then inside the cottage I would draw a warm fire and then a big pot of stew hanging over the fire and then a nice woman who'd been waiting for someone just like the Quinn-like character to come through the door and eat it."

Miss Hekkity keeps staring off. "But he grew up, and I didn't draw on his back for many years. Then he got sick and I did." A small smile forms on Miss Hekkity's lips. "He would close his eyes, and his body would relax, and I could almost feel him slipping off to that place where somebody was waiting behind a red door with a big pot of stew."

Without thinking, Lana says, "You drew him the perfect wish."

"What?" Miss Hekkity says. She seems startled.

"I just meant it was nice you knew exactly what to do to make him feel better about . . . what was happening to him." It's quiet again, and Lana says, "Did you ever finish those big mittens you were knitting?"

Miss Hekkity makes a small laugh. "I did, yes. Finally. I gave them to a neighbor boy who likes the color red. They're too big, but he didn't seem to care. He said they could be his pot holders."

A silence, a calm pleasant silence, then Miss Hekkity looks out the window and points past the opposite buildings. "See that green roof right over there?"

Lana nods. It's the same housetop she saw the crow fly from.

"That's my house," Miss Hekkity says, and Lana suddenly remembers the curlicue *H* on its iron gate.

"I saw that house when I was here before," she says. "It's pretty."

The shopkeeper gives a mild nod. "Pretty *big* is what it is. It's got seven bedrooms. I've just been using the downstairs since Quinn died, but I've kept the house up." She pauses. "It seems like a waste, a big house like that."

Lana feels something faintly expectant rise in her, like seeing a wrapped present in a room without knowing who it's for. She says, "I'm not sure what you're saying."

"I'm saying I've got a track record of sorts. I've got a house. I've worked with the state before as a guardian and every now and then somebody from their agency calls me up to see whether I might be willing to do it again." She's been staring out the window, but she turns now to Lana. "They seem a little desperate for new recruits."

Lana doesn't know what to say, so she sits quiet, and after a moment or two Miss Hekkity smiles and says, "I have the feeling you and I would get along. You're the spunky type, and I've always had a soft spot for the spunky types."

Lana, feeling herself being pulled ahead, suddenly shakes her head. "I couldn't," she says. "I couldn't come by myself. I promised them. . . ." Her voice trails off.

Miss Hekkity's eyes are bright. "I didn't mean just you by yourself. That's why I mentioned the seven rooms."

Lana stares at her. "This wouldn't be a good thing to joke about."

Miss Hekkity lets out a laugh, the same young-sounding laugh Lana remembers from her first visit. "No," she says. "No, I suppose it wouldn't."

Then Miss Hekkity pushes up the sleeve of her sweater and checks her watch. "Well, let me make some calls and we'll see where we stand," she says. She glances down at the street, where the older deputy stands talking to one of the plump gardening women, still wearing her knee pads. "Why don't you see if Carl will come up here," Miss Hekkity says, "then you can join your friends at the park and help keep them out of trouble till we know something. How would that be?"

Lana says that would be fine, and she means it because then she can get right down to the car and see what's on the last sheet of sketch paper. Because what Tilly has drawn will tell her something about what happens next.

59.

The note under the windshield wiper of the Monte Carlo says,

> If you're reading this note, it means (a) you haven't been kidnapped by the ancient shopkeeper or (b) you were kidnapped! but managed a daring escape! We ourselves are walking north to the park. (P.S. The badged man took our keys, so I guess we're more or less busted.)

Lana pulls open the back door to the car. The leather box sits on the backseat, and the flap is open, but the last sheet of paper isn't there. Lana gets in and looks everywhere, frantically, but it's not there.

The park.

Maybe Tilly took it with her to the park.

Almost before she's completed the thought, Lana's jogging in that direction, but as she nears the park, she slows to a walk. Chet has borrowed what looks like a kickball and in a wide section of shady grass he's set up two trash cans as goalposts—the spread is wide—and the

Snicks are trying to kick the ball past him and between the trash cans. Again and again he dives at the ball and misses, and each time it draws gleeful shouts and laughs from the Snicks. It reminds Lana of something Whit might've done, the good Inside Whit, the Whit who wasn't.

A ball rolls Lana's way and she kicks it neatly back. "Glad to see you're letting them score," she says to Chet, and Chet, sprawled on the ground, says, "Who says I'm letting them?"

He calls a time-out and walks over to Lana, with the Snicks not far behind. Lana gives Tilly a close once-over: she isn't holding the sketch paper, but she has pockets. Tilly always has pockets.

"Did someone draw on my sketch paper?" Lana says once they're collected, and all the Snicks go quiet and turn as one to Tilly.

"Me," she says without a trace of remorse. In fact, her face brims with pleasure. "You bet I did!"

The Snicks look from Tilly to Lana, waiting to see what happens next. Hoping for some real fireworks.

But Lana just nods. "Can I see it?"

Tilly works it out of one of her front-leg pockets and hands it folded to Lana.

Lana holds it for a second, feeling its scant weight in her hand, wondering how something so slight can mean so much, and then she unfolds it.

Spreads it open before her.

On the page Tilly has drawn a large circle, with a cluster of small circles drawn inside the larger one. The lines are loose and fluid. What they're meant to suggest is hard to say.

Lana stares at it and keeps staring.

The smaller circles, she notices, are slightly elongated, almost oblong.

Finally Chet speaks. "Tilly says it's a drawing of something in particular, but she won't say what."

Suddenly Lana is through looking at the drawing. She raises her eyes from it and turns to Tilly, who is smiling and staring right back at her. "Guess!" Tilly says.

But Lana doesn't have to guess.

She knows, and with this knowledge a kind of liquid warmth spreads through her. "It's a nest," she says. "A nest with eggs in it."

Tilly's smile cracks wider and her head begins to bob up and down. She seems about to explode with sheer pleasure. "Yes!" she says. "Yes yes yes."

Lana looks again at the drawing. She won't put it in a pocket or store it in a box. She'll smooth it and frame it and hang it wherever she lives so she can always remember the day that divided her life from grim to good. "It's perfect," Lana says, because it is, and then she's grinning at Tilly. "You're perfect."

Tilly falls into her arms. The others pull close, too, even Garth, though he keeps his inches. Only Chet stands clearly to the side.

And then Lana notices something in the drawing.

"There are five eggs," she says. "How come five?"

Tilly is beaming again. "It's me, 'Lito, Garth, Alfred, and you!"

Chet gives Lana a droll look. "You're an honorary Snick," he says.

And Lana, looking at Chet, already feeling the first hint of missing him, thinks that the nest is one egg short.

60.

There is just one more thing.

After the Snicks walk off single file, Tilly in the lead, to investigate the bandstand and gazebo at the center of the park, Lana tells Chet about Miss Hekkity's idea.

Quietly Chet says, "Is there any chance of this actually happening?"

Lana thinks of Tilly's drawing. One nest, five eggs. "Maybe," she says.

Chet is silent for a second or two, then he makes a smile and says, "Well, this is good. This is very good." He says it like he wants to mean it, but Lana can see that just below his wanting to be happy for her is a low-grade sadness of his own.

"You'll get a new and improved Snick House," he says. "One with no Veronica in it."

Lana nods. "That would be good."

"And no Whit," Chet says, letting his eyes settle on hers.

"That would also be good," Lana says. This feels true to her, down-to-the-bones true. She looks off toward Miss Hekkity's house, then back at Chet.

"You know the part I don't like, though?"

He shakes his head, and she says, "The part about your

not being next door." She smiles at him. "I liked being part of Conversations with the Long-leggedy Neighbor Girl."

She wants him to say he could do Conversations with the Long-leggedy Girl in the Next County Over or something like that, but that's not what he says. He just says, "That's all right."

They're quiet for a few seconds, then a small smile appears on Chet's face, and Lana follows his eyes to the gazebo in the center of the park, where Carlito, Alfred, and Garth are pretending to play band instruments while Tilly performs some kind of cheer.

"What's Alfred supposed to be playing?" Chet asks.

Lana gives it her best guess. "Trombone, I think."

A second or two go by, then Chet says, "They're really something."

"Yeah, they are." She turns back to Chet. "We should make them honorary Chetteroids and Chetteristas."

"Why honorary?" He grins. "I say, give them full privileges."

Behind Chet, a black-and-white police cruiser wheels onto the street and heads their way. When it pulls up to the curb, the older deputy gets out, and so does Miss Hekkity. They stand by the car and wait.

Lana looks at the boy in front of her.

He is sad, he is semi-handsome, and he is Chet.

"Quick," Lana says, "do you have a pencil?"

He does. She turns away from him and pulls from her back pocket the piece of paper containing his wish. Next to *Lana,* she adds *& Chet* and draws a quick fluid circle around both names. Then she folds the paper back up and turns around.

She hooks a finger through his belt loop, tugs him

forward, and slides the folded paper into his front pocket. "You've got to promise you won't read that till you get home."

He stares wonderingly at her. Behind him, the older deputy has begun walking their way. Miss Hekkity waits still by the police car. Even from this distance, what you might notice first are the red shoes. She looks small, but she stands at ease with herself, relaxed. The news she bears cannot be all bad.

Lana looks again at Chet. "Promise?"

"Promise," he says, but he still looks confused, so she kisses him on the mouth, once, like she means it, like she has never kissed anyone, because she wants Chet to feel just a fraction of what Tilly felt when she drew her nest and what Lana is feeling right now, which is the pleasure, the pure and gratifying pleasure, of a wish well made.

Acknowledgments

The authors gratefully acknowledge the assistance and inspiration of Laura Orcutt, Lilly Sabel, and the consumers of The Arc of San Diego, who know how to make a good pure wish. Thanks also to Joan Slattery, Allison Wortche, and George Nicholson: first and keenest readers, always.

Laura Rhoton McNeal is a graduate of Brigham Young University with a master's degree in fiction writing from Syracuse University. She taught middle school and high school English before becoming a novelist and journalist.

Tom McNeal graduated from the University of California at Berkeley and was a Wallace Stegner Fellow and Jones Lecturer at Stanford University. His prize-winning stories have been widely anthologized, and his novel *Goodnight, Nebraska* won the James A. Michener Memorial Prize and the California Book Award for Fiction.

Together, Laura and Tom McNeal are the authors of *Crooked*, winner of the California Book Award for Juvenile Literature and an ALA Top Ten Best Book for Young Adults; *Zipped*, winner of the PEN Center USA Literary Award for Children's Literature; and *Crushed*. The McNeals live in Fallbrook, California, with their two sons, Sam and Hank.